Coriander

Coriander

Barbara Victor

DONALD I. FINE, INC.
New York

Library of Congress Cataloging-in-Publication Data
Victor, Barbara.
Coriander / by Barbara Victor.
p.   cm.
ISBN 1-55611-353-6
I. Title.
PS3572.I26C67   1992
813'.54—dc20   92-54470
                        CIP

Manufactured in the United States of America

10 9 8 7 6 5 4 3 2 1

Designed by Irving Perkins Associates

For my parents,
with love.

Acknowledgments

As always, I am grateful to Lennart Sane for his tireless work, steadfast belief, and eternal optimism. Appreciation for Jorge Naveiro who went beyond generous with his time and kindness; Also for David Korsenik for all his help. Special thanks to Dr. Jonathan Paull Gertler for his guidance in trauma and out. And again, to Barbara Taylor Bradford for being such a good friend.

Part I

"Those *Disappeared* are driving me crazy."

ISABEL PERON
Buenos Aires, Argentina, 1975

"I used to go to sleep thinking about shooting or getting shot and when I wake up I'm still thinking about it. You need something that's gonna spit, like an AK-47 that says *pawpawpaw*, not just *pop . . . pop . . . pop*"

RAYMOND, age 15
Trauma patient, Brooklyn General Hospital
Brooklyn, New York, 1992

"Those *Disappeared* are driving me crazy."

ISABEL PERON
Buenos Aires, Argentina, 1975

"I used to go to sleep thinking about shooting or getting shot and when I wake up I'm still thinking about it. You need something that's gonna spit, like an AK-47 that says *pawpawpaw,* not just *pop . . . pop . . . pop*"

RAYMOND, age 15
Trauma patient, Brooklyn General Hospital
Brooklyn, New York, 1992

Chapter One

"Love me . . ." For hours he murmured those words and for hours she did—love him. Nestled against him while he stayed hard inside her, she dozed, breathing with him, a single heartbeat with his, one love, one life. "You're mine forever," he whispered throughout the night.

It was still dark when he made love to her for the last time, street sounds filling the room, prisms of light from the cars and buses reflected off the ceiling beams. He had her by the wrists that last time, pulling her gently to her knees, the covers of the bed kicked aside, drawing her into him, his mouth buried in her hair. "Love me forever," he whispered before his lips found hers. "Don't leave," she whispered back. He kissed her then and went on kissing her, pausing only to look into her eyes, to emit a small sigh when she reached down to touch him. "I'm with you, baby, I'm right here," he said softly, his black eyes crinkling into a small smile. Considering her mouth, he covered it with his own, kissing her again, caressing, burying his face between her breasts, circling her nipples with his tongue, gathering her against him to absorb her trembling and make it his own. Lips pressed against lips, tongues meeting and retreating, he moved on top of her, his knee between her thighs, his body hard, his kisses more urgent.

They both made sounds when he entered her before they lost themselves to a sensation of history that transcended time. He held her so tightly that she could barely breathe, made love to her so intensely that once she cried out in surprise. But when he made her swear that she would love him forever regardless of what happened he filled her without so much as moving a muscle; when he begged her not to leave him ever his touch became almost diffident. An eternity, she swore; forever, he repeated, always and more.

With humor, Coriander told Danny that all he had to do was look at her, touch her, make love to her and she lost all semblance of reason. She intended to launch a study at the hospital, she joked, how usually intelligent and sensible women could be reduced to love-struck by men. She even had a theory that sperm penetrated the rational portion of the brain . . . She used to joke about it, but lately she felt shut out of every other part of his life. She had to read a newspaper to find out if his day had been bad or good; she had nothing to offer him when he talked in circles, avoided issues, or spent sleepless nights pacing and smoking. And even under usual circumstances there was nothing very reassuring about waking up to find your husband dressed up like a cat burglar.

But when she woke up that morning it was especially disturbing to see him standing at the window and smoking, dressed all in black, turtleneck, trousers . . . His profile looked almost surreal etched in the pink light of that summer dawn, his eyes squinting against the haze of smoke curling from his cigarette. Pretending to sleep, she watched him over the top of the covers, debating whether or not to begin the discussion all over again. If she learned anything these past six months it was not to press him on anything that had to do with his business since the answer was always the same. Unlike her business, which thrived regardless of economic and financial developments, his business was sensitive to the most subtle changes throughout the world. The point was that there were more takers for her professional skills than his; more people were getting shot and stabbed than were investing and saving. Eventually, the deal became that if she didn't bore him with donor organs he wouldn't bore her with corporate ones. Except somehow on this particular dawn morning the rules didn't seem to apply.

She waited another minute or two before stirring, as if she had just opened her eyes to switch on a dim light, to glance at the bedside clock, to whisper, "It's only six . . ."

He didn't move although his hand shook as he brought the cigarette to his lips. "Sleep, Coriander," he said, although his tone was not convincing.

Sitting up against the pillows, she ran a hand through her hair before holding it out to him. "What time does your plane leave?"

"Not until six this evening." He turned.

He was the only man she ever loved. "So what's the big rush?" His eyes, she noticed, were red, as if he had been crying, black circles underneath as if he had been without sleep for months.

Instead of answering, he asked, "What time do you have to be at the hospital?"

"Not until noon." He was the first man ever to make love to her.

He posed the next question very seriously. "Did you make a mistake marrying me?"

With Danny there were always subtexts, hidden agendas and double meanings. "What kind of a question?" she asked.

"You could have married anyone, you know, a doctor or a diplomat." He moved toward the bed.

There were times when he broke her heart. "Fate," she said lightly, "it was in the stars."

"In the stars," he repeated softly. "And I suppose everyone

who was in Puesto Vasco prison during the Junta was an Aquarius or everyone in Auschwitz was a Leo . . ."

She leaned closer, still trying not to catch his morbid mood. "After all those years without you, do you think I'm that dumb not to marry you when you finally asked?"

Sitting down on the edge of the bed, his dark eyes glittered. "You don't need all these problems, Coriander. For your own good, you'd probably be better off without me."

She studied him a moment and was struck by all the gray hair that seemed to have appeared only recently, streaked through those thick wavy black sideburns she adored. "Anyone who prefaces advice with the words 'for your own good' is never giving good news." She smiled. "And anyone who starts a sentence with the words 'by the way' is not about to deliver anything good either. Did you know that? It's never 'by the way, I'm leaving my wife' but 'by the way, the affair is over.' " She was chattering even though her stomach was already in knots. " 'It's for your own good that I'm leaving,' never 'I'm staying with you forever, for your own good . . .' " She reached out to smooth a piece of his hair.

He was so serious. "Coriander, don't . . ."

"The last time you pushed me away 'for my own good' you disappeared for ten years."

"You were so young," he murmured, shaking his head, "barely twenty . . ."

"It was in that awful café in Cordoba near the University," she went on.

He took a long drag on his cigarette and exhaled some smoke before he added, "It wasn't bad advice back then . . ."

"Is there a statute of limitations on good advice?"

He looked at her tenderly. "Maybe there should be."

"Are you sorry I didn't take your advice?" she asked.

"Only for you."

"I love you, Danny," she said solemnly.

"Te amo," he responded, reverting to his native Spanish. But for some reason she wasn't reassured, maybe because it sounded like the kind of *te amo* that preceded an *adios.*

"We'll work it out," she said quietly, reaching for his hand, "we'll get through this the way we got through everything else." Her amber eyes sparkled as she touched his lips lightly with the tip of one finger. "Don't go away this weekend and I'll try to get someone to cover for me at the hospital." And when he didn't answer, she persisted, "Come on, darling, we'll drive out to Coney Island and eat hot dogs at Nathan's . . ."

"You'll never find anyone to cover for you at the last minute on a holiday weekend." He reached over for an ashtray on the nightstand and ground out his cigarette. "Anyway, I've got an appointment down there with someone who could bail me out of this mess."

"That's the first time you sound even remotely hopeful . . ."

"It's a question of odds . . ."

"What do you mean?"

"You of all people should understand odds," he said. "A fifty-fifty chance to pull through a difficult surgery means nothing. If a patient survives the odds are one hundred and if he dies they're zero."

"What do you think?"

"Who knows? I'm fighting like hell and every time I think I've cleared one obstacle, two more appear that are even bigger . . ."

"Who's this person who might help?"

"If he comes through I'll tell you everything . . ."

"If he comes through I'll read about it in the financial section of the *Times.*"

"This time I'll tell you everything even if he doesn't come through."

"When?" She hated nagging him.

"When I get back . . ."

"Promise?"

"Swear!" He raised one hand.

She started to say something when she noticed that he was staring at her. "Why are you looking at me like that?"

He leaned forward and kissed her tenderly. "You're more beautiful than when I found you . . ."

She made a face. "Years of worry make a woman more interesting."

"Quiereme para siempre no importe lo que pase," he said the same words again, this time adding a caveat. *Love me forever no matter what happens.* She covered his hand with hers, tears welling. "Of course I'll love you forever and nothing bad will happen . . ." She couldn't help it if she needed one last guarantee before he left for the weekend . . . "It couldn't, could it?"

He didn't exactly answer but he didn't exactly not answer either. "There are so many risks."

"For instance?" Sometimes she barely knew him, this man who seduced her when she was twenty, abandoned her at twenty-one, married her at thirty-one and now at thirty-four made her feel as if he was about to repeat the pattern.

"When I get back," he said wearily, "I'll tell you everything."

The background music was anxious heartbeats. "One question?"

He nodded.

"What if you just walked away and took your losses?"

"A lot of people would suffer."

"Aren't you insured?"

"That's two questions." Again, that serious regard. "My first obligation is to the people who put up the money to buy the bank and my biggest obligation is to my depositors . . ."

What she loved most about him was his sense of decency that made him so committed to what was just and fair. "Just remember something, darling, that even if everything fails it isn't a reflection on your integrity or morality. It's only bank business . . ."

"You don't understand, Coriander, it's the same thing. I am the bank, every last debit, debt, loss, transfer, deposit, everything is my responsibility."

"It's about business, not about you," she insisted.

"It's more than business, *amor mio*, it's about people's lives."

"It's about their lives when it comes to money," she argued.

"Maybe I was too ambitious," he said almost to himself.

"Maybe we should have never come to New York," she said quietly, feeling guilty and angry for all those years of turmoil that they suffered back in Argentina. "Maybe I should have insisted that we go back to Buenos Aires." Her voice took on a pleading tone. "I would have gone anywhere with you."

A look of infinite sorrow crossed his handsome face. "There were too many memories back in Argentina. Anyway, I thought staying in New York was what you wanted because of your career." His eyes filled with tears once again. "I would have done anything to make you happy."

One who was willing to go anywhere, the other who was willing to do anything and yet the feeling persisted that somehow for them the outcome was already decided. Once back at the University in Cordoba when they were professor and student she tried to convince him to stay in academia instead of making the transition into business. There was nothing more pathetic than an urban guerilla without a cause, he argued, nothing sadder than an idealist who didn't know when to hang up his bandana; those were the losers who wandered the rain forests and ecological summits in scraggly beards and knapsacks; the winners were the rebels who brought their terror tactics to the boardrooms and banks, trading in their tired slogans and rhetoric for big salaries and stock options. She never bought it for one minute, not then and not now. Nothing was going to make her believe that he cared about money or power or the corporate world or could ever qualify as a rebel with a lost cause since he wouldn't know a rain forest from a swamp. She touched his face and remarked that a scraggly beard was not part of the package either; she couldn't count the times the skin had been rubbed off her chin because of his tough stubble and kisses.

As she looked at him now he seemed so sad and so anxious that it made her decide to tell him what she had no intention of mentioning until he came back from the weekend. "I'm pregnant," she said without warning, simply, almost apologetically, and waited.

A hundred emotions appeared in his eyes that ranged from shock to sadness to incredible joy and that finished by his gathering her in his arms to murmur over and over, "Thank God, thank God for that . . ." And a hundred thoughts crossed her mind that ranged from bewilderment to uncertainty to relief and that finished by her wondering what exactly he had meant by that, "Thank God . . ." Thank God for what, a baby to replace the father . . .

Chapter Two

Manuel Rojas saw Jesus. It happened yesterday when he was driving on this very same road toward Acapulco International Airport. There He was, just sort of standing on the side of the dirt road that led out of Cerro el Burro next to a sign giving distances; twelve miles to Chilpancingo, fifty to Acapulco. Except that Jesus wasn't exactly standing *on* the side of the dirt road, it was more like He was floating above it. That was one of the first things that Manuel noticed, how His feet in those brown leather sandals were barely touching the ground, and how His arms were outstretched with the palms up but not like He was signaling a car, more like He was blessing everything around him: the dust, chameleons, cactus, even the television antennas on those huts near the highway.

Manuel pulled over and coasted to a stop. Climbing out of his truck, he just stood there and stared, not too close but near enough not to miss a single detail. He wished he had a camera. Jesus just stood there too, right near that road sign, His long white robe billowing in the breeze except there was no breeze, Manuel noticed that right away too. Cerro el Burro in July meant no wind, just a lot of sun, scorching heat, and dust.

When Manuel got back from Acapulco that evening he went directly to church to talk to his priest. Father Ramon was pretty excited about the whole thing even if he tried to act calm, the way he kept hushing Manuel, telling him to start at the beginning of the vision and go real slow so he could write it all down on account of that he needed it for the official record. It wasn't that he doubted Manuel, it was just that sometimes he knew the man could get emotional when it came to his faith. Manuel recounted every detail with surprising composure, how he had been on his way to Acapulco International Airport to answer an ad for a job, the first possibility of work in the six months that he had been without a paycheck, and how when he was just about to say a quick prayer for luck it happened. Manuel was plenty embarrassed about praying to God for favors but times were tough and jobs were scarce. Not that working as an assistant busboy at the Pelicanos Rosas Lounge in the Aeromexico Terminal was ideal as it meant a daily round trip of over one hundred miles. What it also meant was steady income and guaranteed overtime on Mondays when the charters flew in.

Manuel described how Jesus's light brown hair fell to His shoulders and how His beard was so sparse and how His eyes were so kind and forgiving yet so hurt and betrayed at the same time. Father Ramon wanted to know what Manuel did except just stand there like some dumb fool staring and Manuel told him that he had dropped to his knees and wept and how when he looked up Jesus just sort of faded away.

The priest was troubled. There just wasn't anything different about the vision, nothing that set it apart from those fifteen or so other sightings that had been reported around Mexico in the past year. What worried Father Ramon was if the Vatican would take it seriously enough to make Cerro el Burro a holy shrine, maybe even include it on Pope John Paul II's itinerary when he made his pilgrimage to Latin America in the fall. If only Manuel could think of something else before they faxed Rome; maybe he could take a day or two and pray for another sign or even another vision, anything to make the Vatican Committee on Miracles pay attention.

On July 3, two days after it happened, Manuel found himself driving on that same road between Acapulco International Airport and Cerro el Burro and still he hadn't come up with anything new. Not that there was any doubt in his mind that he was touched by a miracle. After all, hadn't he continued on out to the airport to beat those sixty-four other candidates and end up as assistant busboy at the Pelicanos Rosas Lounge at the Aeromexico Terminal. And so what if the manager started him off on the night shift at the same hourly rate as the day guys earned? It didn't matter. There were only two things that mattered to Manuel. He had a job and he saw Jesus.

Manuel's mind was on his new job as he rounded that dangerous curve where Cerro el Burro merged into a two-lane paved highway that continued all the way into Acapulco. It was exactly eleven-fifty-seven on his new glow-in-the-dark digital watch when he saw the explosion. There was no doubt about the hour because Manuel had just checked to see if he was making good time.

The blast was deafening, the flash of fire overhead so startling that Manuel slammed on his brakes only to swerve out of control, hitting his head on the windshield as he did. It took him a full thirty seconds or more before he was able to pull over to the side. Shading his eyes, he watched as a plunging ball of fire lit up the hills surrounding Acapulco. A series of smaller explosions rocked the night as pieces of debris floated down to earth. One final thunderous blast sounded before the sky was still once more, illuminated only by scattered stars and a fine trail of gray-white smoke rising from the peak of one of those distant hills. Manuel crossed himself.

His first thought was that a plane had exploded in mid-flight, shot out of the sky like one of those tin cans he sometimes used for target practice. His next thought was of Jesus even if he was absolutely sure that what he had just seen was not another vision. In fact, he thought about it for a good ten minutes and became even more convinced that what he witnessed was the destruction of both man and machine. Only seconds before it happened he saw a set of flickering lights descending in the direction of the airport. Now he had a dilemma. Unless he hurried he would be late for work and lose his job before it even began. Yet how could he drive off without reporting what he had just seen? The nearest police station was ten miles away off the main road in a town called Chilpancingo. Deep down he knew he had no choice since it all had to do with Jesus. After all, if it weren't for Him he wouldn't have been driving on the road since he wouldn't be going to the airport since he wouldn't have a job to be going to. Manuel struck a deal with his conscience. He decided to report the explosion at the police station at the airport after he finished his shift. It wasn't as if anybody could have survived that inferno; it wasn't as if it was a matter of life and death.

Five hours after the accident at almost six o'clock in the morning, the Chief of Police at Acapulco International Airport finally declared a state of emergency. He listed what turned out to be a private Dassault Falcon out of New York's LaGuardia Airport as missing and presumed down. A Cessna 185 search plane was sent up, reporting upon its return that the remains of what looked like an aircraft had been spotted directly southwest of Chilpancingo at an elevation of approximately seven thousand feet. But given the rough terrain only a police helicopter was able to get close enough to assess the damage and verify that the plane had been completely destroyed with no visible survivors.

The sun was up when Manuel finished his shift, the pink light reflecting off the tall white buildings that lined the beach. The police station at Acapulco International Airport was on the ground floor of the Cocos Condominiums, about two thirds of the way toward Caleta Beach. Manuel walked through the tinted glass sliding panels and stood in a gleaming black marble lobby where a sign indicated that the police station was in the rear through another set of sliding doors. Pushing through a wrought-iron gate, Manuel approached the front desk and told the police-man on duty the reason he had come. He was ushered down a long corridor and into another room where he described what he had seen for the police captain in charge. What baffled him about everybody who listened to his story was their boredom and ap-parent lack of interest. And what was more, nobody seemed to know anything about any accident.

Manuel found himself in a small room with a carved dark-wood desk behind which was a brown leather chair with arms. Three smaller black leather chairs faced the desk and there were three pictures on the wall, one of Pancho Villa, another of Presi-dent Carlos Salinas, and a third of Jesus Christ. Again Manuel crossed himself. On the chair behind the desk sat the captain while on one of the other chairs sat a man wearing a rumpled gray silk suit who appeared to be in his late thirties. Actually, the man could have been younger given the dark curls that framed his cherubic face with features that were small and delicate. On the other chair was a younger man, tall and slim, with sharper features and dark hair that was slicked straight back. Manuel tried not to stare. Instead of hands the man had two metal prostheses.

"Two nights ago you see Jesus and last night you see a plane explode in the sky." The captain leaned across the desk, his mir-rored aviator glasses concealing most of his face.

Manuel shouldn't have mentioned seeing Jesus except that he

wanted them to know how well he knew that road, how often he drove it, how he had seen other sights even more incredible than a mid-air explosion. "It was different last night, Señor Capitán," Manuel said with conviction. "What I saw was a bomb!"

"Why did you wait all night to report it?" the man with the cherubic face asked. He had an accent when he spoke Spanish, softer than the way a Mexican would speak although his tone was arrogant.

"I was afraid I'd be late for work if I stopped, Señor. It was my first night on the job."

"And you didn't tell anyone at work?" It was the man with the metal hooks who spoke. Again, the accent wasn't Mexican, softer like the other man's although his tone sounded almost sympathetic, not at all arrogant.

"I was afraid they would think I was making it up."

"Are you?" the captain asked with a smile, "Maybe you had a little too much tequila?"

Manuel was insulted. "I swear, Señor Capitán, I wasn't drinking. I was driving and I saw a plane explode just like that—bang!" He slammed his fist into the palm of his hand. "I saw it with my own eyes."

The captain sat back in his chair. "There has been no report of any accident or explosion last night," he stated simply.

Just then the door opened and another man entered the room. Stocky and completely bald, he had an uncanny resemblance to Mr. Clean. He glanced around briefly, headed over to the civilian with the cherubic face and whispered something into his ear before taking a seat opposite Manuel. "Perhaps you were inspired by Pope John Paul's upcoming visit?" the man asked. Everyone laughed.

"No, Señor," Manuel barely whispered, his head lowered.

A silence ensued while the captain seemed to consider the situation, adjusting his glasses on the bridge of his nose as he did, shuffling a few more papers before he shrugged slightly and looked up. "I want to thank you for coming here but I'm afraid there's nothing we can do about exploding phantom airplanes." He stood. "Or visions." He walked around his desk. "You can go now," he said. "Go on, you can leave."

Manuel got up slowly, his chair scraping against the floor as he did. "But suppose there's a miracle," he began softly, "and someone survived?"

"There are no miracles Manuel," the captain said simply, "that's the whole problem, there just aren't any miracles." He glanced at the other men.

"And there was no plane crash," the bald man added.

Manuel wanted to ask how they could be so sure about something they hadn't been there to see for themselves but he said nothing.

"What you probably think you saw was a shooting star or a flash of lightning," the cherubic one offered with a smile.

Still, Manuel said nothing, merely studied his shoes.

"Maybe you wanted to make an impression on your boss so he'd switch you to the day shift," the bald man suggested, his black eyes glittering under hairless brows.

The captain held open the door. "If you hurry you can make it back to Cerro el Burro in time for morning Mass."

"If you hear anything," Manuel began, backing away toward the door, "and you want me to come back . . ."

"If we hear anything, we'll call you, don't worry," the captain assured him.

Everybody was standing then, the bald man moving toward the center of the room, the other one leaning against the back of his chair. "Thank you for coming," he said politely. "Drive carefully," someone else added. "And no more visions for a while," the captain advised Manuel with a smile.

❊   ❊   ❊

At seven o'clock on the morning of July 4, Joe Pasinsky was just finishing up his shift as flight watch operator at the Gwenda office in Westchester when the phone rang. Picking it up, Joe listened as someone from the control tower at Acapulco International Airport announced that one of their planes had gone down, somewhere in the hills surrounding Acapulco. Preliminary information indicated that there were no survivors. Pasinsky immediately called Fritz Luckinbill, the owner of Gwenda, who instructed him to do nothing until he got there, assuring him in the next breath that he would leave his home in the neighboring town of Greenwich, Connecticut within five minutes. Twenty minutes later Luckinbill was sitting at his desk at Gwenda and on the phone.

Throughout the morning hours Pasinsky and Luckinbill followed the unfolding situation by phone and fax. Information was sketchy about the accident because Washington was unable to launch an investigation until a formal invitation to participate was extended by the Mexican government. Finally at eleven o'clock in the morning, almost twelve hours after the crash, the Mexicans extended that invitation to proceed to the crash site and collect what remained of the plane, crew and passenger. While Luckinbill was relieved that he could finally participate, he was more concerned about recovering that indestructible black box located in the tail section of all aircraft. Only when he had that device in his possession would he know exactly what happened. The black box contained the flight patterns until the moment of impact as well as tapes of every conversation between cockpit and control towers. What disturbed Luckinbill was that the Mexicans never mentioned finding the box and when he finally asked about it he was informed that so far it was missing. By noon he was on a commercial flight headed for Mexico.

The traffic was heavy going out of Acapulco until that two-lane highway merged into a dirt road that ran between Chilpancingo and Cerro el Burro. Manuel noticed the car only at that point and probably because there were no other cars for miles in either direction. But what surprised him most were the car's occupants, the same two men from the police station. The bald and stocky one drove alongside the truck while the one with the cherubic face motioned him to pull over.

Manuel felt vindicated, convinced that a plane had finally been reported missing and the pair had come after him so he could tell his story for the proper authorities. Signaling that he would comply, Manuel steered toward the shoulder and coasted to a stop. Opening the door, he jumped down from the truck and stood not more than ten feet from the spot where he had seen Jesus. He watched the men get out, noticing that the one with the metal hooks for hands was not with them. For a moment or two Manuel wondered what it was all about. Until he saw the gun.

With one sweeping motion the bald stocky one took it out of his shoulder holster, aimed, and fired three times in rapid succession. Manuel was hit twice in the chest and once in the abdomen before three more bullets were pumped point-blank into his head after he was already slumped on the ground. He died instantly. Together, the men dragged the body back toward the truck, propped it up in the driver's seat, strapped a seat belt around it, and draped its arms over the steering wheel.

The bald one started the ignition and released the hand brake before joining his companion at the back of the vehicle. It took only minimal effort to push the truck over the side and down the ravine. Tumbling and bouncing against rocks and trees, the truck finally landed at the bottom where it burst into flames.

Chapter Three

"Breathe, live, don't die on me, come on, come back." Coriander repeated those words over and over as if they were some kind of mantra. "Breathe, live, don't die on me, come on, come back." Over and over, while Orbison poured out of the overhead speakers singing "Sweet Dreams Baby," she repeated those words, her double-gloved hand reaching inside the flaps of flesh running down the left side of the patient, between the ribs, to massage his unbeating heart. All around Coriander on stretchers in the treatment room, on gurneys in the hall, on litters in the driveway, there were moans, anguished cries, incoherent screams, pleas, all being quieted by loud authoritative voices as if everybody around there was stupid and deaf instead of merely injured and scared. Only a trauma unit could produce such a cacophony of sounds.

"Breathe, live, don't die on me, come on, come back." Coriander said the same thing over and over until the technician who manned the respirator warned, "Stand clear for shock." A pause then to the beat of Roy while everyone took hands off and stood back from the patient except for the young Pakistani nurse who held the electric paddles over his heart. An encouraging blip on the monitor brought sighs of relief throughout the group until someone else announced, "Yeah, all right, doin' it, let's go now!" Coriander resumed the massage, still not prepared to consider it a victory. Not yet. Breathing, living, not dying on her, coming back, almost, maybe . . . "But for how long?" one of the residents also wearing soiled green scrubs dared to wonder. How should she know, Coriander responded silently as she worked, she didn't shoot him, she was only there to pick up the pieces and get blamed if the glue didn't hold. A pressure reading was visible on the screen, good sign, and the pulse—miracle of miracle—was also registering, hovering somewhere around thirty-six, will wonders never cease. "Keep it up," urged the attending physician who had suddenly appeared, encouraging Coriander from somewhere off to the side of the stretcher. "You give one helluva massage, Wyatt. Anyone ever tell you that you could raise the dead . . ."

She understood the irreverence, it was the only way for some not to succumb to that paralyzing fear and anxiety. What she might have preferred was a softer way of communicating that fear and anxiety; a simple, "Can I have a hug," would have elicited a warmer response. "Let's hope so," she said instead, concentrating on the heart that was beginning to beat regularly.

He peered over her shoulder. "Cut an airway, Wyatt, in case he bleeds into his throat."

"Come closer, doctor, it's already in . . ."

"I love how you say that," he replied, leaning over to whisper in her ear.

"Why do you smell of charcoal?" she inquired, ignoring the crack.

"Because I left a barbecue to come in here."

Aren't we just grand, Coriander thought as she massaged; gunshot wound, code blue, potential DOA and so what else is new? It was July 4 at Brooklyn General Hospital in Brooklyn, New York, and it could have been worse. She could have been on duty the night someone opened fire on twenty-seven people sitting in a McDonald's somewhere on Atlantic Avenue. On the other hand it could have been Acapulco with her husband for the weekend.

Ruptured kidney, possible bowel involvement, bullet entry lower back, exit point lower left abdomen. Now that she had the patient beating and breathing and living—and it happened every time she had a success story—she felt the same anger and queasy stomach and uncertainty.

"Don't they have anything better to do with their time for God's sakes?" Coriander wondered out loud to no one in particular as she prepared to close the incision on the left side. "Pulse is fluctuating again so watch his pressure or we'll have to shock," the technician warned. Someone held the thread and curved needle in abeyance while Coriander shoved her hand back inside the gaping hole to reach the heart to massage rhythmically and steadily. When they brought him in, this one had in his bloodied pants pocket a wad of hundred dollar bills, a solid gold lighter and a collection of credit cards. "Wife and brother are outside, pretty upset, want to talk to them?" one of the interns asked. She nodded wearily as she kept massaging. Innocent bystander, the cops announced when they delivered him, rolling their eyes, just coming out of church on the way to visit his mother . . .

She had been across the hall in medical trauma when the attending rushed in. Look at that, he said, his hands firmly gripping her shoulders as he hustled her away from the patient with chest pains. Look at that, Dr. Wyatt, it's a code blue, he announced with what she saw was a glimmer of glee. Not that she was impressed since around there it was always code blue unless it was code coroner. Look at that, Dr. Wyatt, and she did—look at that—which happened to be a naked Black man lying on a table, his penis lying limply to one side and so what of it? What did she expect, that the attending would have said instead, Don't look at that, Dr. Wyatt, before he turned her face and shielded her from the sight? Which was not what she expected although it was what she might have preferred since from the moment she touched him his life was in her hands. Admittedly she was always a bit jarred when she heard the attending inviting her to participate, to touch, to heal, to cure or not to cure as the case might be.

Once her father said those same words—Don't look at that, Coriander—back in Buenos Aires during the military regime in 1978 when an old man was being dragged away by the secret police. Coriander watched the old man begging for help, clinging to passersby, clutching at their lapels. Not one of the many well-dressed and respectable people who witnessed what happened on the Calle Florida that day exhibited any outrage or compassion when he was finally thrown into the waiting car. For years that image haunted her as an example of the horror that was happening in Buenos Aires.

It was back in 1978 under the Junta led by General Videla when more than eight thousand people vanished without a trace, when self-styled fascists drove around in gray Ford Falcons, plucking people from the streets, restaurants, offices, or their beds in the middle of the night and taking them to prisons and torture centers from which they rarely emerged. Coriander was twenty years old and just beginning medical school.

Life had been a series of transfers for Coriander's father, always in South America, and always within the same American oil company until he settled down at the end of his career with a diplomatic reward in Argentina. Palmer Wyatt was appointed Ambassador under Nixon and remained under Ford, staying on as an exception when President Carter was elected in 1976. The State Department decided that because the situation was so critical and Wyatt not only understood the politics but had a cordial working relationship with the Junta it was better to leave things alone. Also in his favor was that his wife came from a prominent family in Argentina. Floria Lucia Sarmiento Wyatt was a descendant of a former president, Domingo Sarmiento, the man who once separated Argentines into civilized "Europeans" and barbaric "caudi-

llos," "gauchos" and "Indians." During the years that Palmer and
Floria occupied the American Embassy there was more business
conducted and diplomacy achieved than during any other period
except during the second coming of Juan Peron back in 1973. It
was only Coriander who found it nearly impossible to bridge both
cultures, constantly finding herself caught somewhere in the middle.

Half American, half Argentine, she was ultimately rejected by
both sides; the Argentines mistrusting her opinions—*gringa*—and
the Americans suspecting her motives—hippie. The best she could
do was try and make herself understood in flawless Spanish until
her words were believed and her actions proven.

Years later in 1984 when she arrived in Brooklyn to do her
training she tried to make herself understood in that way too.
What she noticed most about Brooklyn General were its similari-
ties to Buenos Aires; how mistrust and suspicion were as rampant
as were heartbreak and hopelessness, as were the words in Spanish
for *anger* and *despair.* What was different was that the consonants
were more relaxed in Argentina, not as harsh as the Puerto Rican
or Dominican Spanish heard around Brooklyn. Back in Buenos
Aires the people were more relaxed as well; they took their holidays less seriously, not like the people around Brooklyn who died
to get into trauma on the Fourth of July.

"Catheter in," Coriander announced, measuring the *foley* tube
filling with blood. "My guess is still a ruptured kidney so let's get
him upstairs fast . . ."

The attending had moved to the foot of the bed. "What's the
prognosis for surgery?" he asked, as if there was a better way of
removing that bullet.

"What's the prognosis for no surgery," she replied, absolutely certain of what was coming. "I've never known a bullet to
dissolve, Doctor."

He ignored the sarcasm. "If the patient checks out upstairs we've got a lawsuit. If he expires here in trauma we've got a brief appearance before the mortality committee and an *hasta la vista . . .*" He shrugged, his colorless eyes blinking rapidly behind his pink-framed glasses.

"You're kidding."

"I'm not kidding."

"You're dreaming, Doctor . . ."

"Come on, Wyatt, he's a rotten candidate for surgery."

"He's a worse candidate for death."

"Why's that, Wyatt?"

"Too young . . ."

"Nobody lives forever."

She stopped to look at him. "There're a lot of choices between dying at ninety-five in your sleep and dying at twenty-five from a reparable gunshot wound . . ."

"You're just buying an annuity, Wyatt, he'll be back here again and again . . ."

"Give me a viable option and I'll consider it," she said sweetly.

"Do a scan to make sure there's kidney involvement."

"There's no time . . ."

"Think of the team, Wyatt . . ."

"Do me a favor, Stan, go back to your barbecue."

His voice took on a tone of feigned regret, "Beats me why you picked trauma surgery when you could have avoided these kinds of nasty decisions in dermatology . . ."

The banter didn't come naturally to Coriander even if everything else around there did, bringing back memories from her youth of sirens and protest, of struggle and loss. So, how come you want to be a trauma surgeon and not a dermatologist or pediatrician or gynecologist, those women's professions within those confining confines of male medicine? She craved the intimacy, she never explained, a relic from her childhood perhaps. And how much more intimate could one get than taking care of someone else's trauma; what was more personal than death were answers she never gave. There were other answers she never gave as well, about herself and her virginity, for example, when it became embarrassing to admit that it was still intact at eighteen and nineteen. So she lied and invented lovers. Or, there were answers she never gave about medical school because it made her uncomfortable to admit that she began her first year at barely twenty-one. So she lied and made herself older. And through all the embarrassment and shyness she kept up that habit of distance as it was already embedded by then and too difficult to break.

Once it was a constant series of friendships that ended each time she moved with her family to another country, friendships that never reached the point of intimacy. It was Coriander who caused the sensation when she arrived at the American Embassy in Buenos Aires at fourteen to the cheers and excitement of the Embassy staff. She had the best of both parents; looks, temperament and amazing stamina. Coriander Wyatt was the kind of beautiful woman who looked good even when she looked bad and it was still so now. She had the same thick dark blonde hair that tumbled everywhere, amber eyes flecked with gold when she was happy, specks of black when she was sad, perfectly chiseled features with a little too much mouth, slender body with a little too much bust. Her nose was always shiny and unpowdered with a vague band of freckles across its bridge, her hands were graceful with tapered fingers that moved constantly as she spoke, long limbs unwinding from sitting to standing, eyes sparkling and interested in everything she ever heard or saw or tasted or touched. Her voice could be cultured calm or harsh as a four-wheel-drive truck changing gears on a deserted highway. There were times when bad diction and grammar would make her cringe and other times when she would use a string of profanity that would make a New York cabbie blush.

Within several months of her arrival in Buenos Aires Coriander had already perfected standing for hours in the excruciating heat and cold, listening to boring political speeches and empty political promises. Those were the days when she was forced to participate in one ceremony after another, to watch her father's perfect diplomatic presence and her mother's perfect diplomatic absence. She was expected to replace her mother on her father's arm with little or no notice. In the beginning it was Floria Lucia who created the conflict, in the end it was Floria who offered the solution . . .

Floria Lucia Sarmiento Wyatt was a woman who couldn't live without her sugar whether it was sprinkled on powdered cakes she devoured or laced in cocktails she sipped; whether she got it by licking sticky sweet crumbs from perfectly manicured fingers or by downing whiskey through perfectly outlined lips. Over the years the addiction proved deadly even if Floria Lucia stayed dewy and fresh until the end. Can you get over that, Palmer would say, even in sunlight that blasted woman doesn't look a day over fifty, in candlelight she could pass for forty. And so what if those diamonds as big as Brazil nuts were borrowed or those dresses trimmed in beads were rented or those mantillas made of old lace had been handed down by a squad of departed Sarmiento ladies, Floria Lucia dictated every fashion mode. She was a beauty. She was also a nightmare. She was charming, exciting, amusing, and a lousy mother. On a sober day the woman was unpredictable; on an unsober day she was irrational. Coriander had it all figured out by the time she was fourteen that a daughter who lived in the shadow of a notorious and beautiful mother risked three possible outcomes. Either she could remain in her shadow forever, reject her mercilessly, or put it all aside and get on with her life. Instinctively, Coriander chose the last option although *getting on with her life* had its particular limitations. Coriander wanted to be a doctor and practice trauma medicine in New York while her father always assumed that she would be a doctor and practice in Buenos Aires. In the end the decision was made for her when

Floria Lucia did the only unselfish thing in her entire life. She died. In a pale peach room near the French Clinic in La Rioja in Buenos Aires, behind a beige silk screen trimmed in polished oak, Floria Lucia extinguished like a candle flickering in the warm spring breeze of an Argentine evening.

Coriander was in the hallway outside the trauma unit talking to the wife and brother of the patient who was already upstairs in surgery. She explained, "We've controlled the bleeding and isolated the critical point of damage from the bullet so he's got a very good chance of pulling through."

The woman wept, "God bless you, doctor, we'll never forget you for this . . ."

"You're in our prayers," the brother added.

She would have responded, even if that kind of adulation always embarrassed her, if that young girl hadn't appeared. Wearing a sheer bodysuit and high black boots, blue-spiked hair, smeared black eye shadow, and streaked red lipstick, she approached with a cigarette in one hand. "You got somethin' for my nerves, doc?"

"You can't smoke in here, there's oxygen . . ."

"Fuck you, doc . . ."

Still weeping, the woman was oblivious to the girl. "When can we see him?" she asked.

Still carrying on two conversations at once, Coriander said, "As soon as he's in recovery," before turning to the girl to say, "This is a hospital . . ."

"This ain't no hospital, this is a butcher shop, you got any demerol for my nerves, doc . . ."

Also oblivious, the tearful brother went on, "Is he really out of danger?"

"Let's take it one step at a time," Coriander advised. "So far, he's come through the initial danger in trauma . . ."

"Because of you, doctor, you're the one who pulled him through . . ."

"Come on, doc, one demerol."

"I can't give you any demerol without examining you . . ."

"Drop dead, doc . . ."

Coriander turned back to the couple. "Why don't you have a cup of coffee? It'll be at least three hours until he's out of surgery." Again, she turned, "If you don't put out that cigarette I'm going to call security . . ."

"You're a saint, doctor . . ."

"Butcher . . ."

The security guards arrived then and relieved the girl of her cigarette, escorting her back to the waiting room as she screamed obscenities. Probably the only reason Coriander wasn't particularly rattled was because she viewed that kind of scene as one of those mindless contradictions so typical of real life. Halfway down the hall, one of those tough older scrub nurses approached her, that breed who could have done any surgical procedure better than any first-year resident. "The wife and brother of that gunshot wound are waiting over there." She gestured. Confused, Coriander replied, "But I just spoke to them . . ." The nurse rolled her eyes as she gave Coriander an affectionate shove in the direction of yet another weeping woman and tearful man. "You spoke to the girlfriend and buddy. The wife and brother are over there . . ." As Coriander headed over to the couple she decided not to confront the bogus wife and brother. After all, grief was grief and love was love regardless of status or title. What difference did it make? There were far worse things in life.

Back in Buenos Aires in 1978 the situation was worsening every day. House-to-house searches were made without warning with people arrested on the spot, women and children included. After weeks of torture it usually took only ten days in solitary before a prisoner would talk and denounce his friends and family, anything to survive a few more days or be killed quickly. It was in that atmosphere that Palmer Wyatt withdrew his daughter from the University of Buenos Aires and enrolled her in what he believed to be the relative safety of the University of Cordoba. It was there that Coriander Wyatt met Danny Vidal . . .

The gunshot wound was already ventilated and intubated and hooked up to an array of bottles and tubes in preparation for surgery. Imminent death had now become death from possible infection or surgical error or one time too many passing through those trauma unit doors. Adios one right kidney, Coriander thought as she walked out of surgery and back into triage where there was usually no more than thirty seconds to assess if the case on the table was worth her time and effort and equipment.

Trachea tube in, drainage open, she reminded the team as they wheeled the patient past her; watch his pressure on the way up, watch his pulse on the way in. It was a private club of sorts while everybody was involved in that stage of the emergency. Nobody ever forgot the routine or the rules even when they were in between disasters. You are cordially invited to save a life on the fourth of July—BYOB, Bring Your Own Blood. Until the next time when the same patient showed up with the same excuse, "I was just standin' there, doc, minding my own business."

As she was walking out of trauma, the medics were pushing in a stretcher, this one piled high and wide with a woman with one leg and a half and an expression in her eyes of a frightened and trapped animal. Coriander took the chart from one of the paramedics as they pushed their charge through. Coriander followed the stretcher. "How are you today, Mrs. Rodriguez?" she asked the woman before repeating the question in Spanish, *"Cómo está, Señora Rodriguez?"* Mouth and tongue remarkably swollen, right side visibly immobile, good leg on the right, bad luck.

"Can't talk," the paramedic explained, "she's a CVA, cerebral vascular accident—stroke." As if Coriander didn't understand the terminology. She gave the paramedic a peculiar look; how the emergency teams who brought them in loved to explain things to the doctors on staff. Now what was she supposed to say, Sorry Señora Rodriguez, you've had a cerebral vascular accident but unfortunately it's the wrong kind of accident for this side of the corridor. You see, Señora Rodriguez, you don't belong over here because this side of the hall is reserved for knives and bullets while the other side is reserved for heartbreak. It wasn't that Coriander got emotionally involved with each and every patient who came through her service, it was just that she got involved with each and every one who was hopeless and making a pit stop before being transferred out to the garbage heap of city care. She held the woman's hand and saw her eyes fill with tears. She spoke softly. "Can you write?" The woman nodded. "Write down a phone number of a friend or someone in your family . . ." The tears ran down the woman's cheeks. Coriander produced pen and pencil and waited while the woman wrote the words, NO ONE. Coriander felt her heart lurch. Taking the woman's hand again she spoke directly to one of the nurses, "Put Mrs. Rodriguez on Medical and put me down as both admitting and attending." She turned then, proceeding to the next heartbreak at hand. She didn't have to go very far.

A nurse was calling her, summoning her back into triage. "We've got a knife wound, Dr. Wyatt, not too bad, patient's ambulatory, walked in unassisted, could you call it please?"

Call it please; call it drugs, call it politics, call it anger, call it victim. She was through the door and back in triage to assess although this time there was more than the usual thirty seconds since the knife wound was ambulatory. *Around here they are their injuries; back there they were their politics.*

"Do you need a pen, Dr. Wyatt?" the nurse asked.

Shaking her head, Coriander palpated the patient. Who exactly wrote down notes in a place like this and on what charts? The patient was grinning and why not, he was alive, wasn't he? "Position lower left, possible ruptured spleen, tender. Let's X-ray but don't move him around too much and make sure he's on his left side for the film." She straightened up. "Hook him to a monitor."

"Patient reeks of alcohol," the nurse announced, leaning over the possible ruptured spleen. "Do we mix it with an IV infusion?"

"What's he got to lose," Coriander asked wearily, "except his life?" Not that Coriander didn't suffer for all of them but then she couldn't very well scream and shake them until they understood that life was tough but the alternative was nothing. Breeding, Coriander; manners, Coriander; tact, Dr. Wyatt; decorum, if you please, Doctor; procedure, Dr. Wyatt. "IV infusion or not?" the nurse said, practically yawning.

"Mix it up," Coriander ordered. "Drugs, alcohol, all of it, and when he's stable we'll detox him if he needs it." She suffered because she couldn't change the outcome for most of them, just as she suffered because she could walk away without looking back until another shift began. She felt guilty that she lived in another world high above Fifth Avenue in Manhattan with a view of Central Park from her windows. From a limousine once in Buenos Aires she felt helpless and hopeless and angry for all the children who lived in the slum barrios called San Telmo and Monserrat. Back then the limousine never even slowed or stopped as it sped her to the airport to the plane to take her back to the hospital to do her training.

Look at that, Wyatt, and she had every right to *look at that* particular patient with the perforated kidney even if he was naked since she was the one elected to put her hand inside his chest for God's sake. And after all, wasn't it Danny who taught her about hands on hearts long ago in Argentina before she learned to apply the technique on a more literal level . . . She pushed some hair back from her face and took a deep breath; twenty-seven hours so far with no sleep, only nine more hours to go if she was lucky. It could have been the beach in Acapulco with her husband.

Chapter Four

The cop wanted his hands treated for a minor altercation, doc, nothing serious, except they took a beating and now he was having trouble making a fist.

Coriander listened to the complaint although she was not at all convinced that his hands *took* a beating rather than *gave* one. Things were getting chaotic again after several hours of calm. Usually between two and nine in the morning there was a brief respite after the first wave of drunken or drugged violence was admitted, transferred to the morgue, or released to sleep it off somewhere in the gutter. It was nine-fifteen and a new batch had already ingested and digested whatever it was they took to reach those renewed levels of irrational behavior before they landed in trauma. "How did you injure your hands?" Coriander asked the cop who had extricated himself from the sea of blue uniforms milling around the doors. Whenever she saw all those blue uniforms she imagined that she had just wandered into the middle of a well-armed bowling team. "Bed three," a nurse interrupted, pushing a chart into her hands, "prisoner cuffed to the bed rails needs a quick evaluation." Taking the chart, Coriander read it quickly before turning back to the policeman. "Is that one yours?"

"Resisted arrest, doc . . ."

She continued to flip through the chart before she finally looked up. "He's barely alive," she said in disbelief.

"The guy's an animal, doc, threw his girlfriend down a flight of stairs so he could get out a window with the drugs . . ."

She heard that one so many times that she almost wished they would get a new routine. "Where's the girlfriend?"

"Aw come on, doc, these people bounce they don't bruise . . ."

"Apparently you found one who did," she said before heading toward the prisoner.

The cop trailed after her. "What about my hands, doc?"

"Ask one of the orderlies to take you over to X-ray."

"What about a disability slip?" he pressed.

She stopped only when she reached the bed. "Let's get the results back first."

"What about my prisoner," he gestured, "when can I get him back?"

Her voice was glacial. "Never, if it was up to me . . ." She separated the curtain around the bed and stepped inside.

One of those who bounced and didn't bruise was lying in triage with a lacerated liver, ruptured spleen, split lip, and one eye so swollen that a hematoma covered the entire left side of his face. It would have taken nothing for her to weep. Gently drawing back the covers, she set about examining the man, beginning with his feet and ankles to check for more broken bones, working her way up to his torso to check for more internal injuries. Coriander glanced up when the curtain separated and she saw her closest friend standing next to her, a woman she had known since coming to the hospital and beginning her residency eight years before. "Mugging?" Lottie wondered.

Coriander's attention was once again focused on the patient.

"Resisted arrest," she replied tightly. Out of the corner of her eye Coriander could see an expression of disbelief cross her friend's face.

"Big difference," Lottie said softly.

"I'm tempted to file a report on this one," Coriander said, shaking her head.

"And what if you're out there at three o'clock in the morning and something happens?"

"Do you think it's going to negate that ongoing love affair between us and the police?"

"I don't think you have to be the one to test that relationship," Lottie answered.

Several nurses gathered around the bed. "What do you think, Dr. Wyatt?" one of the nurses asked.

What was she supposed to think, that the system had flaws, that sometimes criminals became victims while victims became statistics while law enforcers became criminals? Her tone sounded more weary than angry. "A fractured left femur is what I think so get a film while he's on the table and put him in a shock suit to get him upstairs." She turned toward Lottie. "You would think after all this time I wouldn't let it get to me."

"When it doesn't you should probably change your specialty to dermatology and learn to cope with the heartbreak of psoriasis."

"You're the second person today who suggested I take up dermatology."

"What I can't believe is how someone could have such a tremendous need for a New York City pension that he's willing to strap on a .38 and patrol the streets of New York." Coriander smiled, grateful for Lottie's predictable dose of irreverent humor. It was dark-haired, voluptuous, always-dieting Lottie who had switched into trauma from orthopedics after her marriage broke up. The idea was that she would work inhuman hours so that by the time she got home she would be too tired to notice she was alone . . . "Look, the guy's alive, he could have gone straight to the morgue. Consider it a blessing . . ."

"Lottie, I've got to tell you something, I may have passed despair on this one but I'm not quite to blessing."

"You've got to stop getting so involved with everyone who passes through," Lottie advised.

"Not everyone," Coriander protested, "just the ones who're homeless and hopeless and have lousy prognoses. About eighty-five percent."

"What's left for you?"

"You should talk."

"What's left for Danny?" Lottie was more precise.

A flicker of pain appeared in her eyes before she managed to blink it away. "More than he seems to want lately."

"Did he go away for the weekend?"

"Business . . ." Coriander answered lightly.

"When are you going to tell him?"

"I told him before he left."

Lottie gave her a narrow look. "Was he thrilled?"

They were standing against the wall in the middle of a busy corridor that separated triage from the two sections of trauma. "Thrilled is pushing it, I'd say he was relieved except I had the feeling he was relieved for me, almost as if I would have something else to worry about besides him."

"What about taking a leave?" Lottie wondered.

"When I can't get close to the operating table to do any good I'll stop for a while," Coriander answered.

Lottie was about to say something else when both women's attention turned toward the swinging doors. They were rushing a stretcher into triage. "Gunshot," Lottie announced while Coriander added, "How unusual!" One of the medics was already shouting the injury above the growing din in the corridor. "Two bullets in the abdomen, someone give me a hand with the bleeding. Both women raced over to the stretcher, Coriander pressing both hands over the bullet hole to quell the flow of blood while Lottie shouted questions at the medic, "What's the caliber?" "Don't know," the medic answered breathlessly as ten or twenty people worked to set up an IV to get fresh blood into the man. "How long?" Lottie yelled over the confusion. "Twenty minutes," the medic shouted back. "Get a ventilator over here," Coriander ordered, aware that one of the policemen had edged over next to her. "Thirty friggin' people in the restaurant and nobody knows nothin'!" was one policeman's summation of events before he made that gesture that was so common around there. Index finger across his own neck, he asked, "Is the patient a likely, doc?" After so much time Coriander had become almost hardened to that question and that gesture. "Can't tell yet," she answered, straightening up to take a clamp from a resident to make a temporary suture. "Hold off before you call homicide," she said as she worked, registering the pulse and pressure. "He's stabilizing," she called out to the others. Before the patient was barely evaluated, before he was even worked on the cops wanted a prediction, before the patient died they wanted a pronouncement. The bleeding was controlled and the man was hooked up to a respirator. "You gonna operate, doc?" one of the cops asked her. "Not me, there's a team upstairs." She took a breath. "For sure this one doesn't look like a *likely* to me."

The policeman shrugged. "I think I'll hang around anyway for a while, these things can turn on a dime . . ."

They were like vultures given their eagerness to advance an assault into a murder. Having brought the patient up to the first plateau of survival, Coriander turned him over to the trauma team who would continue to stabilize him for surgery. Lottie was already on the other side of the room. Glancing over toward one of the examining rooms, Coriander noticed that the smoker with the blue spiked hair and smeared make-up was sitting on one of the tables. Apparently someone had allowed her to smoke because she was holding a cigarette over a small tin ashtray on her lap. "Hey, doc," she waved, "a lot of people get killed around here, right?" Coriander didn't answer. Turning, she headed back into triage when she noticed the attending and two of his residents enter in a rather grand sweep. White coats spread out in the breeze created by those swinging doors, they moved across the floor—three abreast—barely nodding to anyone in their wake, giving the impression of a disaster team in search of a disaster. Coriander had no doubt that he had come down to discuss that gunshot wound with the perforated right kidney who coded on the table this morning. She recalled his warning—it's your baby, Wyatt—that if the man died in surgery instead of in trauma it was a certain lawsuit rather than a brief stint before the mortality committee. Ignoring their entrance, she moved over to that latest gunshot that was about to go up to the OR, rechecking the flow of medication through an IV. "Why don't you let Dr. Bruner finish up," the attending suggested in a surprisingly gentle tone. Coriander glanced up and over to where Lottie stood at the foot of the bed and shrugged. "Let's go inside," the attending said, indicating a small room in the far corner of the unit. Coriander agreed, noticing that the two residents seemed to be having trouble looking her in the eye as they fell in step—single file—toward the rear of the unit. No one spoke. When everybody arrived at the door it was only the attending and Coriander, however, who stepped inside. As if by prearrangement the residents lingered.

It wasn't until they were both seated that the attending spoke. "Coriander, dear," he began with uncharacteristic gentleness and then stopped. He seemed to be having trouble saying what he had obviously come to say. "Look, Stan, I'll make it easier for you," Coriander said impatiently. "I stand responsible regardless of what happened upstairs in surgery. And if it makes you feel better, before I even know what happened I'll state for the record that given the same circumstances and the same indications I'd do the same thing again."

"There's been an accident," he interrupted.

She almost laughed out loud. "So, what else is new around here?" But if she started out flip her tone changed as soon as she noticed the look of pure sorrow on his face. Wary, she asked, "What kind of an accident?"

"There was a call from Acapulco."

It was as if someone cut her open to do heart surgery and forgot to close. She heard the words yet couldn't quite grasp their meaning. "Your husband was in a plane crash, Wyatt," the attending said quietly.

No. She thought the word before she actually said it although when she did say it—No—she whispered it before shaking her head from side to side very slowly to say it louder—No. And then again, hair swinging past her chin and cheekbones and over her neck and shoulders. No. Her eyes were wide and frightened and a lighter shade of amber given all the tears. "How bad?" was all she managed.

The doctor took a deep breath and leaned toward her. "A man called from Acapulco, your brother-in-law he said, Jorge Vidal."

But that wasn't an answer. "How bad?" she barely whispered the question.

"He's dead, Cory, your husband is dead . . ."

Someone else must have screamed because it certainly couldn't have been her. After all, she dealt in violent death on a daily basis which meant that this kind of thing didn't happen to her. She was on the administering end of catastrophe and human suffering and not on the receiving end for God's sake, didn't he know that? She reached for the attending's hand and began quite rationally, that is if you didn't listen to what she was actually saying it sounded rational. "My husband went to Acapulco to meet with someone who was going to help him straighten everything out, don't you see . . ." What occurred to her was that maybe if she explained things calmly he would see that there had been a terrible terrible mistake. Perhaps if she remained in control she might just be able to persuade him to start from the beginning and discuss what he had really come down to discuss, which was obviously that patient who coded on the table this morning—*look at that, Dr. Wyatt.* "Don't you see," she pleaded, "if something happened, someone would have called . . ."

"I'm trying to tell you, Cory, someone did call, your brother-in-law, Jorge Vidal."

"Please, Stan," she begged, having difficulty speaking on account of all the tears, "please don't say that, take it back, take it all back . . ." How could she convince him that there had been a mistake unless she explained how alive Danny was, how he held her all night or was it the night before, certainly not more than forty-three hours ago when she went on duty and he left for Acapulco. How could she tell him how Danny made love to her for hours and hours, staying inside of her while they slept, moving only his lips to say how much he loved her until the very last moment before she left for work. She gave him life and substance, he said; he gave her courage and joy, she told him; he was her obsession, she was his weakness. "I'm sorry, Cory, Christ, I'm sorry . . ." There were tears in his voice.

It was the end of the line and she knew it. There was nothing left to say or do except to keep repeating the words until she believed them herself. "He's dead, my husband is dead." Simply. Just like that except somehow she couldn't quite understand how Danny had gone from being perfectly healthy to being, *He's dead, your husband is dead* . . . No prediction, no pronouncement, not even one *Is he a likely, doc?* Just dead. And what she also couldn't quite understand was how something so horrible could have happened to Danny who had gone through so much to begin all over again.

At some point the residents must have come into the room because one was kneeling next to her and taking her pulse of all things while the other was conferring with the attending that she shouldn't drive home alone. And Lottie was there too, kneeling on the other side of her and crying. How strange, she thought, this kind of scene usually happened in the waiting room to other people, certainly not to her, to other people's husbands, certainly not to her own.

It was decided that Lottie would drive her home and stay with her while she made all the necessary arrangements. Not that she wasn't painfully aware of that undefined order to every tragedy, that peculiar routine for the aftermath of every sudden and not-so-sudden death. There were telephone calls to make, airplane seats to reserve, suitcases to pack, a million details and unwritten lists that kept popping into her head as she took off her scrubs to change into street clothes. She had to call Jorge in Acapulco and her father in Buenos Aires, strange how everyone she needed was out of the country including Danny who was suddenly out of her life.

When she emerged from the room, Lottie and a man whom she didn't recognize were standing in the hall. Coriander's eyes filled with tears that quickly spilled down her cheeks. Hand on her stomach in a protective gesture, she listened as Lottie introduced the man. "Cory, this is Adam Singer and he's with the District Attorney's office." Coriander looked at him, he seemed pleasant enough, in his early forties, with a kind expression in his eyes. Lottie waited for the stranger to explain why he had come, for it was obvious that she had no idea either. "Mrs. Vidal," he began, "I apologize for showing up like this unannounced but it's important that I get in touch with your husband and all I know is that he's in Mexico. I thought you could give me a number." She was aware of Lottie's baffled expression and heard her friend answering, "Don't you know . . ." But Coriander cut her off sharply as if she needed to say the words herself almost as a catharsis, "My husband is dead . . ." The man paled. "What?" Instinctively, Lottie moved closer and put an arm around her. "What's all this about?" she demanded. Perplexed, the man shook his head. "I don't know what to say but I've got a subpoena for

Mr. Vidal," he announced, indicating his pocket, "thirty-four counts of bank fraud and other assorted charges that relate to the disappearance of over fifty million dollars from the Inter Federated Bank."

Chapter Five

Her father held her by the arm. Standing in the shadeless portion of a dusty courtyard inside the compound of the Sanchez Mortuary in Chilpancingo, Mexico, Palmer Wyatt barely blinked. "Coriander, I'm begging you not to go in there, there's no reason for you to see something so horrible . . ."

Coriander turned her head, her face frozen into a beautiful winter expression. Courage, the look said, these people don't know what they're talking about. Danny would never allow himself to end up in pieces—Oh my God—in a dump like this. "I've got to be the one to identify him," she insisted, almost collapsing from the words. She held tighter to her father's arm. "If I don't I'll never know for sure."

"Please, don't torture yourself," Palmer pleaded, "let your brother-in-law take care of it, please dear, there's nothing more for you to do. It's over." A handsome man with a shock of white hair, ruddy complexion and elegant style, his expression pained as he argued quietly with his only child.

"It's not over," she whispered. It's just not happening when Danny's not here, she added silently.

"I can't permit this," Palmer said as with the tip of his finger he caught a tear that was about to run down her cheek. Coriander studied her father. Despite all the years of resentment that he harbored toward her husband he ran to her side the moment she called. As if he read her mind, he said, "I love you and I thought about you every day these past three years and worried if you were all right."

"I was more than all right, I was happy. I loved him, I still love him."

Palmer looked miserable. "How I wish you weren't suffering, how I wish this never happened . . ."

"I didn't want him to go this weekend," Coriander said tearfully, "I told him I wouldn't go in but he said they wouldn't find anyone to replace me at the hospital."

Palmer gathered her against him. "He would have gone anyway, you're not to blame yourself." He stroked her hair. "I'm so sorry you're going through this . . ."

"I'm not going through anything, Danny is the one, look what happened to him . . ." But she was crying too much by then to say anything else.

Palmer continued to comfort her, stroking her hair as she sobbed against him. "In time, you'll get over this, dear, I promise . . ."

It was doubtful that she would ever get over this since she never got over anything that had to do with Danny. She could remember the first time they made love as if it was yesterday, in a room in the farthest reaches of the Tigre Delta in the elegantly faded Hotel el Tropezón. She could still see those five spinster sisters who owned the building and who struggled to maintain a semblance of that 1920s art deco right down to that colored lamppost in the middle of the lawn. She could still smell Danny's lemon cologne when he came out of the shower wrapped in a towel, encircling her with his arms to draw her against him. She could still hear his words before he led her to the bed, "I'll never let you go, Coriander," he promised, "you're mine forever . . ."

Her father's voice brought her back to reality. "He was so damn fatalistic, even back in Buenos Aires when he was plotting against the Junta he thought he was immune," Palmer added.

Coriander disengaged herself from her father's embrace. "He wasn't wrong, was he? He survived everything back then only to end up in some senseless accident." Coriander choked back more tears.

Palmer shifted from one brown cordovan to the other. "I just thank God you weren't on that plane."

"It was fate," she said, remembering his words only hours before when they were making love . . . In the stars, Danny said, as if everyone in Auschwitz and Puesto Vasco was born under the same star; everybody on board that plane as well, she added to herself.

"I keep wondering if Danny had enemies capable of doing such a thing . . ."

"So do I," Coriander said softly, "that's the awful part . . ."

"We can't ever know," Palmer went on. "Danny saw demons everywhere, he had this stubborn twisted view that if someone wasn't willing to risk his life he was automatically the enemy."

Coriander turned her lovely head. "Were you the enemy back then, Daddy?" she asked, aware that she hadn't called him that in years.

"I was in an impossible situation . . ."

Coriander bit her bottom lip to hold back the flood of tears that threatened to spill. "Maybe if you had defended him things would have been different . . ."

"Would you have stayed?" her father pressed.

"How could I have stayed when he was already gone?"

"I blame myself . . ."

"It's a little late for that."

"What do you mean?"

"I'm going to have a baby," she announced without warning.

Palmer's reaction was predictable, as if the news was about a death rather than impending life. "What are you going to do?" he whispered.

"Love it," she said simply.

"My poor Coriander, all alone . . ."

She shook her head. "Not all alone . . ."

"I should never have sent you to Cordoba," Palmer said almost to himself.

"It was the best thing you ever did for me," Coriander said softly, "I met Danny . . ."

Hundreds of people had been taken to an open field not far from the University of Buenos Aires and then shot. The government under General Videla claimed that they were inmates from the Villa Devoto Prison who had been involved in riots where guards and innocent civilians were killed. Members of the left-wing, however, claimed that the victims were *desaparecidos,* the *disappeared,* who had been held incommunicado for months in Villa Devoto. In an unusual move, Washington decided not to take a stand against the Junta for their human rights abuses because of a dangerous situation on the other side of the world. The State Department instructed Ambassador Wyatt that because Islamic Fundamentalists were threatening to topple the Shah of Iran's pro-American throne, it would be imprudent to incur any more anti-American wrath; one more area of the world hostile to Yankee interests was something to avoid. It was in this atmosphere of violence and anti-American sentiment that Palmer Wyatt withdrew his daughter from the University of Buenos Aires and enrolled her in what he believed was the safety of Cordoba.

Cordoba was one of the oldest cities in Argentina, a town with an astounding number of churches, chapels and convents built by Jesuits, Franciscans and Carmelites. The University was

Jesuit-run, the economy was agricultural, the topography was flat pampas and rolling sierras, a glaring juxtaposition of terrain, a harbinger of more serious contradictions to come. What Palmer didn't know about Cordoba was that the University was also the center for anti-government activity and the headquarters for a left-wing guerrilla group called the Montoneros. Still, on the surface it seemed to be a tranquil change from the daily horrors of Buenos Aires. In fact, life was almost uneventful for Coriander in Cordoba until one month to the day of the massacre of the Villa Devoto prisoners.

She was sitting in a small *boliche* near the University listening to a friend play his *bandoneon* while several students danced the tango. She was aware that Hernando stopped playing at about the same time that she noticed the student walk up to her table. Unfortunately, she did not react soon enough to avoid what happened. He spit in her face; *fascista, gringa,* he screamed at her as more students joined in tormenting her. Christian or not she turned the other cheek only to be spit on again. Within seconds there was bedlam with everybody standing on chairs, taking different political positions, yelling, pushing. Hernando had jumped from the stage and was fighting his way toward her when a professor and two Jesuit priests entered the café. They didn't waste any time as they moved through the angry crowd, placating some, physically restraining others; one priest calling for peace and dialogue, the other standing on a table in the middle of the room and whistling through his fingers, the professor making his way over to Coriander who was huddled in a corner. "Come with me," he ordered in an English tinted with a soft Argentine accent. She recognized him immediately. He was her economics professor. Without waiting for a reply, he grabbed her hand and maneuvered her through the room and outside into the quaint cobblestone square. "You're shivering," he said.

"I'm shivering," she agreed and somehow the beginning of a passion was established by that tiny repetition.

He pulled off his sweater and wrapped it around her. "Why do you always sit in the back of my class?"

"I suppose because I'm afraid of blocking everyone's view," she said, surprised that he even knew who she was. And then added, as if he might not have noticed, "I'm tall."

He smiled. "Tell me, would I create a diplomatic incident if I invited you to my office for some *mate?*"

She was even more surprised by the extent of his knowledge. "How do you know who I am?"

"Everyone knows who you are. That kind of news travels fast around here." He looked deep into her eyes.

It occurred to her suddenly. "I was attacked in there because of my father, wasn't I?"

Taking her arm, he began walking with her toward his office in the social science building. "We're passionate about injustice around here . . ."

She stopped walking to look at him. "But why me?"

"You're his daughter."

"Why blame him?"

"Complicity by omission." His dark eyes burned a hole somewhere near her top lip. "Haven't you ever been passionate about anything?"

She felt her face color. "I'm not so sure my capacity for passion includes violence."

He seemed to study her. "You're not really beautiful, you know . . ."

She floundered a moment somewhere between amusement and annoyance. "What exactly does that have to do with anything?"

"If you were less attractive I would have made an effort to meet you when you first arrived a month ago."

"I don't understand . . ."

"I waited until you needed me . . ."

"How did you know that I would?" she asked, aware that he almost knocked the voice out of her.

"It was a question of time until you got yourself into trouble or until trouble found you." He grinned. "At least this way I knew I didn't risk being rebuffed."

Somehow his explanation bothered her. "Does that mean your view of injustice is directly proportionate to your sexual preferences?"

He was the one then who stopped walking to look at her with admiration. "Very good, Señorita Wyatt, you may not be beautiful but you're clever." He took her arm again. "But I suppose that shouldn't surprise me since your father is smart enough to survive three American administrations."

"And which of those administrations was enough reason to spit on me?" Her gaze was unwavering.

"We'll talk about all the reasons that justify what happened," he responded, adjusting his sweater so it better covered her shoulders.

She twisted out of his reach. "Nothing justifies what happened back there . . ."

"If you can't understand the people's fundamental fear and anger then you can't understand the evil that's taken over my country."

"What happened back there was misdirected and useless, it didn't save one innocent victim . . ."

"It's an example of how explosive the situation is . . ."

"And whose fault would it have been if everyone was carted off and thrown into prison?"

"That would have been another example of the evil."

"No," she argued, "it would have been another example of stupidity since I would have been the cause and my only crime is that I'm my father's daughter."

"Whatever the reason, more innocent people would have disappeared at the hands of the regime."

"And you're willing to sacrifice lives as an example of *their* injustice?"

"I'm not willing to do anything, I can't dictate what people should think or how they should feel, I'm only here to support them."

"So, in the end there'd be a plaque on the wall in that café or maybe there'd be a street named after the date the incident took place and maybe if someone wondered why it happened, that is, if the story wasn't changed throughout the years, the truth would come out that someone spit on the daughter of the American Ambassador and caused a riot that brought the police."

"It's better than the incident going unnoticed . . ."

"It's better to save lives than create martyrs . . ."

He seemed amused. "It's very American to be so pragmatic, maybe you should learn about abstractions and symbols . . ."

"There's nothing abstract or symbolic about death, so if abstract anger or symbolic rage costs lives then the Junta wins another round . . ."

"Anyone who doesn't take a stand is suspect, don't you see, that's not an abstraction. The regime has spies everywhere . . ."

"Maybe you should learn not to judge someone's allegiance based on their genetic background." Her eyes flashed anger.

He was watching her with silent admiration. "Why didn't you speak up long ago?"

"Could I have gotten more of a standing ovation?"

He smiled. "Why didn't you come to me? Everyone knows who I am . . ."

"Obviously everybody knows who I am too . . ."

He nodded slowly, his gaze still fixed on her, "We only lost a month, Coriander Wyatt," he said softly, "out of a lifetime, it's not that much . . ."

His name was Danny Vidal and he taught economics at Cordoba when he wasn't plotting the overthrow of the Junta as one of the prominent members of the Montoneros. During his classes or after when he held court in that café, he challenged, taunted, insulted, and reduced his students to tears as quickly as he incited them to heights of brilliance.

He wasn't handsome in any classic sense, that was obvious; rather he had this sensual intensity that burned through whomever happened to be in his presence—even when he took on that practiced air of indifference if anyone got too close. He wasn't particularly tall, barely her height of five feet eight inches, and compactly built with good shoulders and narrow hips, features that were refined and expressive, hands that were surprisingly thick and strong for someone of his stature. His complexion was dusky and his hair was black with tinges of gray here and there that would someday make him look distinguished—if he lived that long. Melodic in English with a soft Argentine accent, lilting in Spanish with those same Argentine sounds, his voice was designed to seduce. He was a man who missed nothing, who denied himself nothing as well, although when it came to women it was rumored that he was unavailable emotionally which only increased his mystique . . .

There was something excruciatingly sexy about a man who happened to be mourning a woman who happened to have been murdered by the Junta. And when that woman also happened to be a famous and beautiful left-wing actress, it made the man even more desirable given his connection to a fallen saint. Alicia Morena had been plucked from the stage of a theatre in Buenos Aires by the police because the government accused her of working to overthrow them. They weren't wrong. Missing for two and a half months before she was suddenly returned like a package that had gone astray in the inefficient Argentine postal system. Raped, beaten, tortured and barely alive, Alicia had been tossed out of a moving Ford Falcon when the regime judged there was nothing left to do with her except use her as an example of what happened to those who opposed them. She died in Danny's arms. Later that night during a candlelight vigil in the Plaza de Mayo Danny made a passionate statement about how everyone who loved Alicia at least knew what had been her fate; unlike thousands of others right there in Buenos Aires who would never know what happened to their friends, family or loved ones . . .

When they got to his office, Danny motioned Coriander into a chair while he set about preparing the *mate*, the typical Argentine drink of herbal tea leaves ground up in a hollow *gourde*, mixed with hot water and sipped through a *bombilla* or straw. When the brew was prepared he carried it over to a table and set it down before pulling up a chair next to hers. He sat down and took a sip before holding the straw to her lips. "Are you warmer now?" he asked.

She nodded, her eyes fixed on him. "Tell me how this whole anti-American thing is so connected to this anti-Wyatt thing."

When he spoke his tone was suddenly weary. "We hoped when Carter was elected that American policy would change regarding all the human rights abuses that are going on down here. But when your father was reassigned as Ambassador and there were no changes it was logical to blame him instead of all those faceless bureaucrats down in Washington . . ."

"Did it ever occur to you that my father was kept on because Washington wanted someone here with access to people who were inaccessible?" She didn't recognize her own voice.

"Are you talking about the people in the Junta or the victims?"

"Both."

"Your father doesn't seem particularly interested in the victims . . ."

"That's not true . . ."

"He hasn't made one official statement against any of the violence."

"He can't speak out as a private citizen, he needs Washington's approval."

"That's another good point, why isn't Washington coming out against the Junta?" He looked at her intensely.

"Haven't you got any contacts that could tell you, people who work at the State Department?"

"Promises is what we've gotten from all our good friends in Washington, which is why we've tried to talk to your father. Unfortunately, he's one of those inaccessible people . . ."

She took a chance. "Would you like to meet him?" she rushed, "because if you would you can come to the Embassy Christmas party."

His tone was vaguely taunting. "Is that a formal invitation?"

"Yes," she barely whispered, not quite sure how she dared without first asking permission.

He scanned her face before his gaze held hers. "On one condition . . ."

"What's that?"

"That you'll dance with me and that you'll be the one to introduce us," he said with an amused twinkle in his eyes.

"That's two conditions . . ."

He smiled, his gaze now settled on her lips. She shivered. "Are you cold again?"

She shook her head.

He stood to move across the room to light several candles on a table against a far wall before he sat down dangerously close to her lips. He touched her cheek. "What do you bet I fall in love with you?"

"You'll lose," she barely whispered.

"I never lose . . ." He leaned over then to press his mouth lightly on hers before withdrawing almost instantly. She kept her eyes closed as she waited for more and when there was no more she opened them to see him looking at her tenderly. She watched as he leaned forward to kiss her again, this time more urgently and with the slightest taste of tongue. She felt herself being drawn into him. "What happens now?" she whispered after their lips separated.

"As long as I'm around, Coriander Wyatt, nothing bad will ever happen to you again, I promise . . ." And it wasn't that he didn't keep that promise, it was only that he wasn't around long enough to make it matter.

By Christmas, General Videla had ordered two thousand more civilians removed to unknown jails and torture centers throughout the country, Palmer Wyatt threw his lavish holiday party, and Danny Vidal became Coriander Wyatt's lover. By spring, women wearing white kerchiefs were picketing the Plaza de Mayo in Buenos Aires, carrying signs with the names of their missing children and grandchildren. *Donde Estan, Where Are They,* the signs read as the mothers and grandmothers walked in circles in view of the generals who sat in the Casa Rosada overlooking the square. Coriander used to say that the Plaza de Mayo had become an outpatient clinic for anybody who suffered anything at the hands of the regime, a meeting place for those who had gone mad from all the brutality that was Argentina. By then, she was helping Danny in the anti-government movement, photocopying leaflets, typing lists of missing students, serving coffee at clandestine meetings, marching. By summer, Danny announced without warning that he was resigning his post at the University to take a job running the Credito de la Plata Bank in Buenos Aires, but not before he announced that the affair was over. For her own good, he said, he was leaving her so she could get on with her life. By the way, he added, he'd always love her. After he left she never heard from him; her phone calls were never answered and her letters were returned unopened. By fall, Coriander heard that the bank had been shut down by the Junta, its officers arrested and accused of laundering money for the Montoneros. Danny managed to escape. There were rumors that he went to Cuba but nobody knew anything for sure or at least they weren't talking.

Years later, in 1984, when Coriander arrived in Brooklyn she came equipped with adequate medical training from Cordoba and an abhorrence for human suffering. She also came with a broken heart since she was still in love with the only man she had ever loved in her life, Danny Vidal. Not that Brooklyn General didn't have its advantages, that much she realized almost immediately; at least in Brooklyn when she was spit on she could do something to make things better instead of just sitting there and not spitting back.

Heading toward that long stucco building in the dusty heat of Mexico in July she could almost taste his mouth, his tongue; she could almost see that lazy smile that started as a curl at the corners of those lips that kissed her inside and out, the smile that flashed perfect white teeth—the better to eat you with my dear. Head held high, hair brushing against her shoulders, wisping on her brow, eyes staring straight ahead from behind dark glasses, Coriander walked in the direction of hell. A basin for God's sake, the image wouldn't quit. Danny was lying in pieces in a basin waiting to be claimed. She choked back a sob that emerged as a gasp.

"I knew this was a bad idea," Palmer said without much conviction.

"It's a terrible idea," she agreed, the tears running down her cheeks. She stopped to take off her sunglasses and rest her head on her father's shoulder.

Heedless dogs barked while people greeted each other much as they might have in a restaurant in elegant Recoleta or along Avenida Corrientes or strolling on the Calle Florida in Buenos Aires. A man moved away from the cluster of official-looking people. He was bent, green-tinted, gray-suited, with a look of professional sorrow. She knew right away. *"Buenos Dias,* Señora Vidal, I am Enrique Sanchez, the undertaker for the city of Chilpancingo."* The man offered a scrawny hand, which she chose to ignore. No takers today, not even any undertakers. Springing into diplomatic action, Palmer extended one weathered and highly experienced hand, proficient at shaking and signing useless friendship treaties. "I'm Ambassador Wyatt, Señora Vidal's father and you can understand what a terrible shock this is for all of us. If you could just spare us as much red tape as possible . . ."

"I spoke to someone in your office," Coriander said, coming to life.

"Yes, you spoke to Anuncio, my clerk . . ."

"He told me there was hardly anything left to identify," she went on, again almost collapsed from her own words.

The man glanced at Palmer and then back to Coriander. Sadly, he replied, "That is true, there is almost nothing."

She began to tremble, beginning with her hands and then throughout her entire body until she felt horribly horribly chilled. She longed for Danny's arms around her. "Please," she began, taking a deep breath, "I need you to explain everything to me, Señor Sanchez."

The man spoke quickly, as if he needed to deliver the information so he could move on to the next stage of this catastrophe. "You see, the accident happened at night and wolves roam the area and of course there are the local peasants who live up there who took whatever they could find." He shrugged. "The interior of the plane was scattered around a fifty mile radius and as for any papers or luggage, well, the elements of the night make it very difficult to find anything . . ."

There was no question in her mind that she was entering insanity by inches. Her voice shook as she asked, "What is there left for me to identify?"

Palmer held her closer, his arm around her shoulders. "Coriander, I wish you wouldn't do this . . ."

But Coriander paid no attention. "Go on, Mr. Sanchez," she said.

Sanchez twitched under Palmer's gaze. "The full inquiry

can't begin until identification is certain." He floundered before he continued, "You see, Señor Jorge Vidal has already identified certain sections of the body but unless we have another person . . ." He paused. "What we hoped was that Señora Vidal could . . ." He looked helplessly at the sky.

It was unbelievable but it was exactly as she thought. "Cast the winning vote, is that it?" she asked incredulously. Thumbs up or down.

"Oh, if you could," Sanchez cried in relief.

Palmer started to say something but again Coriander interrupted. "Whose idea is this, Señor Sanchez?" she asked gently.

"It's Jorge Vidal's idea," the unfortunate undertaker explained before adding, "you see, Señora Wyatt, there are seventy-five pounds of remains that we've divided into three separate sections in three separate basins. Under the circumstances the only way to identify the victims is by elimination."

If Coriander could step back from the situation she would perhaps find the premise fascinating. If she were in on this on a professional basis she might appreciate the idea as rather intriguing. Dividing remains into three equal sections representing three human beings—two pilots, one husband—was clearly quite original. And if by any chance they were divided unequally one could assume that the division was made according to what had been their respective body weights in life. But by then she was operating on overdrive. "Señor Sanchez, I'm a doctor," she said through her tears although she could have been an astronaut for all her failure at objectivity. "How do I know my husband really died in that crash if there're no bone fragments or teeth or fingerprints?" Biting the inside of her cheek until she tasted blood, she remembered kissing Danny once, nibbling, chewing, kissing until they both tasted blood.

"There was one substantial body part," Sanchez barely whispered.

Where were the parts that counted, she wanted to scream,

where were the parts that accounted for that arrogant stare, that I've-got-what-you-want look that never wavered even in the worst of times. "Which part?" she asked.

Palmer was at the helm again, leaning in as if the wind were behind him, but Coriander was there first, "Which part?" she repeated, a tinge of hysteria in her voice.

"The torso," the man barely replied, "the only part that wasn't in pieces . . ."

Want you, need you, love you to pieces and how the hell could Danny have left for Acapulco in a private plane to end up in a private basin. "Based on a torso?" she asked.

"Yes—uh—yes," the man stammered. "All I know is Señor Jorge Vidal has arranged for a cremation so if you could just confirm the identification . . ."

"What?" Palmer bellowed.

"Cremation?" Coriander repeated, certain that she had misheard.

"Only to avoid the red tape," the man said helplessly. "You see, your husband is a foreigner which makes everything complicated in Mexico. To transport a body requires so many forms . . ." He shrugged. "Ashes are," he seemed to search for the word . . .

"Nothing," she whispered, "they're just nothing." She was dazed.

"If my daughter is surprised, I am aghast. How dare you or anyone else make a decision like that without first consulting my daughter? After all, she *is* the wife."

Coriander was pale, even underneath the sunburn that she had caught on the bridge of her nose and across her cheekbones. The decision to cremate went beyond propriety as far as she was concerned, beyond relationships and titles although the irony didn't escape her. For the first time in years her father was defending her status as Danny Vidal's wife, more than defending it he was actually acknowledging it. Although it occurred to her that it was more palatable for him now since the title was about to become obsolete.

"Where are those sections?" she managed to ask.

"In the mortuary, Señora," Sanchez said, backing away, "I'm so very very sorry but I thought you knew . . ." Enrique Sanchez kept backing away, mumbling condolences with each step. There was no doubt in Coriander's mind that the man had done that two-step hundreds of times before since he did it so well; without tripping over tree roots or stones or even that sign post in the ground informing visitors that they had arrived at the Sanchez Mortuary in case anyone might have confused it with Canyon Ranch. When he finally disappeared around the side of the building, Coriander announced in a tearful voice, "I'm going inside."

"At least let me go with you," Palmer pleaded.

"Alone," she said, having trouble breathing. Turning, she walked toward the archway leading to that dilapidated building loosely described as a mortuary.

In a dimly-lit hallway Jorge Vidal rushed over to fumble her into a sloppy embrace, his cherubic face streaked with tears, his curly black hair tousled, his delicate features cloaked in misery. She held back just enough to avoid brushing her cheek against his. Three roaches climbed up one wall near where a pile of dust had been swept neatly into a corner. "Coriander, *querida, que desastre!*" he wept, "I was meeting Danny in Acapulco. We were going to surprise you with the most beautiful villa."

Confused, she responded carefully. "What villa? Danny didn't tell me he was meeting you."

"A surprise, he was going to buy you a villa as a surprise," Jorge said just as carefully. "We decided that I'd meet him when he called from Houston."

"He was meeting someone about the bank . . ."

Jorge looked baffled. "No, *querida*, about a villa . . ."

It was preposterous. Danny would have told her. He never would have surprised her with a house without first discussing it.

And another thing, it was crazy, "What was he doing in Houston?" She was glacial.

"The plane stopped to refuel."

"And he got off to call you?" It made no sense . . .

"*Si, querida,* I was going to take him to the hotel and then in the morning we would go directly to the real estate office."

But what interested her more than villas or phone calls right then were Jorge's efforts to destroy what little was left of her husband. Her tone remained barely polite since theirs was a history that strained the limits of cordiality even under ordinary circumstances. He had lost her respect and admiration when he left a wife and three children for a succession of underage starlets and models, leaving them as well in varying situations that ranged from pregnant to perplexed. "You can't do this," she said, her voice taking on a pleading tone that she heard and hated. "You can't cremate him."

"Didn't Sanchez explain?"

"I don't care about any explanations. You're not touching my husband."

"There's nothing left," he whined.

Whatever control she managed up until then suddenly left her. Her voice was shrill. "Whatever's left or not left makes no difference . . ." She was crying. "You're not going near him."

Still, he insisted. "But Coriander, it's all arranged, it's for you so you don't have to suffer through all the red tape. It saves all the bureaucratic problems and heartache."

If someone had told her that she actually swayed right then she would have believed it. "Based on what," she cried, "how do you know it's Danny?"

"*Por favor querida, no hay nada,* there's nothing left."

"Based on what?"

"On the chest," he mumbled again. "A piece of his chest."

She took a step forward, her head spinning and to her satisfaction she saw her brother-in-law flinch. "You won't do anything, not anything, because it's not up to you, it's up to me." But he just stood there saying nothing, his eyes unblinking and his mouth open slightly as she brushed past him and inside the morgue.

Chapter Six

The smell assaulted her first. It was putrid, worse than formaldehyde, a stench that wasn't unfamiliar given that she had passed
through a burn unit as part of her training. She recognized the
odor of burned flesh that always reminded her of charred lamb
chops. She nearly gagged. Opening her purse, she extracted a
handkerchief and pressed it over her nose and mouth. Looking
around, she took it all in, feeling the weight of the tiled floor and
paint-chipped walls, rusty pipes that covered one entire side of the
room, broken chairs that had been pushed against the other side. It
reminded her of a tenement in Brooklyn where she once super-
vised the removal of a dead baby wrapped in headlines.

Forcing herself to take shallow breaths, she focused on the
long table in the center of the room. There it was. Or, there *they*
were since there were three of them, three basins in basic black-
and-white speckled metal containing chunks of flesh. Tagged as
well, she noted, each basin was tagged with a number, a name, a
signature; three basins, three victims, two pilots, one passenger
and a partridge in a pear tree. Trembling, she raised her eyes
toward the glare of the overhead fluorescent ceiling fixture in an

effort to keep her tears in their respective ducts. She wept quietly, her face buried into a handkerchief until she looked up to notice a man. Across that table holding those basins containing those chunks of flesh was a man, a handkerchief also covering his nose and mouth, his eyes narrowed against the stench. He looked vaguely familiar. "Are you all right?" he asked. What kind of a question . . . "Who are you?" she began, aware that he was motioning her toward the exit. "Out here . . ." But she was no longer paying attention. Instead, her eyes were riveted on the basin to the right, the one holding what appeared to be a torso covered with hair. It was grotesque. Never in her life had she seen anything that prepared her for that. Closing her eyes, she felt on the verge of fainting. In an instant the stranger was around the table and holding her around the waist, in the next instant she felt herself being guided to the door. It was only when they were in the hallway that she recognized him as the man from the District Attorney's office who had come to the hospital with a subpoena for Danny. She still couldn't talk, her senses dulled by those hunks of flesh, all that remained of what had been three human beings, one of whom was meant to be her husband except none of what remained was Danny. She had never seen that torso before in her life and she knew every centimeter of Danny Vidal's body. She took a deep breath. "What are you doing here?"

How could he explain in a sentence or two and even if he could all that was on his mind was how beautiful she looked in black, how vulnerable, even more touching than she looked at the hospital. And what concerned him more than anything else was his own lack of propriety in even allowing himself to think such a thing. "So you remember me?"

"The subpoena," she said, more as an announcement than as a reply, looking up at the fluorescent ceiling fixture in another effort to keep her tears in their ducts. "Isn't it a little late for that?"

He spoke in a voice that sounded perpetually perplexed, "Ordinarily it would be . . ." He shook his head. "Look, I'm sorry about this . . ." And he was, he felt genuinely rotten about confronting her because Adam Singer was a nice man; modest, thoughtful, sensitive, all unusual traits in someone who began his career as a cop and struggled through law school at night to end up as Special Investigator for the District Attorney's office, Southern District—Manhattan.

"This goes beyond apologies," Coriander countered.

There was no argument there. "Could we go outside and talk?"

Concentrating on her black leather pumps as they moved across the filthy linoleum floor, she headed toward the exit with the stranger still at her side. When they finally reached the door and walked out into the courtyard she stopped to listen to what he had to say. "My office isn't convinced that your husband is dead," he said, pausing to hear her reaction. But there was only an intensity in her eyes as she waited to hear more. "They sent me down here to make an official identification of the body and now"—he shrugged—"there doesn't seem to be any body to identify."

"If my husband isn't dead then who's in that basin?"

"I don't know," Adam said honestly, "but that's something I intend to find out . . ."

"And if that's not my husband then what happened to him?" Her hands were shaking, her voice was trembling.

Adam wished he had never gone into this business. "All I know is that your husband had enormous business problems."

The expression on her face said it all, that he was out of his mind to even offer that as an excuse. "That's the reason you think he could be alive?"

Adam took a deep breath. "More than business problems, your husband faced some serious charges for bank fraud and theft."

"And that's enough to assume that he decided to disappear and put me through this . . ." She could feel the emotion rising from within her chest. "It's cruel to suggest such a thing, it's cruel and crazy and a lie," she added, again close to tears. She turned to walk away. But he was right beside her. "I realize this is a shock but at least give me a chance to explain." She kept walking. "I don't think you realize anything." "Look," he said, his hand on her arm to stop her, "I do realize and I'm not minimizing the horror of this thing or the shock . . ."

She withdrew her arm, trying to decide whether to bolt or to hear him out. "What do you want from me?"

He had to restrain himself from taking her in his arms to comfort her and mostly because of that bottom lip of hers that kept trembling as she kept trying not to cry. At the age of forty and after ten years in a profession where cynicism went with the job and regret was a luxury, Adam Singer thought he was immune to good-looking women in distress. Coriander Wyatt Vidal proved that he wasn't. "I want you to help me find out what the truth is and don't ask me why because it's real simple"—he was rushing now because he only had one shot to get to her and he knew it—"If there's one chance in hell that your husband's alive and I can find him or I can prove to you that he's somewhere and not lying in that basin then you're going to take it even if it means an indictment and a trial and a jail sentence." He paused. "Even if it's cruel and crazy because if I find him that's the only way you're going to know the truth."

She took a good look at him. Dressed in jeans and a rumpled seersucker jacket with a necktie stuck in his breast pocket, he had a curious style, a kind of natural chic. He exuded confidence here, and yet he was so out of place. His hair was light brown and longer than was in style, his nose was somewhat pointed, his eyes were a hard light blue and there was never any doubt at whom he was looking or talking because their focus was direct and all-consuming. Looking less like a Special Investigator for the D.A. than a football player, Adam was tall and broad-shouldered, which for some reason made it almost tempting to step into his embrace and block out the rest of the painful world . . . She shook her head. "I can't believe this," she whispered, "not any of it . . ."

"Fifteen minutes," he whispered back, offering his closing argument.

There were tears in her eyes and her voice was unsteady. "Where are you staying?" she finally spoke, sounding completely devastated.

"At the Parador," he said quietly. He had to restrain himself from breathing a sigh of relief, actually he had to restrain himself from reaching out to touch her . . .

Resigned, her voice was small and distant, "Meet me in the restaurant at seven," she said before leaving him standing there looking slightly surprised. Two mangy dogs bounded up to sniff the ground around him. As she walked away it occurred to her that she was grasping at anything even if he was the only person so far who validated her hope. And anyway, just what the hell was all the rush about to cremate remains that she was absolutely certain weren't her husband's . . .

Chapter Seven

Life was full of surprises. One day you were alive and well and bilking a bank of millions of dollars and the next day you were lying in pieces in a speckled metal basin in some hellhole eighty-seven kilometers north of Acapulco. Adam found himself filled with emotion as he wandered out of the courtyard and toward the hotel. The sun was setting and there was a cool, dry breeze coming off the Sierra Madre del Sur in the far distance. He took off his jacket and rolled up his sleeves, thinking that it wouldn't hurt to walk since he reeked of formaldehyde and needed to clear his head. A walk would give him a chance to think about things.

She bothered him—this Coriander Wyatt Vidal and what kind of a name was Coriander anyway—and not just because she was a good-looking woman with an ugly problem. She bothered him because he had this nagging feeling that she knew more than she was letting on and she bothered him because she was destroying his theory that Vidal faked his own death. The guy wasn't stupid enough to leave a wife behind who looked like that unless she knew more than she was letting on, which got back to his original dilemma . . .

Reaching the main road, Adam decided to take the long way around through the pristine town of Chilpancingo with its red-tiled roofs and spotless white sidewalks. The town was certainly different from any other Mexican town he had ever seen; there was no garbage, no slums, no poverty. Not that it would have ever occurred to him to come down here on holiday. There was nothing to do or see except if he wanted to take a course at the University of Guerrero or visit the murals in front of the City Hall immortalizing that brief moment in history when Chilpancingo tried to secede from Mexico. Actually that was probably the last time the morgue had been so busy, back in 1813 when José Luis Morales y Pavon came up with that idea and was shot along with all of his men by Spanish troops. As of this morning the morgue was positively bustling with activity and not only because of the plane crash. Apparently some local resident badly negotiated a curve in the road and incinerated himself and his truck at the bottom of a ravine. As Adam wandered he realized that this case hadn't offered anything easy since the beginning. The problem was that there were just too many answers floating around to the same questions since the investigation began . . .

For instance, did Vidal hire a plane to fly him to Acapulco for the weekend with the intention of bailing out before the plane conveniently crashed. Was he lying on a beach somewhere now with fifty million dollars, a piña colada, and no regrets. Was the plan that Coriander would join him six months or a year from now to live happily ever after in some Latin American haven where there was no extradition? Or, maybe she didn't know anything and the guy really did have an underdeveloped libido and poor eyesight and actually took off without her. Six months, a year later and she'd start all over again with someone else, didn't they all . . . Or, maybe the poor bastard's luck really did run out and he went down in that plane, which still didn't explain what happened to the money. Was it hidden with Coriander or did someone else know where it was . . . Adam shook his head, the whole thing was a series of confusing hypotheses even for him who had lived with it for the past six months. About the only good that came out of it was that it made him forget about his own problems . . .

Not that he still didn't hurt late at night when he was alone or during those moments during the day when he had time to think. Deep down inside, somewhere he couldn't even point to, there was this sick empty feeling that his internist called the beginning of a duodenal ulcer. And what difference did it make what it turned out to be—even after swallowing a glass of chalk and submitting himself to an X-ray—since it wasn't going to change anything or give him back the last ten years of his life . . .

It was all wrong to begin with, now he could say that with absolute certainty even if it didn't make him feel better. If he hadn't gotten shot he never would have met her but getting shot has this way of changing a person's whole perspective on life. Lying there in a gutter and bleeding to death tends to make someone reevaluate his priorities, seeing those flashing red lights upside down and all those horrified faces peering over you while they thanked God it was you and not them gave a guy an instant appreciation for just how tenuous life could be, how senseless to pass through without really feeling anything or loving anyone . . .

When he woke up in the intensive care unit all he saw were beautiful white teeth smiling at him from underneath a mop of black hair and this crisp little white cap. He fell in love. He didn't even know her name or where the hell he was but he fell deeply and profoundly in love. *Eve,* could you get over that, her name was *Eve,* he never would have believed it if it wasn't written on that white plastic name bar clipped above her right breast, the first thing he could read when his eyes finally focused. He was sure he had died and gone to heaven. For the next three weeks Eve changed his catheter tube, rubbed oil on the tip of his penis, changed his sheets more than twice a day, gave him extra alcohol rubs and when he was finally transferred out of intensive care and into a private room she came to visit him every single day.

Never mind about things like gratitude or attraction or timing, it just all seemed so right—Adam and Eve—even down to that Chinese restaurant in Soho—The Garden of Eden—where one of his buddies arranged to have their wedding supper. Six months later Adam was still on disability and taking law courses full-time and Eve was already pregnant. Two years after that and Adam finally got his law degree and left the force permanently when he was hired by the District Attorney to do some low-level investigative work. It was better than trolling the streets as part of the city's front-line force. Penny was a year and a half by then and Eve had quit her job at the hospital to do private-duty work. Life was just coasting along with the usual problems and rewards; the kid was growing up nicely, Eve had time to take cooking lessons, and Adam was enjoying his new position as Special Investigator for the Manhattan D.A. The trouble came at the same time as his big break when he was assigned some major terrorism case and found himself working with a special agent on loan from the FBI's Washington office. They were investigating a cell of the Abu Nidal group that had allegedly set up operations on the Upper East Side. When the case dragged on for months it was only natural that the FBI agent and Adam became friends. By then the guy was hanging out at his house and Eve was trying out her gourmet dinners. They'd hang out around the kitchen table and it was nice, because Adam could see Penny and the guy didn't have to eat all his meals in restaurants or alone in his hotel room. The irony was that eventually the case was put on hold when the suspects did nothing more suspicious than open up a chain of falafel restaurants on Lexington Avenue. Adam and his partner were told they had to wait until something spectacular happened before they could move in; something spectacular did happen only it happened in Adam's kitchen . . .

It was really weird the way Adam first realized what was

going on, not that it didn't take him a while and not that it didn't take a sledgehammer to fall on his head since the affair had been going on for months. They were all sitting around the kitchen table one night—a couple of nights before the case was put on hold—eating pasta and drinking wine and the FBI agent even had a date with him, a woman Eve introduced to him, when Adam saw the look that passed between them—the guy and Eve. What Adam saw in that millisecond changed his life, in that fraction of time that it took for that look to settle in the air over the table before it evaporated when each of them glanced away made him sick. And even though they were all sitting there dressed, laughing and talking and without any flirting or double meanings injected into the conversation, eating pasta and dabbing tomato sauce from the corners of their mouths, sipping wine and spilling drops of it on the table, he knew that these two people had seen each other naked, touched each other's bodies, made love, reached peaks of desire. In the time it took for that fleeting look to cross the table and hang suspended somewhere over the Stella d'Oro bread sticks Adam's entire life flashed before his eyes and with it a history of shared secrets, intimate moments, and all-consuming longings that irrevocably shifted their focus. Adam excused himself, went to the bathroom, and threw up. The scene that followed was almost worse than his realization, with tears and excuses like "We never meant for this to happen" coming from the guy to "I'll always care about you" coming from Eve.

After the separation Adam began sleeping with the woman who had been there that night as witness to the end of his marriage. It was easier to talk about it with someone with whom he could communicate in shorthand without having to explain every detail since she even knew what they were having for dinner that night . . .

Now, a year later and it still hurt like hell and mostly because of Penny but honestly because he had trusted the guy, for Christ's sake they were working together night and day, he was hanging out at his house, playing with his kid, eating his food, guys just didn't do that to each other. Eve was another story, it wasn't exactly a deep sense of betrayal that came out of nowhere because somehow he knew instinctively that they weren't going to last forever. The only thing that still drove him crazy was that every time he thought about her he got that same pain at about the same spot where he took that bullet when it all began . . .

Just off the modern lobby of the Parador el Marques Hotel was a stark restaurant with white stucco walls and unfinished oak tables and chairs. Adam took a table at the far end of the room with a clear view of the entrance. He ordered a beer and when it came he began sipping the froth from over the rim of the glass before he took several long swallows and settled back to review the events of the Vidal case that led up to his trip down to Mexico . . .

Four years ago Danny Vidal arrived in New York with a financial statement listing assets in excess of fifty million dollars in Buenos Aires. Within two months of his arrival Vidal managed to make the right connections and appropriate contacts to put a successful bid on the Inter Federated Bank in New York City.

When Danny Vidal took over Inter Federated Bank it already had a tarnished history of bad loans and undercollateralized mortgages; that was the reason he was able to buy it at such a low price and for so little cash. Nobody wanted another bank failure, least of all the FDIC, which was why Vidal's application to purchase had been so quickly approved by the New York State Banking Commission. Everybody knew that Inter Federated was teetering on the edge of bankruptcy and everybody hoped that the Argentinian would breathe new life into that dying institution. In the two years that Vidal ran the bank it had gone further and further into debt with credit raids, illegal loans and overdrafts. Even more distressing were the large deposits that came out of Argentina as "flight capital" and found their way into Vidal's personal accounts before being transferred out without a trace. In fact, almost all of the money coming from those illegal loans, credit lines and overdrafts went into Vidal's accounts where it remained long enough to show a healthy balance at the end of each month when auditors made routine inspections. A high-tech shell game, Adam judged, now you see it now you don't, except that he couldn't prove anything since all the records and transactions sheets had disappeared along with the cash. What he needed were names, routes the money had taken, and bank statements; what he needed was someone on the inside who was willing to talk.

The break came on the morning of July 4 just as Adam was preparing to take the train down to Washington to visit Penny for the weekend. It seemed that Vidal's assistant, a man who had been unwilling to cooperate since the investigation began, was sufficiently upset about something to want to come downtown to talk. As Adam explained to Eve, he had to be available, holiday or not. Even if the D.A. hadn't already been "airlifted" out to his house in the Hamptons and the others on staff hadn't already left for the country or the beach or made themselves unavailable by hiding behind answering machines in the city, he never would have allowed anyone else to talk to the man. It was his case and he had been working too hard and too long not to follow through. What Adam told Penny was that he would be delayed until the evening.

The air-conditioning in Adam's office was down that July 4 morning. Not only in Adam's office but in the District Attorney's office as well and apparently throughout the entire east wing of the building. Granted that the structure facing the old Criminal Courts on Centre Street was archaic there still was no excuse for an electrical failure. Only last year the building had been completely rewired for individual air-conditioning and heating units in every office. For those who worked weekends, holidays and evenings, there was no longer any problem about suffering through extreme weather without heat or air. Except for this fourth of July, one of the hottest days of the summer with temperatures hovering around ninety-five and recorded humidity off the charts, when the system was down with no one around to fix it.

Fernando Stampa was a small man, perfectly proportioned in miniature and dressed in a slightly worn dark blue suit, white shirt, and maroon tie anchored by an old-fashioned tie bar. On his left hand he wore a wedding ring and a watch with an expansion bracelet, in his right hand he held a crumpled white handkerchief with which he kept mopping his brow. The heat was getting to the man although he may have been perspiring more from sheer nerves.

"Do you have a family here in New York," Adam asked, "because we need a contact number for you today, just routine."

"I have a wife."

"No children?"

Stampa looked anxious. "I had a son once . . ."

"What happened?"

"He was one of the *disappeared,*" the man said quietly.

It didn't quite register. "What do you mean?" Adam asked.

"Fourteen years ago," Stampa began, "during the *Guerra Sucia* or *Dirty War* in Buenos Aires, General Videla and the Junta were responsible for the disappearance of more than eight thousand people. My son was taken away with other students who opposed the Junta."

"What happened to him?"

"We were fortunate, eventually we found his body."

It was hard to find words to comfort the man. "Is that why you left, Mr. Stampa?"

"Too many memories," he said softly.

Adam went on, "You've obviously known Mr. Vidal for years. How long did you actually work for him at the bank in Buenos Aires?"

"Only for about six months but the relationship with Danny

was also a friendship. We came to him when we were trying to find our son."

"And that's when he hired you?"

"Yes, because he knew my son had been picked up by the military and he knew we had no money. He used to pay me even when I didn't come in, when I was out looking for my son."

"Did you ever meet Coriander Wyatt Vidal?"

"Not then, I met her in New York."

"I didn't realize they were married that long."

"They only got married about three and a half years ago but they met when she was his student at the University of Cordoba."

"But she's American, isn't she?"

Stampa nodded. "Her father was the American Ambassador to Argentina."

"Why did the government closed the bank in Buenos Aires."

"They accused the bank of laundering money for the Montoneros."

"Was it?"

"Yes."

"Were you also arrested?"

The man shook his head. "What saved me was that I wasn't officially on the books so the government didn't know I was working there. Also, I didn't happen to be physically at the bank the day the police stormed it."

"Did you know what the bank was doing at the time?" Adam asked, and when Stampa didn't answer added, "Look, I'm not investigating the Credito de la Plata."

Finally, after several minutes, Fernando Stampa described how the Montoneros would embark upon a series of robberies and kidnappings to raise cash to oppose the Junta and how the proceeds would be deposited into accounts in the bank under fictitious names with Danny Vidal overseeing all the financial transactions. "There wasn't anybody who had the least shred of decency who didn't do what they could," Stampa concluded. "It wasn't difficult finding recruits."

"Was your son one of Danny's recruits?"

"My son was an idealist and so became a victim . . ." Again, Stampa fell silent.

Adam tried to piece it all together quickly, to find a connection between a period of violence in the southernmost country in the world, extortion in a New York City bank, and one broken man trying to save the little that was left of his own life. "What about Mrs. Vidal, was she a recruit too?"

"It was different with her," Stampa said quietly, "she was in love with him."

"How did you find out what happened to your son?"

Tears came to the man's eyes. "The government used to drop bodies from helicopters into the Rio de la Plata. We found his body washed up on shore."

"Were the members of the Junta punished?"

Stampa laughed a mirthless laugh. "We have a democracy now in Argentina, which means that our president just pardoned every member of the Junta who had been in jail . . ."

Adam gently steered the conversation back to the point of the man's visit. "I'd like to have your permission to record everything we discuss."

"You promised . . ."

"I promised that nobody would read the transcript unless I asked you first."

He nodded. "Go ahead."

Adam stood. "I've arranged for a stenographer," he said, as he walked toward the door. He was gone only an instant and when he returned he was followed by a woman carrying a small machine covered in heavy plastic. Introductions were made before the woman settled behind Adam's desk, unwrapped the machine, and then waited with fingers poised over the keys. "There are certain formalities, Mr. Stampa," Adam explained, before going on to ask the man if he waived his right to an attorney, to state for the record that he had come down on his own volition without benefit of subpoena or warrant, and to acknowledge that anything he said could and would be used as evidence in a court of law in the event of trial. "Why did you decide to come here? What happened?"

"I'm in trouble," Stampa began, tears welling.

"Why don't you start at the beginning and maybe I can help."

Seemingly hesitant for the moment, Stampa shook his head.

"If you didn't think I could help, Mr. Stampa," Adam coaxed, "you wouldn't have come here."

After a moment or two Stampa took a breath. "A week ago Friday, Danny called me into his office and told me about this deal he was working on in Buenos Aires. But for political reasons his name couldn't appear on any of the papers or checks. He needed a favor."

"Did he explain what the deal was?"

"No, he just said he needed me to sign five blank checks on an account I keep at another bank."

"Would you state the name of the bank, Mr. Stampa."

"Republic Exchange."

"Go on," Adam said, nodding toward the stenographer.

"He said that all he needed was my signature and that he'd make all the necessary deposits in my account to cover any checks he wrote."

"What were you going to gain from this transaction?"

"Nothing," Stampa said quietly. "It was a favor and God knows I owed him a lot of those."

God knows. "Did you sign the checks?"

"Yes."

"What happened then?"

"Nothing happened for five business days and then right before the bank closed for the Fourth of July weekend I was called downstairs by one of the vice presidents."

"Let the record show that was yesterday, July 3, 1992. Please go on, Mr. Stampa."

Stampa looked embarrassed. "All my checks bounced."

"How much money are we talking about?"

"Danny made out each check for two hundred thousand dollars." Again, he looked embarrassed, as if it was his fault.

Adam was stunned, even the stenographer started. "A million dollars?" The man nodded. "The stenographer can't record a nod," Adam managed to say.

"Yes," Stampa replied, "a million dollars."

Adam recovered. "What did the vice president expect you to do?"

"He expected me to cover the checks."

"Did you tell him that it was a transaction between you and Mr. Vidal?"

"I told him there was some mistake."

"Didn't you explain that Mr. Vidal promised to cover those checks by putting money into your account at Republic?"

"No, because then I'd have to give reasons and the deal was confidential, Danny told me not to tell anyone. What I hoped was that there was some kind of mistake and the money was either lost or that it just hadn't cleared my account."

Adam shook his head, finding it hard to grasp, the sheer gall of it all. "Was that the case when you called Republic?"

Stampa took a deep breath. "No," he said softly, "when I called the bank they told me that nothing had been put into my account since I made a deposit several weeks before."

Absolutely unbelievable. "Did you try to reach Mr. Vidal?"

"Yes, but he had already left for the weekend."

"When did he leave?"

"Actually, he never came in at all on the third, he left the bank on the second, at closing time . . ."

"Did you try to reach him at home?"

"Yes, but no one answered the phone."

"And you didn't go over there?"

Stampa looked miserable. "How could I do that? I couldn't just barge in . . ."

The situation was so pathetic that it was almost unbelievable except for someone who knew the man's story. He had already been broken with the disappearance of his son so this latest tragedy merely removed the last shred of trust he had in another human being. "Let's go back a minute, Mr. Stampa, what I don't understand is why Inter Federated called you down when those checks were returned marked 'insufficient funds.' I assume they were returned to Danny Vidal since he was the payee."

"Ordinarily that would have been the case except Danny gave his personal guarantee so the bank cleared my checks for cash."

Adam was visibly shaken. "A million dollars was cleared for cash before Inter Federated got a confirmation of payment from Republic? How did Vidal manage to get someone to do that?"

"He owns the bank, doesn't he? Who was going to refuse him especially since the checks were all made out to him and signed by me, his personal assistant." But his tone suddenly gave way to desperation when he continued, "I owe the bank the money, me, I'm the one who's responsible."

Still, Adam wasn't clear. Something was wrong. "Wait a minute, Mr. Stampa, if Vidal deposits those checks in his accounts at Inter Federated—even as cash—and they bounce five days later, why doesn't Inter Federated simply debit his account and reverse the process to make it as if the transaction never happened so that nobody is out any money."

Stampa smiled sadly. "That would have been the logical thing to do except Danny never deposited the money in any of his accounts."

Adam felt chilled. Carefully, he formulated the words. "Are

you saying that Danny Vidal walked out of the bank before a holiday weekend with a million dollars in cash?"

"It appears so." Stampa asked for some water. Adam filled a paper cup from a cooler that stood in the corner of the room. Adam handed him the cup before sitting down again and asking, "Where is he now?"

"In Mexico."

"Do you know where?"

"Somewhere in Acapulco. He told everybody he was going down to look for a house for tax purposes since he came up with the idea of dividing his time between Acapulco and New York . . ."

A million dollar house no doubt. Still, something was wrong, it made no sense for someone like Vidal to risk everything for a million dollars when he had already bilked the bank for fifty million. Why would he steal what amounted to petty cash from someone who was certain to go to the authorities when he found out that his checks bounced? And continuing on that line of reasoning, why had Vidal done nothing to prevent Stampa from finding out? It made no sense. "What about his wife, is she in Mexico too?"

"No, she's on duty at the hospital."

Adam nodded, gazing off in the distance. "That's right, she's a doctor, touching, he gives heart attacks, she cures them, they're quite a team." What occurred to him then was that perhaps it wouldn't be such a bad idea if he got Stampa to swear out a subpoena for Vidal . . . It also occurred to him that it might not be a bad idea to take a ride out to Brooklyn General and have a word with Vidal's wife . . . Adam wasn't surprised to see Stampa close to tears as he asked, "Will you help me?"

Adam got right to the point, "I'm going to try to make an arrangement to protect you if you give me access to certain bank files and documents. First of all, do you have keys to the bank offices?"

Reaching into his pocket for a handkerchief, the man nodded.

"I assume you also have the names and addresses of most of your depositors."

But this time Stampa proposed a precise deal. "Will you give me immunity if I give you what you want?"

"That's my intention, but I'm going to have to check with the District Attorney." He was being cautious although there was no reason to make the man suffer more than he was already suffering. "Look, you stay here while I try to reach the D.A. at home." It came to Adam suddenly. "Tell me something, what do you think he would have done on Monday if you hadn't come down here today?"

Stampa's color went bad again. "Put me off, told me not to worry, that he'd take care of everything . . ." He shrugged. "Put me on the defensive for not having faith in him. All the usual things . . ."

"He wouldn't be entirely wrong since he seemed always to take care of you in the past." There was something that just wasn't quite right about this whole set-up.

"It was different this time, he betrayed me," the man said through his tears, "he lied to me, he left me no choice."

It was either a question of honor among thieves or misplaced morality. Either situation was a bizarre phenomenon that Adam learned to understand over the years as something that hit most people when their own ass was on the line. But for the moment it was more important that he arrange for that subpoena to be sworn out and the man's statement to be transcribed for signature. Within minutes Adam was on the phone making all the necessary arrangements; within less than an hour the warrant was sworn out and the subpoena was tucked away in his pocket; another half an hour and he was on the *B* train heading for Brooklyn General Hospital to have a word with Coriander Wyatt Vidal . . .

* * *

And now here he was two days later in Chilpancingo, Mexico knowing less than what he knew when he first started this investigation months ago. He heard someone saying his name and looked around to see the agitated owner of Gwenda Charter standing there. Fritz Luckinbill wanted to talk. Didn't everyone, Adam thought, as he stood to shake the man's hand, everybody had a stake in this story and anyway it was only six-twenty. He still had forty minutes until his meeting with the *widow* or the wife—which category she fit into was one of the more fundamental dilemmas in this case . . .

Chapter Eight

Fritz Luckinbill was a large man, lumbering, massive and visibly upset. Red hair flecked with gray, red face etched with blue veins, he appeared devastated by this terrible tragedy that cost him two pilots barely in their prime, a brand-new aircraft, and an unpaid bill of fifteen thousand dollars for the round-trip to Acapulco. The death of the passenger was another matter, one that would undoubtedly bring a lawsuit filed by the family for negligence.

After several minutes of exchanging impressions on the cast of characters, complaining of the heat, and ordering drinks for himself and the charter company owner, Adam finally asked, "Don't you usually get paid in advance?"

There was a tiredness around the man's eyes. "Depends on whether or not I know the customer or if arrangements were made in advance to bill . . ."

"Did you know Danny Vidal?"

"No."

"Why did you extend credit?"

He sighed. "Because the guy ran a bank, how much more solid could you get, and because I was offered the choice of either getting paid up front or getting paid in cash at the other end. The guy's brother was supposedly meeting him in Acapulco with the cash . . ."

"Did you talk to Jorge Vidal since the accident?"

Luckinbill laughed. "Yeah, I talked to him or he talked to me, told me the family was thinking about filing a lawsuit . . ."

"They've got to prove pilot error . . ."

"The Mexicans already put down pilot error on the preliminary report." He leaned forward. "Look, Mr. Singer, I won't waste your time, that's why I wanted to talk to you. Rumor has it that you've got a subpoena for my dead passenger."

Adam was aware of the clattering dishes and two electric fans whirring overhead. "Yeah . . ."

"Which means he's alive and if he's alive the family can't sue for wrongful death," Luckinbill said excitedly.

Adam didn't answer right away, concentrating instead on his beer in front of him. "It's not so simple . . ." He looked up. "Look, why don't you tell me what you found out when you went up to the crash site?"

"How did you know I went up?"

Adam smiled. "Rumor . . ."

Luckinbill took a breath. "I went up there to find the missing black box because without that I can't even prove my pilots' names . . ."

"Don't the Mexicans have it?"

"No, that's the point . . ."

"How can they file a preliminary accident report without it?"

"Because something stinks around here, that's how," Luckinbill said bitterly. "I can't even get my hands on the fucking thing."

"What happened when you went up the mountain?"

Luckinbill sat back in his chair, crossed his arms over his chest and began. "I went up there with *mucho dinero,* spread the word around that I was willing to buy back anything those peasants found."

"Any takers?"

Luckinbill nodded. "Unbelievable the way they grabbed everything they could get their hands on. For a couple of bucks I bought back the air speed indicator and for a twenty I bought one of the chrome hydraulic cylinders and the flex lines." His expression turned suddenly tense. "And here's the best . . ."

"The black box?" Adam prodded.

Luckinbill pulled out a high shrug. "Seems somebody was already up there poking around and walked off with pieces of it . . ."

Adam felt his interest tighten like a cord. "How do you know?"

"An old woman up there told me, even described the magnetic tape wrapped around a metal spool and some silver foil, close enough to what the flight recorder and voice tape look like. Anyway, some guy bought it from her for fifty bucks . . ."

"Do you know who?"

"No idea except according to those mountain people he's a gringo and doesn't have a hair on his head . . ." Luckinbill shrugged. "It's not much to go on I suppose but that's all I could find out."

Adam reached into his pocket for a small pad and a pen. He made a couple of notes. "Did you recognize any of those body parts as either of your pilots?"

Luckinbill made a face. "It's hard to tell for sure but that's why I went over to the morgue." He looked at Adam closely. "That's when I heard about the cremation."

"What cremation?"

"A couple of the Red Cross workers over there told me that Vidal's brother put the remains in the furnace . . ."

What Adam felt was sick disbelief. "What's all the rush about?"

"Something about saving the family all the heartache and red tape when it comes to getting a body out of Mexico . . ."

"Calling what was left in there a *body* is stretching it . . ."

"I gather you went to the morgue . . ."

"Calling that a morgue is stretching it too." He could see Coriander's face suddenly, more than just her face he recalled every tear and blemish and intonation of her voice, every expression, every gesture. He glanced at his watch; she'd be here any minute unless she decided not to show. "Was the widow in on this cremation?"

"I'm not even sure she knows about it. The last I heard she forbid the brother from touching anything. Seems he cremated a torso and seems she swears it's not her husband . . ."

Adam remembered the horrified expression on Coriander's face when she saw the basin on the right. "Did you see the torso?"

Luckinbill nodded.

"What do you remember about it?"

Luckinbill didn't even hesitate. "A lot of black matted hair."

"Are you in a position to say if that torso was one of your pilots?"

"I can swear that it wasn't."

"How?"

"Because both pilots spent some weekend layovers at my house in Greenwich," Luckinbill went on just as matter-of-factly, "They were both fair . . ."

It was tough now but it was going to be even tougher if it ever went to trial. "Are you absolutely certain that Vidal boarded that plane in New York?"

"Absolutely, we've got witnesses who saw him . . ."

"I understand the plane stopped to refuel in Houston . . ."

"I'm checking that out now, trying to find out who was on duty that night . . ."

"What's your best guess?"

"Hard to say since there's not much to latch onto. All that's left of my plane is the outer shell and a couple of pieces of useless equipment that I bought back from those mountain people. And then there's that bald guy who appears out of nowhere and buys back what sounds like pieces of the black box." He seemed to consider if it made sense to go on. Apparently it did. "The only thing I'm sure of is my theory about those trees."

"What trees?"

"The ones on top of the mountain." He leaned forward. "You see, if the plane really plowed into that peak the way the Mexicans claim so they can substantiate pilot error, those trees would've broken in two like so many matchsticks . . ."

"And the trees are still standing," Adam said thoughtfully, "is that it?"

Luckinbill nodded.

Adam tried to make the obvious conclusion sound deliberately dull. "So, judging from those trees the plane exploded in mid-air and landed in pieces on that mountain?"

The message was complete and Luckinbill seemed to relax for the first time since he sat down. "That's the only explanation that keeps coming into my head."

"What's the only explanation, Mr. Luckinbill . . ." Adam needed to hear it from someone else.

"A bomb."

"And what about that poor sonofabitch burning away in that furnace, what's your best guess there?"

Luckinbill shrugged. "Nobody I know, that's for sure . . ."

It still wasn't enough, not even close. What Adam needed was hard evidence—names and accident reports and witnesses—and judging from the rules and regulations around that exclusive club called Mexico that wasn't going to be easy to get. What he also needed was to go to Houston and talk to anyone who had come in contact with the plane, crew, and passenger when it touched down to refuel; he needed to talk to Enrique Sanchez and Jorge Vidal and just about anybody else who was even peripherally involved in this mess. But the most important thing that he needed to do was to remember that everybody was a suspect, including Coriander who had just walked into the restaurant . . .

Chapter Nine

Coriander glanced around the restaurant briefly before she spotted Adam. He was already standing, watching her as she headed over to his table. As she walked, her mind whirled in a million confused directions. The only thing about which she grew more certain with each passing hour was her unwillingness to make the transition to *widow*. She remained wife-in-waiting, waiting for answers to questions that hadn't even been asked, which was why she agreed to meet the man-with-the-subpoena-in-his-pocket.

Adam offered his hand. "Welcome to my office," he said.

She clasped it briefly. "Why?"

"I was going to ask you the same question . . ."

She sat down and crossed her legs under the table. "You should know, you're the one with the subpoena."

"I was asking about the cremation. Why were you refusing to accept those remains as your husband's?"

She went pale on him. What do you mean, *were* refusing? I'm still refusing . . ."

"*Were*," Adam repeated, watching her closely. "Your brother-in-law ordered them into the furnace about an hour ago."

She tensed. "How do you know?"

"The owner of the charter company told me and he found out because he came from the mortuary right before he met me here." If she was lying, she was one hell of an actress. "Look, I'm sorry about this . . ."

She sat there in silence for several moments, her forehead resting on her hands, before she took a deep breath. "It wasn't up to him," she said dully, "it was up to me and I told him not to cremate."

"Well, apparently he didn't listen . . ."

She frowned. "Nothing, nothing was Danny . . ." Danny. Jesus, it was incredible but true that a human being could survive almost anything.

"If you like I could take you over there . . ."

"I can't put out the fire, can I?"

"No, you can't put out the fire," he agreed, feeling incredibly sad.

She wondered, "What about the owner of the charter company, could he identify his pilots?"

This was tough. "I'm not sure," he evaded.

"What about that torso?"

"He didn't recognize it." Adam looked up gratefully when the waiter appeared, then asked Coriander, "Would you like something to eat?"

"My body seems to be going into gastrointestinal shock very nicely on its own, thank you . . ."

He would have smiled if the situation wasn't so desperate. "A drink?"

She folded her hands across her stomach. "Just some tea." She gazed off in the distance as Adam ordered a Coke for himself, no ice, and a tea for her in a flat, idiomatic Spanish. When he finished and the waiter had gone, she went back to her original question. "Why?"

"Because it's just too convenient for someone to get himself killed on the eve of an indictment."

"And I find it incredibly convenient that you showed up to serve a subpoena now . . ." She gestured toward the window and the mountains in the distance.

"There wasn't enough to go on before this."

"I don't understand," she said, shaking her head. "Whatever happened at the bank didn't happen overnight."

Everything they taught him when he started out in this business was useless when it came to her. Weaken them, they taught him, keep them off balance with questions that followed no particular pattern before apologizing for the trouble only to begin questioning them again, all the while deciding if they were worth cultivating or sacrificing. In her case the rules didn't apply from the beginning . . . "Do you want me to explain?"

"If I had my choice I'd want you to go away."

"I don't blame you," he said kindly.

She shrugged. "I'm here to understand . . ."

He didn't hesitate. "Every bank that's chartered in New York State has routine audits. Last month the auditors found a series of irregularities and overdrafts. It seems your husband kept shifting money around so he was always one step ahead of the auditors . . ."

"Except for last month," she interrupted.

Adam nodded. "Either he didn't care any more or he got sloppy but by the end of June there was fifty million dollars missing on the books."

She was beside herself. "It's impossible. If you knew my husband you'd understand that he could never do such a thing." There were tears in her eyes. "How do you know he was even aware of what was going on?"

On the one hand he wanted to explain it to her, on the other he wanted to get up and walk away. And take her with him . . .

"Right before I came to see you at the hospital I met with

someone who offered us partial proof with the promise of more." For the moment Adam decided not to mention Stampa and that million dollars.

"Who?"

"I'm afraid I can't tell you that."

"No," she said softly, "I didn't think you could."

The waiter was back to serve the tea and Coke. When he left again, Adam changed tracks. "Do you really believe your husband is dead?"

"Nobody could have survived that crash," she evaded, her mind still racing. She had no allies, even among those who were trying to prove Danny was alive, there was no one . . .

"Nobody who was actually in it could have survived," Adam agreed.

"Do you have proof that my husband wasn't on that plane?" She clasped her hands together on her lap. Still, they trembled.

"Obviously we've got enough to go on," he bluffed, aware that it was one thing to mislead about evidence and another to mislead about lives.

"That's not an answer."

He leaned forward. "Don't you think I've got better things to do than chase a dead man?"

Right then she detested him, she detested all of them. "I'm not sure," she replied evenly, "because you can put a rubber stamp on anything and make it look official." Courage baby, Danny always told her, when it comes to mindless bureaucrats there is nothing more effective than courage.

"If your husband hadn't gotten himself killed, Mrs. Vidal, the bank would've been closed down by Monday morning and not reopened until all the accounts were balanced and the records audited. And we're talking about thirty-four counts of unlawful loans and fourteen counts of unlawful deposits."

She was more angry than upset. "Where's all the money?"

He was hoping she wouldn't ask, at least not yet. "That's one of the big mysteries unless you can tell me . . ."

It was getting more unbelievable all the time. She began, "You come to the hospital with a subpoena for my husband only minutes after I learned about the accident and then you show up here hoping that I can supply you with the proof you need to make a case." She took a breath and continued, talking even though she saw that he wanted to say something. "It's painful enough that you're accusing my husband of abandoning me but it's inhuman to accuse him of staging his own death by killing two innocent men just to avoid a business crisis."

What was he supposed to say, that if her husband did abandon her he didn't deserve the fifty million dollars that he got away with? What Adam wished was that he had all the answers; what he really wished was that the questions didn't apply to her husband; what he wished even more was that they hadn't met under these circumstances. "Do you want me to explain how the money disappeared?"

Her expression was anything but friendly. "I suppose it's better than asking me to help you figure out where it went."

Adam wondered briefly how it happened that he was suddenly on the defensive. "Your husband opened several accounts at Inter Federated with deposits sometimes as small as a couple of hundred dollars before he exceeded the legal lending limits imposed on every officer of every bank. What he did was write bad checks that overdrew those accounts by thousands and borrow through credit lines that overextended them by hundreds of thousands." The best was about to come, which was certain to evoke an instant response from her. "For the past six months he's been transferring that money out of those accounts, leaving no visible trace of where the money went, and putting the bank and his depositors at risk as well as his position with the New York State Banking Commission . . ."

Not to mention their lives. She sprang to his defense. "It's impossible," she exclaimed passionately, "money means nothing to him, he would never do anything like that . . ."

"Maybe he's got expenses you don't know about it," Adam suggested, suddenly hating what he did for a living.

She had no intention of letting him get away with that. "Like what?" she dared him.

What touched Adam was her vulnerability; what baffled him was that husband of hers and just what the hell he was doing. "There're a lot of possibilities in this case," he began, and was surprised when she interrupted.

"Even if I was willing to assume that my husband had another life"—she paused—"another wife or a mistress"—she paused again—"isn't fifty million dollars a little extravagant?"

It wasn't that her logic was faulty it was just that he had seen too much in his life to be surprised by anything. He told himself to sound concerned. "It's a little irresponsible . . ." Irresponsible, as in "Call me irresponsible . . ." For some reason right then he noticed that she was still wearing black and except for her hair, which she had gathered into a clip at the nape of her neck, she hadn't changed. "Probably the first thing to do is to find out what really happened to the plane."

She said, "If your thesis is correct and my husband extorted all that money he's certainly worth more alive than dead."

"I was thinking more along the lines of his having planted a bomb on board before he got off, say, in Houston . . ."

"My husband isn't a murderer."

"Are you sure about that?"

She was furious. "Of course I'm sure."

And he was pushing it. "Tell me something, what do you stand to gain from your husband's death?"

"We never discussed it."

"Why?"

"We just never did. My husband is . . ." Again, those tenses. "He's only twelve years older and there were always other things to worry about." What she didn't explain was after all they had gone through she was unable to discuss death when it came to him. And as unable as she was to discuss death Danny was unwilling to discuss its opposite. When we get settled in New York we'll talk about having a baby; after the apartment is finished we'll see about getting pregnant; when business at the bank improves, when hours normalize at the hospital, when the Rio de la Plata freezes over, when, when, when . . . "There's something you should know," she began in a halting voice. She took a breath. "As much as I want to believe that my husband's alive it's not possible."

Adam waited, feeling a combination of frustration and fury that this woman was in this position. Coriander stopped to swallow her tears before her words came out in a rush of emotion, "I'm pregnant and we loved each other and it would take a monster to do something like this." She couldn't go on but she didn't really have to since it was clear by Adam's expression that he understood. He thought about Eve and he realized it was the second time in his life that he found himself emotionally distressed to the point of nausea . . . "I don't know what to say," he said and then, as if it was the most natural thing to do, reached across the table to take her hand. To his surprise she didn't withdraw but rather seemed to gather comfort from those several moments of contact. "Neither do I," she finally said before she reclaimed her hand to wipe away more tears.

"Are you sure he knew?"

"Yes," she said quietly and with great dignity, "he absolutely knew."

Adam just sat there lost in thought before he finally spoke. "Look, I don't know anything about your relationship except sometimes people get themselves into a bind where they become temporarily insane and do things they would never do if they were thinking clearly . . ."

"Danny would never do this, he'd never leave me in this position," she said quietly.

Adam answered in a low voice, "I need your help, I started to explain back in the mortuary . . ." He gestured toward the window.

"I'm well aware," she said, "You want me to help you build a case against my husband . . ."

He felt like hell. "You've got a bigger stake in this than anybody. Don't you want to find out if your husband is alive and if he is where and why and all the other questions that go along with it?"

That was quite a package. Did she want to find out if her husband was alive and be forced to confront him so she could understand how he could have done such a thing to her, to them . . . But the answer was clear in her mind. "Yes," she said simply.

Still, it wasn't quite enough. After coming this far he knew enough to turn it around again. "Even if it means he ends up in jail?"

Even if it meant that it ended with her heart broken and her life in shambles. "Yes," she said again before settling back in her chair.

"Can I ask you a few questions now?" he asked gently.

She nodded.

"Did you know the plane stopped to refuel in Houston?"

"Yes."

"Who told you?"

"My brother-in-law."

"How did he know?"

"Because my husband called him from Houston, at least that's what he said."

"Did your husband call you from Houston?"

"I was on duty all weekend at the hospital."

"Did he call you there?"

"No."

"Is there an answering machine at your apartment?"

"Yes."

"Did you get any messages that weekend?"

"Only a couple of hang-up calls but Danny would never hang up, he'd leave a message."

If he weren't playing dead he'd leave a message . . . "Why didn't you go with him to Acapulco?"

"A holiday weekend in trauma is like combat duty. Nobody would voluntarily change to take on that shift."

He decided to risk it . . . "I understand you met your husband during the Junta in Argentina . . ."

She went along with it . . . "I was his student."

"And I understand your husband was involved in the opposition against the military."

Her expression was wise. "Is that your mystery witness?"

"When you do an investigation you talk to everyone."

She looked at him a few moments before she spoke. "Fernando Stampa never got over the loss of his son . . ."

"Do you blame him?"

"Of course I don't blame him but he also never forgave Danny for not finding him . . ."

"How do you know that?"

"Because we all live with the guilt that we survived while people we loved didn't."

"Did you lose anybody close to you?"

"I lost my best friend." She smiled sadly. "The irony is that if I hadn't lost Hernando I probably would have never married Danny." Adam listened as she began the story.

She met Hernando in that same *boliche* near the University where she would meet Danny several weeks later. She had wandered in to study one afternoon to try and get through Borges's essay on Don Quixote and Hernando was playing tango music on his *bandoneon*, rehearsing for the evening's performance. He lingered at her table and what began as idle conversation about Borges and the tango ended with dinner and an intense political discussion on the situation in Argentina.

Hernando Sykes was editor of the University newspaper, a daily that systematically attacked the regime and for which he wrote an editorial listing names, ages and all available details of every person arrested by the secret police. He held to the notion that giving the *disappeared* an identity not only made them real people rather than statistics but also gave their family and friends the support to demand their condition and crime. As time went on the mothers and grandmothers of the Plaza de Mayo did more than just name their missing children and grandchildren, they supplied photographs that Hernando also printed in his newspaper.

From the beginning Coriander and Hernando shared an attraction that transcended the physical, more a recognition of each other's appeal without any expectation for either to act upon it. Although they genuinely loved each other, neither held any illusion about the limitations of their relationship. It turned out to be moot anyway since several weeks later Coriander met Danny and several weeks after that began a love affair.

Hernando was a pretty boy with dark hair and dark eyes, quiet and intense, tall and lanky, giving the impression of wisdom beyond his years. He had the patrician features of his Argentinian mother—dark hair, slim nose, high cheekbones, sculptured mouth and the candid brown eyes and ruddy complexion of his Scottish father. He and Coriander met when he was already a member of the Montoneros, one of Danny's disciples, a militant Marxist who believed in violence as the only way to achieve democracy. Even the beret and beard he wore were to cultivate the image of Ché . . .

One weekend in late summer Coriander, Danny and Hernando decided to drive to Buenos Aires. Danny had a meeting at one of the Montonero safe houses in La Boca, the working class neighborhood along the Riachuelo Canal, while Coriander and Hernando went to hear tango music and dance at a club called La

Verduleria on Avenida Corrientes. The understanding was that if Danny didn't show up before the club closed they would all meet back at the house in La Boca.

Avenida Corrientes was one of the busiest thoroughfares in Buenos Aires, known as the "Avenue that never sleeps," similar to Times Square, Pigalle, Piccadilly. Neon lights, fast-food restaurants and illuminated tubes known as "kioscos" lined the street; movie theatres were everywhere as were those postage-stamp size bookstalls with cafés tucked in the back that sold everything from foreign newspapers to vintage editions to the latest bestsellers—all government approved and censored.

Once a mariner's hang-out, La Verduleria had been renovated with upscale pretensions. A dwarf minded the door, guiding people to their tables while a singer opened the show with an abysmal imitation of Frank Sinatra, and a band played *cumbias, sambas* and *tangos* beginning at three in the morning. Coriander and Hernando arrived in time to dance.

Those were dangerous times in Argentina. The government hardly needed an excuse for violence, a few lines recited from a Pablo Neruda poem on armed struggle or a passage or two from Mao might be enough. More than two people together was considered a conspiracy, a threat to national security, which meant that gatherings in private houses were avoided. Instead, people met in public places—restaurants, the race track, soccer games, the opera, movies, on street corners, buses—anywhere that was blatant and obvious and didn't arouse suspicion. By five-thirty, Coriander was growing anxious about Danny and what was going on with his meeting back in La Boca. She asked Hernando to take her home.

They had just exited La Verduleria and were crossing Corrientes, walking arm in arm, when it happened. A gray Ford Falcon screeched to a halt next to them and three men piled out, rushing forward to surround them. Out of the shadows and silence came the sound of leather soles trampling the pavement, heavy breathing and grunts as those monsters began wielding their fists and clubs. Even the dwarf had taken refuge inside La Verduleria at the first screech of brakes, closing the door behind him. The bouncer locked it. Days later someone who had been inside when everything was going on mentioned to someone else, who told Danny, that through it all the music played on to drown out the screams of a woman in the street.

It took only an instant for Coriander to realize that Hernando was their target and not her. Already down, he was writhing in pain as the men worked him over, one holding him by the hair and slapping him repeatedly in the face, another removing his shoes and belt, yet another kicking him—*whomp* went the leather boot into Hernando's ribs.

Coriander was right in the middle of the melee, grabbing Hernando's shirt, clutching his arm, hanging onto him as he was beaten. And through it all, half out of hysteria and half out of instinct, she kept screaming his name over and over as if by giving him an identity she could guarantee his future existence. Within the first ten seconds of the skirmish she lost her shoes and ripped her dress; within the next thirty seconds she was punched in the right cheek and in the mouth, kicked in the stomach and flung off to the side where she bounced into a group of on-lookers who immediately disengaged themselves and moved away. Nobody wanted anything to do with her . . . Once more she was back in the fray, clawing and scratching and pleading, ducking to avoid the blows and the clubs, wrapping herself around the boy, clinging to him as he was pulled nearer to the car. It was useless. Shoved again, she landed in a heap in the street, realizing that this was not a random attack and that they must have known Hernando would be in Buenos Aires for the weekend. It was only after the car had screeched off, leaving an atmosphere of terror and relief in its wake, that Coriander managed to stand. People came to life then, daring to move about and whisper among themselves, traffic was once again in motion and even the policemen who had been patroling Corrientes peeked out from doorways where they had ducked when it all began.

Coriander refused help from everybody who offered her either a lift home or to a hospital. Disgusted by their sudden concern, she ignored them all and concentrated on finding her shoes, which she eventually located underneath a car. She sat on the edge of the curb to put them on. Her mind raced with a thousand alternatives until, without any thought to time or distance, she started off in the direction of La Boca, carried along more by anger than energy. But it was miles away and already the sun was coming up over the buildings on Avenida Corrientes. Clothes torn, hair wild, bruised and beaten, she kept walking, ignoring the cars that slowed and their occupants who leaned out windows to stare. After ten blocks or so, she finally gave in when a *collectivo* stopped along its regular route. She got on. Her fatigue was overwhelming, a pain cut through her in the middle of her chest. She watched out the window as the bus drove down Avenida Pedro de Mendozo and across Nicolas Avellaneda Bridge. On the Calle Necochea she got out and continued on foot along the Riachuelo Canal toward Danny's safe house. Past the rowdy cantinas and flashing lights, she kept on going, stepping over stereo speakers that had been placed out on the sidewalk and that blasted rock music, past the hawkers who tried to lure her into the strip joints, past the sheet-iron houses painted in bright colors—orange, blue, red—with metal birdcages hung over New-Orleans-style balconies, all backdropped by murals of dark, stooped figures scurrying like ants against florid scenes of the docks.

When Danny opened the door and saw her standing there in that condition he almost collapsed from the shock. Falling upon her, he cradled her in his arms, kissing the bruises, gathering her up to carry her inside the house. It took only a sentence to explain what had happened, that the Junta had taken Hernando; another sentence to say that their only hope was to go to the Embassy and enlist her father's help. Danny agreed that it was only because of

Palmer's good standing with the Junta that Coriander's life had been spared. What none of them knew that night was that a tape had been running in the house in La Boca and everything discussed during Danny's meeting had been recorded, which meant that the generals sitting in the Casa Rosada had already informed Palmer Wyatt that his daughter was injured. Even before Danny and Coriander got into the car for the drive across the city, Palmer was already waiting for them.

In silence they drove, Coriander sitting very close to Danny, her head on his shoulder, her hand on his thigh. The car approached the Embassy gate and Danny coasted to a stop. Two guards emerged, one walking over to the driver's side, the other over to Coriander, both shining lights just as Palmer came rushing out of the house.

Without a word Coriander opened the door and stepped out of the car while Danny got out as well to lean over the roof. Within seconds Palmer was next to her, caressing her face and pressing her hand to his lips, too overcome with emotion to speak. All he could manage at first were disjointed exclamations of horror before he began mumbling over and over, "This wasn't supposed to happen to you, oh God, this wasn't supposed to happen." But Coriander was already out of his embrace and with tears streaming down her face accused, "You knew, even before we got here, you knew . . ." Later, Danny would admit that he had never seen such raw emotion on the man's face as when he took out a handkerchief to wipe the blood from Coriander's mouth. "Thank God you're safe," was all the man could manage in a trembling voice.

"They took Hernando," she cried, "they beat him and took him away in a car. Please find him, do something . . ."

What was clear was that Palmer was less prepared for his daughter's request than he was for her physical condition. He looked past her then, across the top of the car toward Danny. "How could you let this happen?"

"I could ask you the same question," Danny said, glaring at Palmer.

"Stop this," Coriander cried, "you're wasting time."

Still, Palmer was reluctant to commit himself. "What makes you think I've got the power to do anything?" he argued. "I'm only a guest here . . ."

"If you didn't have any power I'd be where Hernando is right now," she said through clenched teeth. "Please find him and save his life."

Palmer seemed to consider before turning to walk into the sentry hut to pick up the phone. Coriander and Danny's eyes met over the top of the car; one call was all it took . . . Within minutes Palmer was back in the courtyard. "He's in Puesto Vasco . . ."

She gasped. Puesto Vasco, the prison in the basement of the Naval Engineering School. "It's over," she wept, "he's dead."

"Not necessarily," Palmer said comfortingly, "he's only been charged . . ."

She whirled around. "Charged? As if he'll get a fair trial or be allowed even to make a phone call . . ." She clutched at her father's shirt, "Stop treating me as if I'm stupid . . ."

The man seemed suddenly to gain control. "Come home," he bargained, "promise that you'll never see him again"—he gestured toward Danny—"and I'll try to help, just come home."

"Home?" she cried, "I have no home."

They argued for several minutes more, Palmer begging her to return and Coriander refusing to comply. Finally, Palmer simply gave up. "There's nothing I can do for your friend," he said sadly.

As Danny and Coriander drove through the gates and out of the compound the last image in the rearview mirror was of Palmer Wyatt looking helpless and dejected, as if he had just lost a child. Coriander kept saying the same thing over and over, how her father knew what had happened even before they got there.

Danny didn't argue. The problem was that neither knew just how much Palmer had been told.

When they got back to La Boca they began calling everybody they could think of to enlist their help. Predictably, they came up against the same reaction every time—where people turned deaf and dumb, hanging up telephones quickly, pretending not to be home, begging not to be involved. They remained at La Boca for the next several days, all their time and thought consumed with finding Hernando and saving his life, until the initial shock subsided. When they returned to Cordoba they kept trying although after a while Hernando became part of the growing list of the *disappeared* until he and the others faded into a painful abstraction.

The official reason given for Hernando's arrest was his subversive activities connected to that newspaper at the University of Cordoba. The public trial was for the benefit of the world while the verdict was for the benefit only of Argentina. The sentence was for Hernando alone. He was paraded before a panel of judges, found guilty, sentenced to death, and whisked back to prison. Six months later Danny left Cordoba for Buenos Aires to run the Credito de la Plata Bank, only to vanish himself the following winter.

Years later she regretted that moment more than any other, as if she had chosen her own life over Hernando's, abandoning him by refusing to relinquish Danny.

"So Hernando is one of the *disappeared*, which is a polite way of saying he's dead," Adam said.

That was the moment she probably should have told Adam the rest of the story, but leaving it in a suspended state of ambiguity was something that had already become a habit. She thought about it now, what Danny told her, how only days before the Junta closed the bank and before he left her, Hernando reappeared. Minus his hands and with a *bandoneon* strapped around him, he was deposited in front of La Verduleria one night. It was Danny who Hernando called and Danny who raced to Avenida Corrientes. The club was mobbed that night. The dwarf had a new uniform.

"Hernando was more than just another victim of the regime, he was my victim . . ." Even if she had wanted to explain then, she couldn't. Turning when someone called her name, she saw her father. Freshly shaven with traces of white talc on his face, showered with his hair still damp and combed straight back, Palmer Wyatt kissed his daughter on the top of her head before introducing himself to Adam. He sat down next to his daughter. "This is pretty unusual," he said, "isn't it—carrying a subpoena around for a dead man?"

"Very," Adam admitted.

"Then why are you doing it?"

"Because he doesn't believe Danny is dead," Coriander answered, her eyes on Adam.

"Do you have a reason to believe that?"

"Enough." Adam left it vague.

Glancing at his daughter, Palmer asked gently, "Is there anything I can do to help?"

Coriander shook her head. "I don't think so."

Palmer seemed troubled. "Look, I'm afraid I've got some bad news," he began. "It seems Jorge ordered the remains into the furnace."

"I know," she said, "Mr. Singer told me."

"Who told you about the cremation?" Adam asked.

"Jorge Vidal," Palmer replied.

Adam merely nodded. The waiter appeared and Adam asked for the check, looking distracted as he did so. After the waiter left, Adam turned his attention back to Palmer Wyatt. "Did Jorge Vidal mention anything else?"

Palmer shook his head. "We don't exactly have the kind of relationship where he confides in me . . ."

"Nothing about the black box?"

"Nothing," Palmer said as the waiter returned with the check. "I hope you're not leaving on my account . . ."

Adam shook his head. "No, as a matter of fact I've got an appointment with a priest," he said, reaching into his pocket for some money.

Coriander asked, "What priest?"

Adam looked at Palmer before answering. "It seems one of the local residents had a vision"—he purposely left it vague—"Saw Jesus on the side of the road between Cerro el Burro and Chilpancingo."

"What does that have to do with anything?"

Adam stood. "I'm always interested in the spiritual side of things." Palmer stood as well and extended his hand. "It was nice meeting you." The men shook hands.

She surprised him, "Will I hear from you?"

He said, "I'll be in touch." Their eyes met.

She surprised him again, "Did that local resident who saw Jesus also see the accident?"

"I honestly don't know what he saw," Adam answered as he reached into his pocket for a card. Turning to Palmer, he asked, "Are you going to be in New York for a while?"

"Yes and in Washington," he answered, also reaching into his pocket for a card. He turned it over to scribble something on the back. "Here are all my numbers in Buenos Aires as well as in Washington and New York."

Adam slipped the card into his pocket. "Take care of yourself," he said, looking at Coriander, vowing not to get caught up in any emotional booby traps from now on. He might as well have vowed to stop breathing since this case was mined from start to finish—ever since he saw her in that trauma unit. "I'll talk to you in New York." He hoped his words sounded the way he intended, a vague suggestion of an official promise that held only professional motives. He walked across the room and out the door. When he was gone Palmer finally spoke. "I don't trust him."

"You don't have to trust him," Coriander said gently.

"I don't trust what he's doing," Palmer amended.

"He's trying to find Danny."

"I don't like his reasons."

"The reasons don't really matter."

Palmer reached over to take her hand. "He's dead, Coriander."

A small muscle worked in her jaw. "I'll believe it when I've got something, anything, that proves he was on that plane."

Palmer lowered his voice. "At least for the sake of your child, Coriander," he whispered, "you should be aware of the repercussions. Don't you realize that D.A. can keep the subpoena open indefinitely and you'll never collect one penny after you sue the charter company. As long as there's any doubt that Danny died in that crash, you won't even be able to bring a suit against them."

She was only mildly surprised. "I have no intention of suing the charter company," she said before asking, "And how did you happen to know about that subpoena anyway?"

"Jorge told me."

The annoyance was evident. "What else did he tell you?"

"He told me that the bank is insolvent so it might be wise not to dismiss your option about suing so quickly. More than insolvent, he tells me that it's about to be shut down on Monday by the New York State Banking Commission, which means whatever assets your husband had will be seized." Palmer looked concerned. "How do you expect to maintain that apartment?"

"I don't," she said simply.

Palmer tried a different approach. "Danny wouldn't approve of this alliance you seem to be forming with this man."

"Danny isn't here," she retorted. Not that the thought hadn't already occurred to her. But as quickly as it had she dismissed it.

She wasn't the least concerned about approval or permission, especially from her father but more especially from her husband. The only thing that mattered was finding out if their life together had been a complete and total lie and that was incentive enough to form an alliance with just about anybody.

"Jorge intends to give you the urn filled with Danny's ashes."

"Tell him not to bother."

"It's protocol, Coriander," Palmer insisted gently.

"Then you take it," she said, "that's your department."

"You've got to start facing reality and thinking with your head instead of your heart."

She turned so he wouldn't see the tears. The point was that she *was* facing reality or she would be willing to behave as the perfect grieving Argentine wife and take that bloody urn filled with those unknown ashes. But even Danny would know better than to expect her to do something like that. What was strange was that her emotions kept flipping back to the beginning when she first loved him and lost him. Somehow she kept imagining herself among those women who marched in the Plaza de Mayo so long ago, the ones whose husbands and sons had *disappeared . . .*

Part II

"Shootin' the gun, it made me feel the whole madness comin' out. The whole neighborhood is full of guys like me, fathers and killers: make a life, take a life . . ."

ANTHONY, age 17
Trauma unit patient, Brooklyn General Hospital, 1992

"First we kill all the subversives; then we kill their collaborators; then . . . their sympathizers; then . . . those who remain indifferent; and finally we kill the timid."

GENERAL IBÉRICO SAINT-JEAN
Governor, Buenos Aires, 1975

Chapter Ten

It was payday in Patagonia. Forty-six million four hundred thousand dollars in large denomination bills were being transported in a twin-engine Cessna that was just touching down on a makeshift landing strip on an *estancia* along the banks of the Beagle Channel near Ushuaia. Charles Darwin wandered Patagonia all the way down to the southernmost city on earth, Ushuaia, to study the terrain and the Indians. After eight years of suffering the desolation of that remote country he returned to England to give the world his theory of evolution, which somehow didn't include God . . .

In the distance the jagged peak of Monte Olivia rose one or two thousand feet surrounded by the five rounded hills known as the Cinco Hermanos, all capped with snow and overlooking the densely wooded forest on either side of the Beagle Channel.

The money had been packed in forty-one shoe boxes, divided so that one million fit tightly into one without the bills getting damaged or torn. The boxes themselves came from all over the world, some from Gucci and Weston, others bearing the mark of Florsheim and Bally, still others from discount shoe chains called

Eram in France and Fayva in America, all contained in two suitcases made of parachute material that expanded with their contents.

The aircraft was piloted by an old Yugoslav who years before had settled within a small Yugoslavian community in Porvenir, a town on the Chilean side of the Straits of Magellan. Once the pilot's dream had been to fly for Aerolineas Argentinas and save enough money to return a hero to his native town in Croatia. Failure was undoubtedly the reason why the man got drunk in the same bar near a Chilean naval base after each short hop across the Straits. Afterward, almost as a ritual, he would drive down to the ferry dock in Porvenir to read the sign pointing out that Yugoslavia was a mere 18,662 kilometers from the Chilean Tierra del Fuego.

Near the landing strip on that estancia where the plane touched down was a pebbled beach, deserted except for one man who waited, standing amidst a flock of sea birds, his hiking boots crunching over mussel and crab shells each time that he shifted impatiently from one foot to the other. Nearby a pair of black-and-white plovers shrieked and strutted in circles around a community of fallen penguins, the dead birds resembling small children dressed in formal burial suits. The man himself was stocky, with a body of fallen muscles, a ruddy complexion and head, face, brows and eyelids devoid of any hair. The weapon slung over his shoulder was a Belgian FNL assault rifle, the pistol in the waistband of his pants was a Halçon.

MacKinley Swayze was many things to a select group of people around Latin America, even though his career as a mercenary began on the other side of the world. His love of war and weapons had led him from a factory job in Altoona, Pennsylvania to Cuba in the fifties and then to Vietnam in 1969 where he worked as an airplane mechanic for the Viet Cong, servicing the Soviet transport planes that ferried North Vietnam troops in and out of Hanoi. He distinguished himself, however, in the field of munitions by concocting an altimeter bomb made from trotyl trinitrotoluene, or TNT, a material usually used for blasting in artillery shells. Swayze discovered that the chemical, in big enough quantities, was capable of blowing up a plane, specifically an American 707 that was leased from a stateside charter company that flew almost half of the 101st Airborne out of Saigon one weekend. Swayze bought the altimeter for the bomb in a PX on an American Army base, concealed it together with the explosives in a mess kit and set the timer so the plane blew up as it was in an ascent pattern over the South China Sea. To his credit there wasn't a single civilian casualty.

He wasn't unattractive, despite the ravages of alopecia. In fact, his glittering black eyes set in that perfectly hairless face and head were almost sensual, the way they took everything in, to heart, to mind, to memory. Clinging to the memory of his teenage Cuban bride who died in childbirth on the eve of Batista's fall, Swayze had long since given up on women. Or, perhaps that skinny Cubana with missing teeth and bruised knees died from an advanced case of gonorrhea, it was hard to say. Whatever the cause, Swayze disappeared shortly after her death and the death of the boy infant. Between Cuba and El Salvador, Swayze dropped out of sight; out of commission some claimed, out of his mind others argued, sick and demented with grief, while a few swore he was none of those things, certainly somewhere in Latin America training commandos for revolutions to come. Sometime in the early seventies he turned up in Argentina where, along with several militant Jesuit priests, a few former right-wing Catholic pro-Peronists and a couple of upper-middle class intellectuals with a fascination for violence, he founded the Montoneros. Or, more precisely, refounded the Montoneros since they had been around for a hundred years before Peron as *gauchos* and *caudillos* who clashed with Spanish troops over the liberation of Argentina.

* * *

Standing on the Patagonian beach on that freezing July 6 day in the middle of a typical Argentine winter, Swayze's eyes never left the door of the Cessna. His expression alternated between truculence and quiet despair as he watched the plane's engines shut down. The wind howled, carrying gusts of water from the sea that pelted the craft's windows. A canvas staircase swung down from the open hatch, dangling back and forth in the wind. A solitary passenger appeared. In one hand the man carried a black attaché case while the other hand gripped the twisted rope banister. Reaching the last rung on the ladder, he stepped onto the matted sand, shoving his free hand into the pocket of his trenchcoat. With his head buried in his turned-up collar, he walked backward several steps, forward several more, sideways to avoid the wind and water, making his way toward the welcoming committee of one.

Swayze greeted him with pure joy, shifting his rifle to the side to gather him up in a bear hug. "Fancy meeting you here at the end of the earth, Danny Vidal." Laughing and slapping his back, Swayze released him to reach for his attaché case.

Danny swung the case out of reach, his dark eyes sparkling as he looked deeply into Swayze's. "It's been a long time, Mac," he said, speaking in a soft lilting accent, a small smile playing at the corners of his mouth. *"Mucho tiempo,"* he added, his eyes focused over the man's head, searching the beach as far as he could see for unexpected complications.

"Stampa went to the District Attorney," Swayze announced.

"That wasn't completely unexpected," Danny said easily. "How do you know?"

"A Special Investigator for the D.A. went down to Chilpancingo with a subpoena in his pocket addressed to you."

At first it was almost comical although when he responded there was neither mirth nor levity in his tone. "A subpoena about what?"

"That million dollars," Swayze replied, motioning ahead toward the Cherokee jeep parked on the sand several feet away.

"He's been hanging around your wife too," he added, casting a sideways glance.

She was too smart, his Coriander, too tough, too trusting to believe he could have arranged his own death, she wouldn't buy it for a minute. Danny said nothing as he followed Swayze toward the jeep. "You're usually so careful, Danny boy," the man said, "but this was a big mistake." Swayze paused, nodding toward the old Yugoslav who approached with a suitcase in either hand. "We'll talk about it in the car." Setting one of the valises down at the back of the Cherokee, the pilot hoisted the other inside next to it before he waited to be paid. Swayze reached inside a pocket and took out an envelope, handing it over to the man. "I'll be in touch, Milos," he said. The Yugoslav nodded, shoved the envelope into his belt, barely looking at either man before turning to head back to his plane. Unstrapping his weapon, Swayze leaned inside the jeep to place it on the rear seat before straightening up to hold open the door for Danny. He adopted a tone of paternal regard when he asked, "What the hell did you do that for, *hombre,* a million dollars . . ."

"For Coriander," Danny said simply before climbing into the car.

Swayze shook his head as he walked around to the other side, opened the door and climbed in. He just sat there for a moment without touching the keys or the ignition. "How is she supposed to get the money?" he finally asked. "You can't send it in monthly payments with a return address on the envelope for Christ's sake, *hombre.*" Shaking his head again, he reached over to tousle Danny's hair. "Maybe you intend to deduct it as alimony on your tax return." He smiled.

"It's all arranged," Danny said, before gazing off with vague uncertainty across the choppy waters.

"You know, Danny, I love you like a son and I know these kinds of feelings for a woman, you know I do, but this involves more than just us, this involves a lot of other people." He paused before reverting once again to a more jocular tone. "So, what's it all about, a farewell gift of a million, is that it? A little generous even for you, isn't it?"

"What difference does it make? I'm dead, remember."

"Danny, listen to me," Swayze said seriously, "leaving behind a trail of emotion is going to make people wonder if you're really dead. It only takes one ambitious D.A.'s assistant to sit on this thing. He'll watch Coriander for as long as it takes, he'll do it in his off-hours and believe me, it's no hardship and no trouble." He rolled down the window to spit before rolling it up again. "There're worse jobs, *hombre,* than calling on a beautiful woman every once in a while for questioning. Believe me, he's got no reason to let go of this thing if he feels there's the slightest doubt. You just better not even think about contacting her, you hear me? Just forget it," he said again, "or everything we've worked for will be ruined."

Everything would be ruined . . . They had been on the verge of ruin so many times that Danny couldn't even count and every time he had come up with a solution to save them . . . The last time was in the late seventies when he found the means to generate enough income for the group for years to come. He decided back then that what was needed was a bank through which all revenues from kidnappings and robberies could be laundered. But banks cost money, which was how Danny came up with an idea that not only produced enough cash to buy that bank but also made a political statement that was heard throughout Argentina.

The director of a leading grain and flour monopoly with mills throughout the world and headquartered in Buenos Aires was followed as he left his house one morning. Diverted from the main road by "policemen" holding a battery-operated traffic light, he was ambushed further along by about twenty "telephone repairmen," in reality four combat platoons from the Eva Peron column of the Montoneros. Within hours Swayze had composed a "war communiqué" announcing that the man would be put on trial for "crimes against the workers." The main charge was that the government was hoarding goods to force prices up to benefit the corporation which in turn gave kickbacks to several highly placed members of the Junta. It was Danny who set the price on the man's head of sixty million dollars, the largest ransom in history, and which the conglomerate paid within one week in return for the safe release of the executive. That accomplished, the Montoneros went on an aggressive publicity campaign, putting up giant billboards around Buenos Aires, taking out ads in Western newspapers, and distributing dozens of truckloads of food and clothing to the residents of those working class barrios and *villas miserias*, announcing to the world that the people's money was finally being returned to its rightful owners.

Of the sixty million paid as ransom, ten million was used not only to feed the people and for advertising but also to buy arms, ammunition, and to replenish Montonero safe houses and *estancias* scattered throughout the country. The remaining fifty million was used as payment for the Credito de la Plata bank. The Montoneros were back in business. Danny Vidal had a new career. Coriander was another story . . .

The good times lasted until 1976 when General Videla came to power. It took only months before the Junta shut down the bank and arrested its officers. Danny was the only one who managed to escape, to Havana with most of the cash. Ten years, six months, three weeks, and fourteen days later and the money was almost gone, used to support a dying revolution. The Soviet Union was bankrupt with Communism deemed a bad investment. Cuba stood alone . . . That was when Danny appeared in New York to start all over again, to resuscitate the Montoneros for yet another round.

While he was still in Havana, Danny learned that the Inter Federated Bank in New York was for sale. He made the right contacts in certain financial circles to negotiate successfully for its purchase while devising a five-year plan to raise another fifty million dollars. Every month Fernando Stampa would carry a briefcase containing six hundred thousand dollars in cash to Havana, interest from depositors' accounts. Swayze would be waiting to deposit the money into the Cuban National Bank where it would be available to buy arms, feed troops and support ideology. Unfortunately, the arrangement lasted only six months before Inter Federated plunged into irreparable financial disaster. There was only three million six hundred thousand dollars in the Montonero coffers in Havana, only forty-six million four hundred thousand needed to reach that fifty million . . .

As time went on and the bank slumped further into the red, the only solution left for Danny was to use depositors' *capital* instead of *interest* to finance the Montonero base of operations in Cuba. Revolution didn't come cheap. There were just no bargains when it came to saving the world. After a short while misappropriating money and bouncing checks became a daily routine in order to accumulate those millions.

Months before that July 4 weekend Danny was already aware that the New York State Banking Commission and the District Attorney's office were conducting an investigation that would eventually lead to his indictment. Weeks before that final holiday weekend he was also aware that the bank would never survive that investigation. For him, either outcome would mean personal humiliation, arrest, and even possible deportation back to Argentina. Disappearing was the only solution. When he finally made the decision and actually walked out of the bank before that July 4 weekend, all those millions had already been transferred to Houston by Hernando. That extra million was in Danny's briefcase to hand over to Hernando in Houston who would give it to Jorge who would deliver it to Coriander.

Swayze said it again, "Foolish, Danny, taking that last million was a foolish mistake."

"On the list of foolish mistakes killing that Mexican ranks right up there."

Hand on the clutch as he shifted into second, Swayze accelerated over a dune. "He saw the explosion, showed up at the police station while Jorge and I were still making arrangements and claimed he saw a plane blow up in the sky."

"And if he saw it how many others saw it too? What were you going to do, wipe out the whole area?"

"We were going to take it one at a time and with that one there was no choice. Your brother and Hernando had just gotten the police captain to agree on a price to hold off reporting the crash for at least four hours. I needed time to reach the site and find the black box. Besides . . .

Danny nodded slowly. "You needed another body at the morgue, is that it?"

Swayze laughed. "Parts and pieces were acceptable . . ."

He thought about Coriander in the morgue in Chilpancingo identifying parts and pieces . . . "Where's the black box now?" he said, changing the subject and with it those images . . .

"That's another problem. I've got most of it, bought it off some old woman up at the crash site, but I don't have it all yet."

"That's great," Danny said sarcastically.

"Don't worry, we'll get it, those peasants up there don't even know what they've got, they just grabbed everything they could get their hands on. Jorge's working on it . . ."

Again, Danny answered sarcastically, "That's a relief." Reaching into his pocket, Danny took out a pair of sunglasses and put them on. "That black box was your second mistake," he admonished calmly, "the third was forgetting to have me paged in the airport at Houston. What happened?"

"Jorge got involved with something else," he replied evasively.

Danny looked disgusted. "Something underage no doubt. You should have seen to it that he didn't forget anything."

"I had my hands full with the police."

"It was close . . ."

"What did you do when you realized that Jorge forgot to page you?" Swayze asked, anxious to change the subject.

"I made several calls to numbers I knew wouldn't answer." He shrugged. "Then I told the pilot I had a business emergency in Houston."

"Did he offer to wait?"

"He stopped offering when I reminded him that my brother was waiting in Acapulco with his money."

Swayze kept his eyes on the road. "Who did you call?"

He needed to hear her voice one last time. "I called home and hung up on the machine."

Swayze looked momentarily disturbed. "Well, it's almost over now if that D.A. decides he's got better things to do than tangle with Mexican bureaucracy and if he decides there's no percentage in tangling with your widow."

"She can take care of herself."

"I'm not so sure."

There was no point in belaboring it. He didn't care to make her the subject of their discussion. "Jorge hates the sight of blood," he said suddenly.

Swayze understood. "It was good for him, my killing that Mexican upset him enough so he looked like a man whose brother just blew up in a plane." Shifting, Swayze accelerated around a curve in the road, the jeep lurching forward as it hit a pile of rocks. "Up until then he was having too much fun, he loved being part of the intrigue—wasting that Mexican got his mind off those *muchachas* for a while." Swayze squinted against the rays of sunlight peeking out from between the gray clouds. "Although I'm not so sure how much he likes what's going on now."

"What do you mean?"

"He's got his hands full with the cremation and the bank and all those other problems."

"What other problems?"

"Your widow, for instance . . ."

For instance. A liar, a thief, a murderer, and now this, a man who abandoned his wife without so much as a note and she would never know why. For most of his life Danny had been all of the above for a variety of reasons, some political, most financial, some by duty, most by choice. What he was above all was a man with an utter disregard for convention and morality, someone with a surprisingly accurate instinct about politics, allegiances and money. More, he was a man who possessed an extraordinary sensitivity about danger, about what to do and where to go to keep alive and functioning. Without his charm and grace, his wit and intelligence, things would have been even more difficult.

He could see her now, his Coriander, on the way to the crematorium, standing like a good little soldier dressed all in black complete with a Sarmiento heirloom black lace mantilla draped around her head and shoulders, receiving the urn, her amber eyes filled with despair, her lips trembling, the perfect, grieving Argentine wife. Except he knew better.

Swayze was talking again. "You'll be safer here than in Cuba for a while. There're too many CIA and FBI agents swarming around Havana and anyway, Danny boy, you need the rest to get your mind off things. It's man's country in Ushuaia, make you forget all about women." Women, as if there was ever anyone else but her . . . He turned to pat him on the shoulder. "When things die down and when that subpoena is dropped and the investigation in New York dies down you'll leave for Cuba. Fidel is waiting for you with open arms . . ."

"Has he changed?"

"He hasn't changed at all, which will probably be his downfall in the end," Swayze predicted. "He's grayer and heavier and doesn't have the same stamina to talk for hours but he'll never let go, he'll hang on forever until they carry him out of the People's Palace." Swayze settled back behind the wheel. "At least you had her for three years, *hombre,* while the rest of us were sitting it out in the jungle or in jail. Some men never have a woman like that."

Not that he didn't pay dearly for his Coriander. Shutting his eyes, he remembered that Christmas party in 1978 after their first encounter at the University in Cordoba. Ambassador Palmer Wyatt could have been a corrugated box salesman for all his charm and culture; lace-up shoes and button-down collars were his trademark, that and a penchant for old whiskey and young women. A good old boy Republican, just what the people needed in Buenos Aires to help the Junta make even greater right-wing strides and practice more torture and terrorism, he thought bitterly. But Swayze was right about one thing, not everyone had a woman like Coriander and that Christmas night was just one example of how everyone who met her felt the same way . . .

He could still see her standing on that receiving line wearing a dusty rose velvet gown, a dusty rose velvet ribbon woven through her long hair. She looked so shy, so vulnerable, so lovely with one shoulder bare, her hands making what he would learn were typical nervous gestures to that prominent collar bone of hers just above that prominent cleavage. Security was exceptionally tight that night and understandably so following a slew of death threats received by the Embassy after Wyatt defended the Junta for that Villa Devoto massacre. Fifteen extra guards armed with Uzis surrounded the Ambassador and his daughter. Not quite enough artillery to have prevented Danny and several other perfectly respectable businessmen who belonged to the Montoneros from receiving invitations. Danny got his from Coriander while the others were on the regular guest list. But that was both the beauty and the danger of the group, that its members could penetrate the very fiber of Argentine society at the same time they were plotting its demise.

Leaning against a marble pillar, Danny's eyes never left her, watching as she tried to keep up conversations with all the guests who passed down the line to shake hands, compliment, inquire about school, or mention they had a son, nephew, cousin, grandson, friend of a friend who might be passing through Cordoba. Perhaps the young man could ring her up . . . She looked so ill at ease, as if she hated every minute of the evening . . .

Swayze was talking again, interrupting his reverie to bring up that bloody million dollars. "For that kind of money, *hombre,* you could have your choice of any virgin or whore in all of Patagonia for the rest of your life, twenty lives, *amigo,* a hundred lives." He laughed. "And for a man beginning his second go-around, who knows how many virgins you'll need? Or whores, for that matter, *quien sabe, hombre, quien sabe?*"

Stretching out his legs, Danny feigned sleep behind his dark glasses. Virgin or whore, once he had both in the same woman, from the very first his Coriander had been both without even knowing her potential or effect. What he taught her was to know the difference, what he nurtured was her instinct to go even further than she ever imagined until it was still not enough. Danny recalled every last detail of that Christmas back in 1978.

On the night of the party Danny clocked the distance and time it took for the Ambassador's motorcade to reach the Embassy from the Chancery. Somebody had an idea to test it out in case they decided to kidnap the Ambassador's daughter and hold her for ransom. Using a walkie-talkie and keeping in constant touch with two of his comrades, Danny watched from the edge of the park along the route, having been warned when the cars screeched out of the driveway of the official residence to head for the party. The lead car carried one machine gun and four guards armed with M-16 rifles, the middle car carried the family, two bodyguards with two-way radios and automatic weapons cradled on their laps, an extra man positioned in the back of the limousine with a machine gun sticking out the rear window. The tail car followed with five more guards, all fully armed as well, machine guns protruding from the windows. Forty miles an hour was the precisely designated speed that the three-car motorcade drove—no more no less—until it reached the electronic gates of the Embassy, programmed to swing open automatically according to a pre-set timer. That was what he needed to find out—time and distance—before he stepped into his own car to make his appearance at the party.

Before the last guest had passed along the receiving line, Coriander drifted over to one of the gilted gold loveseats in the corner of the grand ballroom, Velasquez's *Los borrachos* on loan from the Prado taking up most of the wall behind where she stood. What Danny would have preferred was to lead her by the hand away from there and make love to her; what he did instead was to catch her eye and nod slightly, not surprised when she nodded slightly in response, a shy smile playing on her lovely mouth. "I didn't think you'd come."

"How could I not come?"

"I thought you'd decide it wasn't worth it."

"On the contrary, I'm an optimist . . ."

"I would have guessed the opposite."

"Maybe you changed me . . ."

She looked embarrassed. "Have you met my father yet?"

"Not yet but you promised me a dance and you promised that you'd introduce us."

She looked around. "How about if I keep one of those promises?"

"Which one?"

"The one that means the most to you." She turned then to walk away. He watched for several moments as she moved in the direction of the adjoining room, half a dozen or so potential lovers, escorts, dance partners trailing her as she did, before he followed at a discreet distance.

A French laquered buffet table was set with gold cutlery and blue cobalt china plates, gold-trimmed goblets, pink damask napkins, all centered under a pink-crystal chandelier, each bulb covered by its own pink satin shade, silver buckets holding champagne at either end of the table, platters of smoked salmon, paté, caviar, petits fours, fruit, sides of Argentine beef, all attended and served and poured by waiters in cutaways and waitresses wearing black uniforms, starched white aprons and pleated caps. Enough to feed his men for a month, a year, certainly long enough for them to drive out General Videla and turn the American Embassy into their own private Casa Rosada.

Surrounded by guests, Coriander kept glancing over to where Danny stood. To his amusement, he saw that she noticed his feigned interest in a certain blonde, an older woman whose dress got right to the point. If only his Coriander knew how much he didn't care. A waltz played in the background—*"Mis Noches Sin Ti"*—which the blonde took as a cue to dance and which Danny took as a cue to edge away. Coriander was directly in his sights. The dash around the buffet table was almost predictable and so comical that Danny had to contain a smile; the blonde following Danny, an array of eligible men following Coriander. Everything happened in slow motion until there she was again, Coriander with the fabulous eyes and delicious lips, suddenly animated as she talked and laughed with several young friends and all for his benefit. As if he wouldn't have noticed her had she never uttered a word.

"Do you waltz?" he asked when she momentarily wound down. She considered ever so briefly, the expression in her eyes almost regretful. "Yes," she answered. So serious his Coriander, so innocent back then. Offering his arm, he invited, "May I have this dance?" Her amber eyes sparkled when she asked, "Have you met the Ambassador yet?" He understood. "Not yet." She smiled slightly. "I promised this dance," she replied, before turning her back to accept a dance with a pudgy man with black-framed glasses and a signet ring on his middle finger.

Moments later Danny ambled over to where the Ambassador stood, a circle of men gathered around him to hear his views on inflation, devaluation of the *austral*, democracy, communism and a terrorist group called the Montoneros.

What happened next happened unexpectedly, before Danny could hear the rest of something about the current pro-democracy, anti-communist, God-loving Junta . . . One moment there was nothing very interesting and the next there was everything to live for, to breathe for. Coriander appeared out of nowhere to interrupt her father's diatribe, her arm linked through his, her gaze focused on Danny. Palmer may have been a lot of things but one of them wasn't dumb when it came to his only child. "Have we met?" he said to Danny, "I'm Palmer Wyatt."

"This is my economics professor, Danny Vidal," Coriander said, introducing them.

Palmer glanced at his daughter before turning his gaze toward Danny. In a charming tone and with his hand extended he said, "I want to thank you for helping Coriander out of an ugly situation."

"The situation was less ugly than the reason . . ."

Palmer only hesitated a moment before his expression turned to jovial and he laughed one of those diplomatic laughs that signified everything but humor. "Did you know, my dear, that this man is trying to teach you a social science that has been imitating a fundamental mathematics for decades?"

She smiled, her eyes still fixed on Danny. "It takes talent to turn abstraction into a reality . . ."

"Or unreality into a political abstraction," Palmer replied smoothly.

Small talk ensued, the weather, summer plans at Punta del Este across the river in Uruguay, more about the guerrillas, the economy, until after the prescribed and courteous period of time Danny excused himself. But even as he walked away he could still feel her on the back of his neck and in the pit of his stomach; it was hard to remember when he wanted someone so much. A breath of air was what he needed before he left, since in those circles timing was everything. Again, she appeared out of no-where, stepping out onto that granite balcony where he stood, the terrace that was an extension of the grand ballroom that wrapped around the entire second floor of the Embassy. Without a word, she approached and stood with her back against the railing, her face somewhere between him and the moon.

In a small voice she asked, "Do you waltz?" A look of amusement crossed his face as he studied her to weigh the risks before he stopped weighing anything and took her in his arms. They waltzed to non-existent music, around and around until he stopped with her in his arms, his hand on the back of her head, her lips under his control. He didn't bother to inquire if she did or if he could or if she might, he just pressed his mouth against hers, lightly at first brush, even chastely and certainly without overt passion before he drew her closer, his mouth nibbling hers, his tongue edging between her lips. She kissed like a whore, the way she responded without any inhibition, only a whore kissed like that. Or a virgin.

Again, Swayze was back on the subject of the money. "Hernando has everything set up on the computer including how much money goes where and for whose campaign. The way we figure it is there are at least fourteen candidates who have a chance, who are running on socialist or communist tickets in about eighteen cities in Latin America. After that, we can start thinking about moving into Miami on a local basis . . ."

"Take it easy, Mac, and don't get too ambitious." Danny turned his head to open one eye and smile. "Let Hernando do the political analyses and you worry about the military. Get the ammunition together and give me a plan about all the foreign installations and embassies in Argentina that are vulnerable. Remember Mac, you're in charge of making something spectacular happen," Danny went on good-humoredly, "Let Hernando worry about long-range plans and let me worry about money . . ."

But Swayze was barely listening. "This is it," he continued excitedly, "this time we can't fail regardless of what idiot is in the Casa Rosada or the White House . . ."

"Nothing is sure," Danny warned, "just remember that anything can happen anywhere to knock everything off balance. Unemployment could suddenly be wiped out in Argentina or new social welfare programs could be implemented in the States or there could finally be a peace plan in the Middle East. The important thing is never to underestimate the opposition."

"We've suffered enough loss and casualties so that this time we won't fail . . ."

"What happened in the past has nothing to do with what's going on now." After so many failures Danny knew that a successful outcome would depend mostly on a solid financial base with correct statistical information. The rest was window dressing. An attack here, a bomb there, a kidnapping, a murder, Swayze could plan all the attacks he wanted and carry them out until eventually they wouldn't make an impression, until once again the world would grow weary of violence as a way to send a message. People were getting more sophisticated, plans had to be more original. True, there was always that initial flurry of media attention after a terrorist attack, several days of follow-up reports giving the condition of the victims, which led to human interest stories that occasionally produced an anniversary special and another three-minute mention of the attack as part of a year-end round-up of global atrocities . . . Still, governments were rarely toppled nor were candidates elected as a result of violence. Danny always believed that what was needed was a financial network that would support candidates and provide money for public relations campaigns, advertising, and the dredging up of scandal against adversaries. It was an ambitious plan that would take all of his time, energy, and devotion—at the expense and sacrifice of everything else.

He could see his Coriander on her way back from the crematorium, clinging to her father's arm and clutching the urn filled with her husband's ashes. He could see her returning to New York to carry on with her life, packing up the apartment for sale— the art, silver, antiques, paintings, books, everything bought for the rising star on the New York banking scene and his beautiful and charming wife who didn't give a damn about any of it.

So unspoiled his Coriander, so simple in so many ways. She didn't care about his business or money or even the wine he loved so much. He once held up a bottle of Mouton Rothschild, a magnum, and offered it to her in honor of the year of her birth, 1958. She couldn't have cared less. Wine by the *month* would be fine, she laughed, her eyes twinkling in delight, her nude body glistening on the sheets, her skin still damp from him, her mouth still moist from his. How unimpressed she was by most luxuries, this girl who grew up with every last luxury that money and power could buy. She had no taste, he teased lovingly, his *gringa,* she only knew about Coca-Cola and hamburgers and baseball. He was wrong. Coriander knew about lots of things even if they didn't come under the heading of the usual luxuries. Wine by the *month,* Chianti in July, would do just fine as long as she could drink it from his mouth, wine by the *mouth,* and to prove her point and show what she knew, she rolled on top of him, straddling, leaning over his face so that her hair brushed against his chest, his mouth. Covering his eyes, nose and neck with kisses, she worked her way down, slowly, languidly, pressing her lips on each rib, pausing to count, nibbling until her mouth reached its mark to take him all in, her tongue running the length and width of his erection. He stopped her then, taking her face between his hands to pull her up so her lips were almost on his. Her voice deepened when she asked him why, her expression changed from passionate to perplexed, her eyes demanded an explanation. But any reason was redundant by then since he had already been overwhelmed by the obvious— love. He studied her carefully, committing every inch of her face and body to memory before he read something familiar in her eyes, a look of reproach rather than anger, something he understood better than she could have ever imagined. What the look said was that she had depended on him and he had let her down because together they had broken the rules and gotten caught up in that whole notion of love. Losing her virginity at twenty had been a conscious decision that made her the hunter, while falling in love with the man who took it made her the prey. Still, the job was done and the deed accomplished in record speed. She fell in love with him and in return he taught her everything to make her perfect for someone else.

The body if you please, gentlemen, he could just hear that demanding tone of hers before it would escalate into pure banshee when she wanted, no demanded, to know where the hell was the body or if not the entire body then at least a tooth or a bone or a fingerprint or anything at all to prove that her husband had indeed perished in that plane crash. He could even hear that imperious inflection in her voice when she made those demands that would launch an inquisition, challenging anyone who had the gall to try and placate her with condolences and assurances instead of hard facts and evidence. The only thing that worried him was that man from the District Attorney's office and how she would get around his doubts . . .

Danny opened his eyes and sat straight up in the seat, a movement that Swayze interpreted as an invitation to continue the conversation. "The only thing that worries me is that those Islamic

Fundamentalists will jump in to take credit for any attack we make."

"Use them," Danny interrupted sleepily.

"What do you mean?"

"Make a deal. What's the difference who takes credit if it serves the same purpose, use them in the suicide missions, pay them. After all, we're destroying a common enemy in the end."

"And what about the message to the world?"

"It doesn't matter, Mac, since every legitimate group or lunatic faction denies or admits everything anyway. Who knows for sure who does what? The only message that makes an impression are the debris and the bodies that come across the television screens."

"But what we want is the Montoneros' name on everyone's lips . . ."

"Glory doesn't buy elections, Mac."

Danny said nothing more, his psyche shattered by all the memories of Coriander, as if he had been making love to her for hours without a single sensation reaching any of his nerve endings. He missed her like hell.

More sun was breaking through the clouds, glimmers of light were reflecting off the water and the sand. Morosely, he glanced out the window to watch the splendor of the snow-capped mountains in the distance, a scene not unlike an Antarctic version of Cairns or Brighton with the many lakes and glaciers dipping and rising on the horizon. The jeep held the winding road, continuing toward what would be his new home for a while, toward the southernmost tip of nowhere, the end of the earth, a town at the bottom of Patagonia called Ushuaia. He was desperate to see her again, only forty-eight hours and he needed to touch her, to feel her, to explain. What had been an abstraction for years was now a reality. It was over. The only two women he loved in his life were gone; Alicia was dead and Coriander was widowed.

He drifted off again as the jeep bumped along. In the distance hundreds of sheep were grazing inside a paddock; the site of a ranch was marked by twin gables leading to the entrance of a corrugated house with a high pitched roof. A man dressed in a kilt plodded along with a walking stick. This was Scotch and Welsh country, these were the tough ones who were brave enough to endure a Patagonian winter.

He thought of the picture of them together in his wallet. "Together forever" she had written on the back. Pictures don't lie, Coriander always said, only people lie. Keep my pictures, *querida,* Danny thought, keep them forever, *mi amor,* because pictures don't lie, the words pounded in his head, only people lie.

Chapter Eleven

Coriander came back from Chilpancingo on a Tuesday, spent the evening with her father before he took the last shuttle down to Washington. After he left she threw herself into the shower, standing there with her head leaning against the cool tiles, not quite sure where the water began and her tears ended. Hair dripping, Coriander reached over to turn off the faucets, wrap herself in a towel, make a turban for her hair before she stepped out. She stood in front of the mirror and looked beyond her own reflection. It took time to adjust, she reasoned, it took time to forget and courage to remember. After all, it just happened that she was married for three years, pregnant for three months, and widowed for three days.

Slowly, she made her way to the bedroom, stopping to dump out her suitcase and make a pot of tea before she got into bed with a pile of mail and the television turned on just for the sound. She fell asleep with the mail strewn everywhere, the screen flickering, and her hair half-wrapped in that turban, lying sideways across the bed as if she had been sleeping alone for years.

It was already morning when she awoke, startled and disoriented, not quite sure for the first few seconds where she was, her body still positioned crossways on the bed. She sat up slowly and surveyed the disorder, the tea tray on the floor, the mail still strewn over the sheets, a morning talk show going full-blast on the television. Leaning back against the pillows with her hand stretched out on the empty space of white sheet that was once Danny's side of the bed, she remembered that he wouldn't be coming back anytime soon, that all she had left of their life together was this baby growing inside of her. Just like that in about three seconds flat she took inventory of her entire past, present and future. And what kept coming in and out of her head as she sat there were two separate moments with Danny that spanned a decade but that always seemed to be one long conversation . . .

It was in Cordoba, at the University, right before he left for Buenos Aires to run the bank, when he had already told her that she should forget about him and go on with her life . . . It was the last time she saw him.

Coriander looked beautiful that morning. Her hair was loose and she had on no makeup and there was a wildness about her, a gleam in her eye that came from the anticipation of waging war to stop him from leaving. Dressed all in black, sweater and slacks, boots and black leather jacket, she blocked his way as he emerged from the classroom that day. "I love you," she said simply. He just stood there, searching her face, as if she might supply him with the proper response. "Please, Coriander, don't do this . . ." She took a step closer, near enough to touch his arm. "Take me with you . . ." He stood there another moment before he turned to take long strides in the direction of the exit. But she was right beside him, keeping up although not daring to take his arm.

They walked in silence through the long portico with its rust-colored ceramic floor before emerging from under the white stucco arch and stopping in the cobblestone square, a tiny church with a bell tower in the distance. "I can't give you anything . . ." There were tears in his eyes.

"I don't want anything except you . . ."

"There's nothing left."

"Whatever there is, it's enough . . ." And despite all her efforts to the contrary a tear rolled down her cheek.

He took her hand. "Not here," he said, leading her to his office.

There were no candles then nor did he set about brewing any *mate,* merely gestured her to a chair before he turned around to sit facing her with his arms leaning over its back. "I've already given my resignation."

She was silent, dying inside but determined not to plead her case until he had exhausted his own.

He waited for the argument. Still, she said nothing. "This is something that's been in the works for months . . ." Again, he paused and still she said nothing. "You know what's going on, Coriander, every day more people are *disappearing,* more bodies are washing up on the beaches and the world doesn't seem to give a damn, they're killing the best and the brightest . . ." When he paused once more, however, she reached over to take his hands, to press them to her lips and whisper, "Let me be there with you to help . . ." There was an interminable silence for several moments before he shook his head slowly. "I can't . . ."

Coriander didn't move, her eyes filling with pain as she desperately tried not to cry. Something Floria Lucia always said came to mind, how a woman should look her best when she was leaving or being left as it was the image that lasted forever in their minds . . . "You're the one who made me understand," she began, fighting to retain her composure. "It's because of you that there's still hope to find Hernando and all the others. Please, Danny, take me with you and whatever you're doing let me be a part of it . . ."

"You deserve better . . ."

"I love you, it's not a question of better, you could be the worst thing in the world for me but I want you . . ."

His eyes filled with regret. "You're so young, so innocent," he began, but she cut him off. "You're my whole life," she said, the tears evident in her voice.

"I'm in this thing already, don't you see, it's my whole life. I belong to something that goes beyond my own feelings . . ."

"Tell me that you don't love me . . ."

"I can't tell you that," he said softly.

She was crying by then but she didn't care, not about appearances or images or about anything except losing him. "Don't do this, Danny, please, take me with you . . ."

He sighed before withdrawing his hands to get up and pace. "You don't understand . . ."

"I understand more than you know," she argued fiercely. "You're the one who doesn't understand that you don't have to reject me to do the other, both parts of your life can survive nicely together. Loving me isn't going to make you impotent for whatever else you're doing . . ."

He stopped pacing to look at her. "I'll always love you, Coriander . . ."

She got up to stand very close to him. "That's not enough . . ."

"That's all I can do . . ."

She was the one who instigated it, not him. "Make love to me," she said softly. He hesitated only an instant before he took her face tenderly in his hands and kissed her, before he wrapped his arms around her and kissed her harder, his tongue slipping into her mouth, crushing her breasts against his chest. Only then did her fragility disappear along with his indecision, when they stood nibbling and kissing and chewing each other's lips until both tasted blood. Again, she was the one to initiate as she led him to the sofa to kneel over him, unfastening his pants, opening his shirt, throwing off her own clothes as well, her tongue running the length of his erection, over his abdomen, up and down his thighs, across his chest, her mouth pausing over each nipple. More, she needed to bury herself inside him, to draw him inside of her. In a frenzied flutter of limbs she rushed him between her legs, her mouth closing over his, all other images and reasons disappearing as together they crept higher and higher. And through it all, that last time, unknown to both of them, a hidden tape in his office played on, recording the sorrows and passions and sounds for the generals in the Casa Rosada and the American Ambassador in his Embassy . . .

Afterwards he held her although neither said a word until that church bell pealed in the distance signifying that it was noon. She held no illusions as she got up to dress, aware that he watched her every move. At the last moment he got up, threw on his clothes and announced that he would walk her to class. It occurred to her to refuse but she didn't. Arms wrapped around each other they started out in the direction of the social science building, across the cobblestone square where that tiny church with the bell tower stood, under the white stucco arch, through the long portico and over the rust-colored ceramic floor until they stopped in front of his classroom. It wasn't happening, she thought to herself, he wasn't going to turn around, walk away and leave her there alone. She was wrong. He left her standing there without even looking back as he walked away. There was one other conversation by telephone when she called him at the bank in Buenos Aires to tell him that she was planning to go to New York. He wished her well . . .

For the ten years that it took Coriander to finish her residency and go on staff at Brooklyn General, she lived alone on the Upper West Side in a brownstone near Central Park. The neighborhood was unusual for Manhattan with trees that lined the street, garbage cans that were chained to an entire block of freshly-painted metal gates. An English actress of about eighty or so owned the building and the apartment was a find, a floor-through with one large room with high ceilings and a working fireplace, an alcove just big enough for a double bed and an ironing board that Coriander used mostly as a clothes tree. The kitchen was adequate considering that Coriander was rarely home, taking most of her meals in the hospital cafeteria, and the bathroom was ancient with a tub on ball and claw feet and with faucets that dripped. She needed ear plugs to sleep.

Charming and dotty with a talent for reading tea leaves and cards, Miranda Malone not only owned the building but lived in the basement apartment with about eight or nine cats who wandered in and out and through scattered litter boxes. The bedroom walls were covered with old theatre bills and photographs taken in every stage of Miranda's career. The parlor was cluttered as well, with makeup of all kinds, a collection of feather boas, dressmaker busts on which were an array of sequined gowns, and wig stands holding different wigs in various shades of Miranda's signature red hair. Overhead hung a colored glass Venetian chandelier with a fine layer of dust on the crystal and bulbs. A permanently unmade sleigh bed with rumpled satin sheets, where Miranda usually held forth, stood in the center of the room. She was a character who lived blatantly and unapologetically in a past that included a husband or two and countless lovers. The memories kept her alive since Miranda had done it all and through it all had invested wisely in that brownstone, which was why she always lectured, "Nothing wrong with getting caught with your knickers down, luv, as long as you've got a place to hang them when that part is over . . ."

Coriander started out as her favorite tenant, less because she paid the rent on time than for her portable dopler that checked the woman's circulation and a blood-pressure cuff to monitor her hypertension. They became friends after the second or third "professional" visit when Coriander realized that loneliness was an illness too. They grew attached as only two women could whose lives were in varying stages of transition.

It was Miranda who convinced Coriander to go to that party at the home of Remi and Luis Botero, an Argentinian couple who kept an apartment in New York. And despite Coriander's fatigue after one of those marathon shifts at the hospital she managed to pull herself together and make the trip across town. It was a freezing winter night that offered the perfect excuse not to wear anything flimsy and which allowed her to stand out even more than usual in a crowd of women dressed in designer gowns. Coriander wore black slacks, boots and a turtleneck sweater, her long dark blonde hair tumbling over her shoulders and down her back, gathered on each side of her face by black combs. Her lips were painted peach, her cheeks blushed peach as well, her eyes luminous and moist from lack of sleep.

Remi Botero swooped down on Coriander the moment she entered the apartment, fluttering long lashes and dangerously waving a sterling silver cigarette holder around the crowded foyer. A striking woman, she was ageless, tall and reed-thin with jet black hair, large black eyes and a sense of theatre that she used even in simple conversation. Remi had the money while Luis was the intellectual. She designed jewelry that was sold only at one or two exclusive boutiques around the world and at prices that only one or two people could afford; Luis wrote sexually explicit poetry that he published himself and gave to the one or two people in the world who enjoyed it. "I was afraid you wouldn't come," Remi exclaimed, embracing Coriander on each cheek as she lifted a glass of champagne from a passing tray. "There's someone I want you to meet," she announced, propelling Coriander through the crowd.

Coriander couldn't quite explain the feeling in the pit of her stomach, a combination of fear and excitement, as she followed her hostess through the rooms, stopping to greet people along the way, some she recognized and some she didn't although she wouldn't have been able to identify any of the faces afterwards even if her life depended on it. It was only when they reached that white baby grand piano in the corner of the room that her heart began pounding in her chest.

There he was, just standing there, his head tilted to one side as he listened to something someone was saying, his beautiful hand holding that familiar Gitanes cigarette. He had hardly changed although perhaps his hair was shorter with more gray and perhaps there were a few more lines around his eyes when he smiled. She felt weak, she wished she was wearing something more feminine, she hoped her smile wouldn't be too bright or her voice too shrill or a hundred other things that would show she was still marked by him.

"Coriander," Remi was saying, holding her hand, "I want you to meet Danny Vidal . . ."

Coriander was no more than two feet from his lips, frozen as Danny crossed the distance to take her in his arms. "I missed you like hell," he whispered, his mouth pressed against her hair.

Remi was surprised. "Don't tell me you already know each other," Coriander heard her hostess say from somewhere on another planet, "and I wanted to be the one to introduce you," she added before she was pulled away by one of the other guests.

Coriander and Danny were alone in the middle of fifty or sixty people.

What she should have done was bury her emotions, wipe that look of sheer astonishment from her face and say a simple, "Nice to see you again after so many years," which he could have taken as a reproach. Or, she should have pretended that she didn't know exactly who he was although his face looked somewhat familiar, "Remind me where we met," which he would have taken as an insult. Or, she could have acted upon her instincts after so many years and asked quite simply, "What the hell happened to you while I loved you and waited and still love you," which would have created quite a scene that would have found its way all the way back to Buenos Aires within days. Instead, she had no time to say a word or pretend memory loss or ignorance or insult because he gathered her in his arms, kissed her on the lips, and said, "I've never stopped loving you for ten years . . ."

There it was, their whole story right out there in the open in the middle of a party for the entire Argentine community in New York City. But Coriander was splendid, smiling one of her best smiles, mustering every last ounce of charm that she never even knew she possessed. "What are you doing in New York?" she asked in perfect party pitch.

"Finding you again," he said, looking into her eyes.

Whatever she might have said would have been pointless since the years had changed nothing when it came to her feelings for him. Still, she tried, "How long will you be here?" she asked, ignoring his words, his lips, his eyes. That was the moment when he made it clear that he had no intention of putting up with another moment of her facade of indifference. He took her by the arm and moved her across the room—nodding and smiling at a blur of faceless people as he did. "I'm taking you home," he informed her. But that was when something snapped. Stopping dead in her tracks, she asked "And where is that exactly, where the hell is home after ten years, six months, three weeks, and fourteen days?"

He studied her, a small smile beginning at the corners of his mouth. "You look the same," he said tenderly, "you're even wearing the same clothes . . ." She looked down and remembered she was dressed all in black that last day in Cordoba. When she looked up there were tears in her eyes. "It's not enough," she said quietly.

"Would it make a difference if I accounted for these past ten years? Would you forgive me then?" Ten years, six months, three weeks, and fourteen days of her life and he wondered if an apology or an accounting would make a difference. "Could we go somewhere and talk?"

If nothing else it was natural curiosity that made her agree, not to mention that she had never gotten over him. Without saying anything to anybody they left. They ended up at her apartment, sitting on the floor and talking well into the night. Welcome to humility, she thought as she sipped brandy from a snifter, the flickering light from an array of candles casting shadows across his handsome face, listening as he made excuses and amends. A last stab at pride, she considered as the journey began . . .

"I came to New York hoping I'd find you . . ."

"You could have found me long ago."

"My life was impossible until I came here."

"You owe me reasons . . ."

"There are so many reasons, darling, I don't know where to begin . . ."

"At the beginning, from the day I never saw you again . . ."

"I was involved getting money to the opposition, negotiating arms and supplies and then the bank failed . . ."

"In the beginning, maybe, but ten years for God's sake, Danny . . ."

"My life was committed to other people's tragedies," he said as if that explained it.

"Is there someone else?" she asked, holding her breath.

"There's never been anyone else," he said quietly.

"Why don't you ask me?"

"I don't have to . . ."

"How can you be so arrogant?"

"I'm not arrogant, I just know that when you love the way we do there can never been anyone else. I thought about you every minute . . ." He had somehow managed to reduce their separation into minutes. Not that it mattered since the years apart could have been centuries as far as she was concerned. "You could have done something to let me know that you were alive or that you wanted me to wait for you."

He began to explain and his face seemed pinched, nearer to pain than she had ever seen it before, his mouth set in a way she had never noticed before either. "I thought about it in the very beginning until everybody got arrested and I got away. After that it was impossible, you couldn't come where I was."

"Where were you?"

"Havana."

"Then the rumors were true?"

"There were so many that some of them took on the proportion of myths . . ."

"What we heard was that you were laundering money for the Montoneros through the bank in Buenos Aires. After the Junta closed the bank you managed to escape to Cuba with the money where you supported the revolution . . ."

"It was the only place we could keep everything going, otherwise there wouldn't have been any hope for anyone. People were still missing, we never gave up."

It was too grand a notion for her to comprehend although what was in his favor once again was the nobility of his excuse. He left her neither for a woman nor for money nor adventure but rather to try and stop a horror that she herself had lived through if only on the periphery. Still, she argued through her tears. "What if I told you that I don't love anymore? What if I told you that I'm too angry and hurt to ever feel that way about you again? Did you ever consider that possibility?"

"Marry me," he said without warning. Forever. At last. She wanted to laugh out loud except that she wasn't quite sure if it was out of joy or anger or the gall of it all. "I can't go through this again . . ." Her voice held a warning.

"I swear, you'll never have to, please, just give me another chance . . ."

"And now?"

"I'm going to take over the Inter Federated Bank."

Her eyes went wide. "Again?"

He laughed. "No, darling, I've become a capitalist," he said, moving closer to her.

"How can you go from one extreme to the other?"

"There were reasons back then. When I went away I believed it was my responsibility to change things and if I had felt any other way you wouldn't have fallen in love with me." He paused. "I suppose I succeeded because now there's no reason to fight anymore . . ."

It was comforting to accept his explanation since it included a promise for the rest of their lives. Anyway, it would have been useless to resist because he was kissing her, his tongue slipping in between her lips, his hands cupping her face. He followed her moan with a tremendous shiver and no sooner had their lips parted than he was removing her clothes while fumbling with his own. Slipping out of his suspenders, taking off his shirt, bow tie, kicking off his shoes, socks, he was completely naked and lying next to her on the floor. Their eyes met across her body. Let him, she thought, let him do it all since it had already gone beyond any threat of abandonment. It couldn't happen twice and carry the same impact . . .

Afterwards they talked about her work at the hospital and his plans for the Inter Federated Bank; they talked about her father and his brother before she asked about Hernando.

"Is he alive?"

Danny was vague. "You know that his greatest love was playing that *bandoneon.*"

"It *was*, then you know for certain that he's dead . . ."

"I only saw him once more . . ."

"Where? What happened?"

"They cut off his hands . . ."

She gasped. "But where is he?" she repeated.

Danny took her in his arms. "He was so despondent, *querida,* that he killed himself . . ."

She wept quietly while Danny held her although her tears were not just for Hernando but for everyone who had suffered during those years. And when she stopped crying they talked some more about old friends in Buenos Aires and new friends here in New York and how much he loved her and how much she loved him before they agreed to try it again together for the rest of their lives.

Eventually Miranda Malone met Danny Vidal and not too long afterwards offered Coriander a negative observation on him and some general advice on life and love. "You're not the main event, dearie."

"Another woman?"

"Too simple."

"We're getting married next month," Coriander announced as if that explained everything.

"It's too bad some women marry their first love for all the wrong reasons," Miranda observed, "the excitement, possessiveness, the passion, before they end up suffering the humiliation."

It was an odd comment to someone starting out in a marriage.

About a week before the wedding Danny took Coriander to see their new Fifth Avenue apartment. Taking her by the hand, he walked her through ten large rooms that faced the Metropolitan Museum of Art. It was disquieting, as if the apartment were part of a higher plan, the way Danny explained what the decorator had designed, how he introduced her to the painters who were striating the walls and to the marble craftsman who was patching up the fireplaces, the wood craftsman who was staining the oak panels and ceilings. And then there were those leather-bound books that Danny ordered by the yard and all those antiques that arrived from a Greenwich Village auction house. Coriander had the impression that everything was designed to create an instant past, each eighteenth century possession and first edition that entered their lives was there to invent a history. Had she not been so involved in her work or had she been the type of woman who was interested in decorating she might have had more of a hand in it.

Danny wore a cream-colored turtleneck that afternoon, with gray slacks and a navy blazer. Wrap-around sunglasses protruded from his breast pocket. Coriander wore a gray suit with a fitted jacket and a frozen smile. He sensed something was wrong because he came up to her while she stood at one of the windows and gathered her against him, his chin brushing her cheek as he looked over her shoulder, talking soothingly in her ear. "Why so sad, *querida?*"

"Not sad, overwhelmed."

"Look," he pointed, "you can see the park where the children will play."

"Whose children?"

"Our children. You'll be happy here, I promise you, *amor mio.*"

"It reminds me of the Embassy."

"This is ours, *querida.*"

She wanted to point out that nothing in that apartment was theirs. This was the first time she had even seen what would be their new home; he had done it alone and all for the stranger he had somehow become in New York. "You know, darling," she tried, "I'd be happy living in Miranda's as long as we were together."

He smiled a hard-edged smile, one that she had never seen before. "How can the owner of a major New York bank and his new wife live in a brownstone." He kissed her nose. "Unless Miranda wants to sell it . . ." And when she didn't respond, he kissed her eyes and then her lips. Involuntarily she stiffened. "What's this about?"

"I'm frightened," she said simply.

He took her in his arms again. "Of what, *querida,* we're going to have a wonderful life . . ."

"This isn't me, it isn't even you . . ."

"It's important for my business to have this. I need it to attract bank customers."

And who was she to argue about what had become his life's work? She would have resented it like hell if he made her change her specialty and her hours . . . Still, she wanted it all ways. "What happened to all the idealism?"

"It's all here," he said, touching his heart, "but times have changed, darling, my life isn't about a tattered bunch of idealists anymore discussing revolution in a university cafe or teaching abstract economic theories. I promised you, *querida,* no more politics, just business."

"Yes," she said softly, "You promised me . . ."

"It's the beginning of a wonderful life," he said softly as he walked her away from the window, his arm supporting her around the waist, his lips brushing her cheek again before he stopped under the massive crystal chandelier that hung from the sculptured ceiling in the living room. He drew her close to him. Lovingly, longingly, and with great passion he kissed her once more and that time it took nothing to light the fire, the ache of desire was there. His tongue traced its way around her lips before it slipped inside her mouth to cause a pleasant tingling sensation, that familiar rush ending somewhere between her thighs. "It's your day," he whispered, "tell me what you want . . ." Alarmed, she didn't tell him what she wanted most was for that intruder—whoever he was—to go away.

Chapter Twelve

It was early morning and the woman who waited in the emergency room wore a sleeveless dress and kerchief tied around her head. Her arms were flabby and white, her face was covered with a fine mist of perspiration, and vague traces of a heat rash crept down one side of her neck to disappear underneath her collar. She was one of the religious ones whose five children ranging in age from three to eight needed booster shots. The old guy who hung around looked lost and excruciatingly lonely as he watched everything with a hawk-like intensity, unglueing his eyes only to remove a nylon cap and rub his damp head, his toothless mouth constantly chewing. There were a pair of out-of-towners waiting for a friend who was hauled in after he fell off a bar stool and cracked open his head. They dozed, their legs stretched out so that hospital workers pushing carts tripped over their feet. A couple of hookers were sleeping it off in a corner; one of them had a nice body and bright red heels, the other was listening to a compact disc player, swaying to the beat blasting in her ear.

Near the swinging doors that separated emergency from trauma a man leaned against the wall. He wore a khaki suit with a light blue shirt open at the neck, and he had a tie shoved into a breast pocket; his hair was slicked back and not yet dry from his morning shower and he was freshly shaved and smelling of lemon. He looked out of place.

It was Coriander's first day back at work. She wore jeans and a white T-shirt underneath a starched white hospital coat. Her hair was pulled back, features cleanly defined, and she hadn't bothered to put on any makeup. She had parked her car in the lot, crossed over the suspension walking bridge that linked the hospital with the laboratories and blood bank, and then continued through the labyrinth of underground corridors. Now she walked briskly through the emergency room and approached those swinging doors leading to trauma. She stopped dead when she saw him. "What are you doing here?" she asked, remembering the message he left on her machine when she came back last night from Chilpancingo. "I'm sorry, I should have called you," she apologized, "but we got back late and . . ."

Adam shrugged. "You probably had nothing to tell me."

"That's no excuse. You obviously had something to tell me . . ."

"Nothing that couldn't wait until morning." He smiled. "Can I buy you breakfast?"

There was something about Adam Singer that made her feel instantly secure. It was probably his boyish good-looks and easy manner because it certainly wasn't what he did for a living.

She glanced at her watch. It was eight-thirty, if she pushed it she could spare fifteen minutes . . . "Can we do it at the Greek diner across the street?"

After the light changed and they were already in the middle of the street, he asked, "Are you on duty all day?"

"And all night and all day tomorrow." She glanced over. "Thirty-six hours."

"Do you look as beautiful at the end of thirty-six hours as you do now?"

She might have taken offense if the light hadn't changed, prompting a distant screeching of tires as Adam took her arm to run to the safety of the other side. "The problem with you is that you're so genuinely nice it's almost impossible to get angry."

He held her arm tighter. "So, maybe nice guys don't always finish last."

They walked in silence until they entered the small coffee shop where the owner greeted her by name and one of the waiters called out, "Table for two in the back, doc . . ." She turned around to ask, "Is this all right?" Adam nodded, following close behind.

They didn't start a conversation until the waiter finished pouring coffee into mugs that were already on the table. She wasn't quite sure for which of the million possible reasons but she felt uncomfortable. Take your pick, she thought to herself. "So, why did you call me?"

"Basically to find out how you were doing . . ."

She set down the mug. "We left Mexico yesterday afternoon . . ." She couldn't bring herself to say the name of the town that she would remember for the rest of her life.

"Did your father come back with you?"

"Yes, but he left for Washington last night."

"You were smart to go right back to work, you know."

"I had no choice even if I would've preferred to hide under the covers. We're short-staffed."

He decided to do what he had come to do right away. Reaching into his pocket, he produced two photographs. He handed one to her. It was a picture of a man standing in front of a ramshackle shanty, grinning into a camera, his black hair long and unkempt and falling over his brow, a thick gold chain with an amazing collection of medals gleaming on his bare chest that was covered with matted black hair. "Do you recognize him?"

Coriander studied the man before looking up, "No, who is he?"

Instead of answering, Adam handed her the second picture. "What about this?" It was the same shot except only the man's bare chest was visible, blown up to take up the whole frame. She went pale as she studied it. "What is this?" she whispered, trying to put it all together as she listened to Adam explain.

"When you were so sure that the torso wasn't your husband I began thinking that there had to be another body to account for those remains divided into those three sections in the basins." He watched her carefully to see if she could take it. As if she read his mind she said, "It's all right, go on . . ." He did. "When I talked to Luckinbill he told me that your brother-in-law was rushing to cremate that torso and he swore that he couldn't identify it as belonging to either of his pilots—seems he has a pool up in Connecticut and both guys used to go swimming on weekends. Anyway, I began thinking that somewhere someone got another body to fill that third basin." He paused. "You all right?" She nodded. "After I met you at the hotel I went back to the mortuary and talked to that pathetic little undertaker who told me how they weren't equipped for a lot of bodies on account of the heat." Adam shook his head. "You'd think they would have caught on by now that they weren't living and dying in Juneau . . . Anyway, he told me how the last time the morgue was so busy was in 1813 when somebody had the bright idea of seceding from Mexico and everybody got shot . . . So, he was complaining how he could barely handle all the business and I asked him what business since as far as I knew there was only the plane crash. That's when he told about the truck accident where some guy from the next town drove his truck off the road." He paused. "The damn thing blew up at the bottom of a ravine, nothing left, at least that's what the undertaker said." Adam studied her another moment before going on, "The guy was really nervous and upset so I bought him a beer and he relaxed a little and started telling me how the Pope might be making a stop in Cerro el Burro, that's the name of the next town, during his Latin American trip . . ."

She found her voice. "Why?"

"That's exactly what I asked and, would you believe it, a couple of days before the truck accident this guy in the picture, the one who got killed, claimed he saw Jesus almost at the same spot on the road."

"So you went and talked to the local priest about a vision."

Adam nodded. "Father Ramon, and he took me to the guy's house and introduced me to his wife who gave me the photograph. I had the chest portion blown up because it struck me that it certainly looked like that torso. What do you think?"

She looked at the photograph of the torso again before looking at Adam and asking if he thought it was a coincidence that the man was killed or if someone had gone out and purposely murdered him just to have another body.

"That gets back to the original problem. If your brother-in-law hadn't rushed to cremate I wouldn't have bothered about someone who drove a truck off the road because I would've been too busy getting the remains out of there and over to a lab for analysis and identification. And while I was doing that I might have made it my business to find out if there was any bullet wound or anything else that could've told me the exact cause of death after I found out that the torso hadn't been in a plane crash . . ."

She thought about how much time she had already spent swallowing her rage that Danny had left her in this position. "Now what?" She was still pale as a sheet and looked as if she might faint.

"Unfortunately, there isn't any physical evidence left so I'm going to have to plod through flight logs and bank records and talk to as many people as I can who either saw the plane before it crashed or saw your husband or knew what was going on at the bank in the days and weeks before . . ."

She held the picture. "It's unbelievable how this man, someone I never met and will never meet, can be the reason to make me wonder if my whole life has been a lie."

"Has it?"

"I don't know anymore," she said honestly.

"Did your husband ever confide in you about any problems he was having?"

"Not really." She met his gaze. "Except for that last day . . ."

"What about?"

"Just vague innuendos, almost as if he wanted me to figure things out for myself."

"Can I ask you a personal question?"

"What would you like to know?"

"What was it about him that made you take another chance?"

There was a wise expression in her eyes. "You know everything, don't you?"

That's when he told her that it was his job to know everything because he was involved and had to understand the people closest to Danny if there was any possibility of ever learning the truth. He told her that he would never betray her, that he was right there with her and would stay with her until there were answers to all her questions; he told her she could trust him. What he didn't tell her was that he had already fallen a little in love with her . . .

"Danny was an idealist and I loved that about him. He genuinely cared about people. He was the most generous and kind person I ever knew, tough and committed and brave . . ." She stopped, a strange expression on her face. "Maybe I should start by being honest with myself."

"What do you mean?"

"The truth is that we had this incredible physical attraction . . ."

He hoped his voice wouldn't crack. "And the rest of it . . ."

"It's all true but I guess it worked the opposite from the way it usually does. I was a child when I first met him. The initial attraction back in Argentina were all those things I just mentioned."

"Yet he left you twice," he stated rather than asked.

"I guess he preferred the child to the woman."

Maybe it was because Adam had nothing to lose that he went off on a tangent. "Here's what I had in mind, that you'd call me if you needed to talk, I mean, even if it wasn't about the case." The card was in his hand and he was already scribbling down numbers before he handed it to her. "I want to give you my home number and my private line at the office in case you need me."

She hadn't been prepared for that . . . "I don't know how good I am about doing something like that, I mean, just calling to talk about things that bother me."

"Will you try?"

"I'll try . . ."

"Will you have dinner with me sometime?"

She looked at him a moment. "I won't ask if you're married."

"Okay . . ."

"Are you?"

"I was—my wife left me for an FBI agent."

She said, "I'm sorry . . ."

"Yeah, well, so was I . . ."

"Will you tell me about it," she said before adding, "at dinner?"

"The memory is fading very quickly." He grinned. "So we'd better have dinner soon."

She smiled back before glancing at her watch. "I've got to get to work." She stood. "Thanks for the coffee."

Standing as well, he spoke softly. "Keep in touch with me, Coriander Wyatt Vidal."

"I'm going to try and learn how to do that." She turned around before he could say anything else, taking long strides across the coffee shop floor and out the door.

* * *

Coriander had a dream. Two gray birds in the middle of a country road, one lying crumpled and still while the other nudged its life-less companion along with its beak, pushing it over to the side. Look at that, Coriander said to Danny in the dream, she's protect-ing him, even in death the little bird is looking out for her mate. Why *he* and not *she* Danny asked in the dream, why is the dead bird so surely a male? She couldn't answer. Not in the dream and not now. She just knew.

It was seven-fifteen in the morning, coffee with Adam had been almost twenty-four hours ago and Coriander was just wak-ing up from a brief nap and another disturbing dream. As always when she thought sleep would never come, when she reached that point beyond exhaustion when the tears came instead, she would finally drift off and dream—disturbing vignettes that starred only the two of them. These past forty minutes were no exception. But however bad she felt it was better to be feeling bad at work than staying at home and feeling worse.

Most people just stared when they saw her back yesterday, concern etched on their faces although they were unable to think of anything to say. A few approached her, mumbling things about God and strength and if she needed anything not to hesitate to ask . . . Better than the sympathy notes where people actually de-scribed how she was supposed to feel; how sad, how devastated, how enormous her loss, how irreconcilable her grief. More than anything she wished that everybody would stop trying to reflect her pain in their eyes or describing in writing how her husband's death was affecting her. Unfortunately she knew all too well on her own . . .

Lottie was one of the few who hadn't pushed her into admit-ting her grief or accepting her sorrow. Not that she wasn't sup-portive, although perhaps a bit too determined to keep Coriander aware of how those male members of that macho fraternity called "surgery" were waiting for her to flounder and fall because of a personal tragedy—a typical excuse for barring women from that last bastion of male medicine. As Coriander wrote up her reports from the first twenty-four hours, she reflected on Lottie's last effort when she did flounder and almost fall. The incident happened only several hours ago . . .

Somewhere in Brooklyn, not far from the hospital, a young woman awoke to find a burglar in her apartment. The first mistake was that she sat up in bed and screamed, the second was that the telephone was on the right side of her bed. In an attempt to call the police she tried to reach the phone with her left arm, which the intruder grabbed in mid-air as he plunged a knife underneath and into her chest. Thanks to her neighbors who heard her screams and called 911, the woman arrived in trauma some twenty minutes later where Coriander and her team had been alerted and were waiting to receive her. The initial picture told the whole story; neck veins distended, heart inaudible, blood pressure desperately low. The woman was near death. The sac surrounding the heart was filled with blood, which prevented fresh blood from reaching the heart.

The rush around the woman's stretcher in triage was impressive, the ABC's of trauma were implemented without delay: *airway, breathing, crack the chest,* rather than the usual *accuse, blame, criticize.* Within ten minutes after arriving, the woman was wheeled upstairs to surgery where her heart stopped. Coriander was with the patient from trauma to the OR and she went inside the chest to do a manual maneuver of the heart that caused the blood, with the first contraction, to hit the ceiling. Putting her finger over the hole in the left ventricle, she managed to stop the blood flow while another surgeon clamped a major bleeder in the lung. What happened next was what caused Coriander, in the words of that young resident, to "lose it." That was also when Lottie walked into the operating room from the theatre next door where she had just set a broken femur on a suspected victim of child-abuse.

As Coriander was about to sew up that left ventricular wound she discovered that there was no adequate needle—the standard needle was too small and the big needle was too thick although she opted for the latter to prevent further tearing of the muscle. And while that little mishap was happening, one of the nurses sent the surgical resident over to the blood bank, which was equivalent to two city blocks away from trauma, to bring back uncrossed blood (non type specific). As fate would have it the clerk refused to release any blood until the resident filled out the necessary disclaimer forms, given that the blood was un-crossed and there had been no time to cross-match the patient. Twenty minutes later the near hysterical resident arrived back in the operating room with the blood at the exact moment that the patient went into ventricular fibrillation (V Fib known in the biz, as one of the vascular surgeons explained when he popped his head in the door). Shocked back to life or as Coriander put it, "shocked back to near death," surgery continued. After several transfusions plus more shock the patient did come back for a while although after repeated episodes of V Fib, repeated rounds of drugs, and more blood, it became obvious that nothing was going to reverse the damage that had already been done, some-thing that seemed obvious to everyone except Coriander. She was like a wild woman as she ordered, "Let's get every available pint into her . . ." "Let her go, Cory," Lottie urged gently. "That was a good piece of surgery, Wyatt," the vascular surgeon added. "Nice try, Doctor," the resident offered, which was when Corian-der turned around to say through clenched teeth, "This isn't a fucking tennis match." Lottie moved closer, a hand on Corian-der's arm. "It's useless, Cory," she pleaded, "the patient's gone."

But Coriander wasn't interested in anyone's opinion and re-fused to face the eventual realities. "I want this patient transfused," she ordered, "and now. Let's go, we've got seven or eight units of blood left in this operating room so move it!"

Everybody moved, or at least the frightened underlings like the OR nurse and that hapless resident did, one of them attaching the plasma to the tubes to run into the dying girl's veins. Coriander was right beside them, massaging the heart, beating the patient back to life when life flickered out, tasting her own tears as she labored, getting a heartbeat, losing a heartbeat, exhausted and sweaty and bordering on outburst after outburst until finally she reached a level of complete desperation. Lottie just stood there helplessly, listening to Coriander issuing orders that made no sense, watching the operating room staff rebound more out of fear than duty.

"There's no pulse," a nurse announced.

"We've lost her," the resident confirmed.

Lottie took a step forward, her hand resting lightly on Coriander's arm. "Cory, please, don't do this . . ."

But Coriander wasn't interested in anything except that dying girl. "Get a heart and lung machine in here *stat*," she ordered, shaking Lottie away, "and hook her up, let's go, fast, move it, come on." And when nobody moved, her voice rose, "IS EVERY-BODY DEAF?" she yelled, glancing around, "get a machine in here now!"

"Coriander, stop this," Lottie commanded, "it's senseless, the patient is dead."

Coriander whirled around. "This isn't your operating room so your opinion isn't under consideration." Lottie backed away while someone made the mistake of asking where a heart and lung machine might be at the same time as someone else listed more reasons why it was fruitless. But Coriander was already in the hallway, pushing in the machine all by herself. "Hook it up," she commanded breathlessly, "fast, let's go, hook it up!" Within two or three seconds the machine was functional and within thirty seconds the patient was attached. Coriander dragged over a stool and sat down, watching the numbers on the respirator, the heart-beat and blood pressure, listening to the *whooshing* sound of the pump as it breathed for the girl. Again, Lottie tried to get her away. "Cory, you can't bring her back again, let her go peacefully," she pleaded. "Go away," Coriander whispered, her eyes fixed on the patient, "just leave us alone." But it was useless, even the machine couldn't sustain her. The girl died about an hour later, twenty-two years old, a nursing student it was learned, who wanted nothing more than to work in trauma at Brooklyn General, which wasn't far from where she lived.

Coriander was still with her when they took her off the machine; nobody could get her away, not even Lottie. "They've got to remove the body, Cory," Lottie tried again, "let me take you downstairs, please." Eyes overflowing with tears, Coriander finally stood up to cover the girl gently with a sheet. Still, she hovered over the body, shielding it from everyone else. Lottie was desperate. "Cory, they need the operating room," she begged. It was then that Coriander nodded to the orderlies who had been waiting with a collapsible stretcher to remove the body to the morgue. At least everyone had the sense not to impose upon her as she walked out of the operating room alone. Eyes unblinking, staring straight ahead, she made her way downstairs and into that small lounge. Entering, she closed the door, lay down on the cot in fetal position and cried as if her heart would break, for the first time since hearing about Danny.

Coriander finally finished writing up all the reports just as someone knocked on the door. "Come in," she called out.

The door opened. It was Lottie looking wary and concerned and disheveled, her scrubs stained with a combination of betadine and marinara sauce. "Are you all right?" she asked tentatively.

Coriander turned around in her chair. "I'm sorry," she said simply. "I'm really sorry."

Lottie shook her head. "I didn't come here for an apology."

"Sit," Coriander said, motioning Lottie to another chair.

"You've got to grieve, Cory . . ."

"For what, my marriage or my husband or both . . ."

"You picked a lost cause up there."

"I would've fought like hell to save her regardless of Danny," she protested.

"You tried too hard, Cory."

"Or not hard enough."

"That's another discussion . . ."

"Then don't blame what happened up there on what happened to Danny."

"It's not about *blame,* it's about your confusing issues and letting your emotions cloud your judgment."

"A perfectly healthy young woman woke up in her own bed to get murdered."

"It's never easy losing a patient."

"That wasn't just losing a patient, that was a total waste of life . . ."

"So are the gunshot wounds that come in and the children with broken femurs and just about every single case that's wheeled in through those doors."

"I can't make value judgments anymore," Coriander said wearily.

"Then at least try and accept things the way they are and don't take it upon yourself to change something that can't be changed."

Her eyes filled with tears. "I used to know when to give up. Don't you remember, Lottie, when I used to know it was useless . . . Now I can't tell the difference anymore . . . She waved her hand in front of her face as if to dismiss the grief.

"He's dead, Cory, and you've got to grieve."

"People grieve over a body, that's why we have funerals in

the civilized world." She looked at Lottie through her tears. "I've got nothing except doubt . . ."

"Maybe you're the one creating all the doubt."

"No, Lottie, there's nothing except an urn filled with ashes that don't even belong to Danny . . ."

She reached for her hand. "What can I do, I want to help and I hate people who say that but I really do."

Coriander didn't say anything, she just sat there for a moment or two, her eyes focused on a large crack in the wall near the desk. Containing more tears, she changed the subject. "What's it like out there?"

"Like working in the lingerie department at Bloomingdale's, most of the time you can't predict the walk-in business." Better to discuss random death.

"It was unbelievable last night, wasn't it?"

"Come outside and meet my four new fractures and see how unbelievable it is this morning."

"Where was I when they came in?"

"Up in surgery . . ."

"Another MVA?"

"Three cars and the paramedics brought them all here. They must have thought we were running a special on plaster splints," Lottie replied, rubbing her eyes.

Coriander was about to say something when the phone rang. Both women started as she reached over to answer. She motioned to Lottie to wait. It was Jorge and he got right to the point—he wouldn't have called her at the hospital except that he had been trying to reach her all night with no success and he was afraid he'd miss her before he went back down to *Mexico* on *business*. *Mexico? Business?* Events at the bank had detained him in New York. It seemed that Danny left her some money in case something happened to him. Money, she repeated the word, aware that Lottie was watching her from across the small room. It was all arranged without having been included in any will since Danny didn't have a will although he was very aware of his *obligation. Obligation*—since when was she an obligation? It seemed Danny left her a million dollars in cash, which meant it wasn't subject to taxes, which shouldn't have come as any *surprise* since Danny disapproved of government controls and bureaucratic red tape, which explained the reason for that hurried cremation. The arrogance . . . Actually, *surprise* wasn't the word she would have chosen to describe how the news struck her; *shocked* would have been more accurate and mainly because Danny had never discussed anything with her about money or wills . . . A million dollars, she said the words out loud before asking a million questions; where did it come from, where was it now, where had Danny kept it and for how long, what was she supposed to do with it and how was it that Jorge came to have it—the whole thing was inconceivable. Jorge assured her that he would be in touch in a few days either before he left for Mexico or in a few weeks after he returned. After she hung up, she turned to Lottie. "That was my brother-in-law . . ."

Stunned, all Lottie could say was, "A million dollars . . ."

Coriander was pale. "It seems Danny left it to me in cash. Can you believe that?"

"Can you?"

"Why would Jorge tell me such a fantastic lie?"

"I don't know, why would he?"

"It makes no sense."

"At least if it's true you can afford to stay in the apartment."

"If it's true I can afford to move out without getting into more debt to pay the movers. You don't know how many unpaid bills keep surfacing since this whole thing began . . ."

"Unbelievable," Lottie murmured, still not recovered from the news, "a million dollars . . ."

She looked at her friend. "I can't imagine why Danny thought of doing that . . ."

Lottie stood. "I can't get over it."

"Neither can I."

"What are you going to do now?"

Coriander shook her head. "I've got to digest it before I even know what to think or say about it let alone do . . ." She looked at her watch. It was a bit past three in the afternoon. "How much longer are you on duty?"

"Until six."

"Go on, don't wait for me, I'll join you in a minute. I've got to make a quick call."

Her hand on the knob, Lottie repeated, "A million dollars . . ."

When Lottie left and the door was once again closed, Coriander picked up the phone to call Adam. After being passed through a receptionist and a secretary, she heard him answer with obvious anxiety. "What happened?" he said.

"What makes you think . . ." she began.

"Because it's too soon for you to call for nothing."

"Something very strange," she began and then thought better of it. "Can I come down to your office to talk or could we meet somewhere?"

"Of course, anytime."

"I'm probably going to run a little late this evening so it would be better tomorrow."

"I'm going to worry if you don't give me an idea what it's about."

She hardly hesitated. "Do you remember when you asked me down in Mexico what I stood to gain from my husband's death?"

"Yes, and you said you never discussed it."

"Well, I was wrong."

"You mean, you did discuss it?"

"No, what I mean is apparently my husband discussed it because he made certain provisions."

Adam didn't miss a beat. "How much?"

"A million dollars," she said, "in cash."

Bingo. "How'd you find out?" he asked, containing his excitement.

"That's why I prefer to talk about this in person and not on the phone."

"Would you like to have dinner with me tonight?"

"I'd love to."

"I'll pick you up."

"Would you really be willing to come back out here?"

"Just tell me what time you're finished."

"About nine."

"Do you have a car there?"

"Yes."

"Then I won't bring mine. We can drive back to the city together."

"All right," she said, before adding, "And thanks, Adam."

The conversation ended. Coriander thought about it briefly as she draped her stethoscope around her neck, stuck the small flashlight and several pens in her breast pocket, clipped on her name bar and headed back into triage for the next round. Dinner. Breakfast. It was anything she wanted to make it. It was up to her. After all, he was the Special Investigator for the District Attorney and she was the wife of the object of his investigation. Or widow . . .

Adam thought about it awhile. There he was busting his ass to prove that her husband was alive, which made an already complicated situation even more complicated from a purely personal point of view. The whole thing was so completely confusing except for certain feelings that were very clear and which had only to do with her. He imagined how it would be . . .

Nine would become nine-thirty before they would finally leave the hospital; it would be ten-thirty by the time they reached the other side of the Brooklyn Bridge, which also happened to be near Chinatown where they would probably end up in one of those crowded and cluttered dives. A million dollars cash, the words reverberated in his head, there was no doubt that the money had everything to do with Fernando Stampa's five bounced checks. Everything in this case was so blatant that it almost went beyond proof.

What Adam hadn't told Coriander was that her father had telephoned from Washington only the day before to request a meeting with him in New York. Palmer Wyatt was due in his office in just under an hour. Although the former Ambassador assured Adam that Coriander knew he was in Washington and on his way to Buenos Aires via New York, he asked that Adam not mention the meeting. Apparently the man had certain things to discuss that could help the investigation but that could also contribute to Coriander's unhappiness. There was no point creating more conflict and pain than there was already. Adam agreed to keep everything confidential—at least for the moment—since he had fully intended to question Wyatt anyway before the man left the country. He tried not to think about Coriander as he waited for her father to arrive.

Chapter Thirteen

Palmer Wyatt entered Adam's office looking fit, tanned and rested, doing for khaki pants, a light blue shirt and navy linen jacket what most men would have done for a tuxedo. "I appreciate your seeing me," Palmer said, shaking hands with Adam.

"And I'm glad we've got a chance to talk before you go back," Adam answered, motioning him to the sofa. "Can I offer you some coffee?"

"Just some water," Palmer replied, taking a look around the cluttered room before sitting down. He got right to the point. "I hope you intend to keep your word, Mr. Singer, and not discuss this meeting with my daughter."

Carrying two glasses and two bottles of Perrier from the small refrigerator in the corner of the office, Adam set them down on the coffee table before taking a chair opposite the man. "I'd prefer it if you let me use my judgment on that one . . ."

"She's been hurt enough . . ."

"She's also stronger than you think."

"I think I know my daughter better than you do, Mr. Singer,

and she's got enough to cope with now without going back in time . . ."

"How about if I promise not to do anything unless I discuss it with you?"

The man nodded before he began. "I love my daughter and I find myself in a very difficult position, not that it's the first time I find myself in a difficult position when it comes to my daughter and her husband."

"Why don't you start at the beginning."

Palmer settled back. "One of the reasons I tried to keep up good relations with the Junta when I was Ambassador was to protect Coriander. It seems I failed at everything I tried to do for her, but those were bad times in Argentina, terrible times . . ."

"That's one of the things that surprises me, how you managed to stay on as Ambassador even when the Administration changed."

"If there's such a thing in government as being indispensable that's what I tried to be. I inundated Washington with reports showing that replacing me would have harmed American relations with the Junta. You see, at least I was able to keep a dialogue going."

"Then it wasn't only because of your daughter that you wanted to stay . . ."

"It was a very bizarre situation."

"In what way?"

"As long as I was there as Ambassador, Coriander was safe, and as much as I didn't approve of Danny, he protected her from the Montoneros and the constant threat of kidnapping."

"Were you ever worried that your daughter might involve herself in any of his activities?"

"I would have worried even if she wasn't involved with him. Most of the young people would have done anything against the Junta during those years. As far as I was concerned the threat was greater from the Montoneros because they always needed money and would do anything spectacular for cash or publicity . . ."

"Was it the spectacular that attracted Coriander to him?" That question had been bothering him for a while . . .

"Danny was older and attractive, you probably know he was her professor, and a kind of hero within the movement. Compared to him people her own age were just kids. He was a man who did more than just talk about getting rid of those monsters, he acted on it."

"From what I'm hearing you didn't disagree with him."

Palmer smiled slightly. "Nothing is black and white when it comes to diplomacy . . . What I didn't agree with were his methods."

"The violence?"

Palmer nodded. "I lived in fear that somebody would decide to kill him when she was with him and kill her unintentionally."

"What are you afraid of now?"

"I didn't come here because I'm afraid. I came here because I've got information about Danny Vidal that might help you. You see, Mr. Singer, he's a murderer."

"We're back to blowing up that plane . . ."

"That's another story, what I'm talking about is a murder he committed back in Argentina."

"Considering what he did back then he must have committed more than one murder."

"I'm talking about a specific murder." The man paused a moment before continuing. "Danny Vidal murdered the United States Honorary Consul in Cordoba, a man who was my mentor and who held that position on his first tour of duty in Argentina back in 1955 when I was fresh out of graduate school." Wyatt reached for a manila envelope that he had set down beside him when he first came in. He handed it to Adam who opened it. It was a Supreme Court document with the official seal of the United States of America in the upper left-hand corner. Without saying a word, he began reading. It was a subpoena issued by the United States Supreme Court for the extradition of several men who were residents of Buenos Aires, members of the Montoneros. The charges had to do with the abduction and murder of Matthew Johnson, the United States Honorary Consul in Cordoba. Adam glanced at Wyatt before turning the page to read the particulars of the charge.

On November 12, 1977, the men in question burst into Johnson's office and took him captive, writing anti-American slogans on the office walls with an aerosol can before throwing their victim into a Peugeot 303 that waited outside the building. Later that day a Montonero "war report" accused Johnson of being the "direct representative of Yankee interests in our province." Johnson was condemned to death by shooting but, in an additional statement issued by the Montoneros, his sentence would be "commuted" if the Junta could show before nineteen hundred hours on November 13 that five "missing" Montoneros were alive. Glancing over the pages, Adam looked at Palmer before glancing back down to read the last portion of the document. It was a copy of a handwritten letter from Johnson to the American Ambassador in Buenos Aires.

> Dear Palmer,
>
> I know that you have enough power to get the Argentine Government to meet the Montonero demands. If these missing members of the group are not dead, please use all your influence to insure that they show up at the designated time and hour.

Adam finished reading. "Did you?"

"My hands were tied," Palmer answered quietly. "There was nothing I could do. If I had responded to the letter it would have discredited the Junta and made them look like a tool of the United

States. You can understand how terrified I was to do anything to anger the Junta so that my daughter would suffer."

"But Danny Vidal isn't named in this subpoena . . ."

"He's not named because the government knew they had a better chance of prosecuting the two other men who participated in the murder. By the time the police knew anything Danny had already left for Cuba. But he was the one who actually shot Matthew Johnson in the head."

"How do you know that?"

"Because he talked about it afterwards."

"To whom?"

"He talked about it to someone named MacKinley Swayze."

Confused, Adam pressed on. "Well, there're two things I don't understand, first of all who's MacKinley Swayze and secondly how did you happen to overhear the conversation?"

Wyatt sighed. "The Junta put a bug in a Montonero safe house in La Boca as well as in Danny's office at the University at Cordoba. The reason I got to overhear the conversation was because I had contacts in the Junta who gave me copies of every tape that implicated Coriander." A look of pain crossed his face. "It was an ugly business since the tape where he talked about murdering Matthew Johnson also included things that I should never have heard . . ."

"What do you mean?"

Again, Wyatt sighed. "Obviously my daughter was in love with him and they had a life together but it was one thing knowing about it and another thing hearing it. The night that Danny talked about murdering Matthew Johnson he was in that house in La Boca. That was the night when she came out of a club in Buenos Aires and her friend was picked up by the secret police. She ran back to the house in La Boca to get Danny and they both showed up at the Embassy. They wanted me to get the boy out."

"Hernando . . ."

"She told you?"

"She still feels it's her fault . . ."

"There was nothing I could do . . ."

"Was Coriander aware of Matthew Johnson's murder?"

"It was all in the newspaper and of course she knew that Johnson was a close friend of mine."

"Did she have any idea that Danny was the one who killed him?"

"Not to my knowledge, at least there was nothing on the tape to suggest she did."

"Do you have that tape?" Adam asked carefully.

Without answering Palmer reached into his jacket pocket and took out a cassette. He held it a moment before handing it to Adam. "It's all here."

There was more discussion then about that period in Argentina during the Junta, background that Adam already knew but that he didn't mind hearing again from yet another person's perspective. When Palmer finished speaking, Adam asked, "Let's get back to this Swayze."

"Swayze was one of the leaders of the Montoneros who was and is still very close to Castro. It was Swayze who took Danny in and Swayze who arranged for him to run the Credito de la Plata in Buenos Aires. Swayze was also in Cuba with Danny after the bank was shut down."

"Do you think Swayze is involved with Danny now or has anything to do with the missing money scheme at Inter Federated?"

"I realize it's all conjecture on my part but that's exactly what I think."

"What would be his motive since there's no more Junta in Argentina and communism is just about obsolete."

"Don't forget Swayze has a particular fondness for Fidel and communism isn't obsolete in Cuba. But who knows if it has anything to do with politics? After all, fifty million is enough money to make people forget about idealism or revolution." Palmer took a sip of water. "But there's something else that keeps coming into my head . . ."

"What's that?"

"Swayze happens to be an expert at blowing up airplanes using altimeter bombs."

"That, Ambassador Wyatt, is probably the most relevant point you've mentioned today." He smiled. "Tell me more about this Swayze."

Handing over several FBI and Justice Department reports as well as photographs that had been taken of the man over the years, Wyatt talked briefly about Swayze's actions in Vietnam and his experience with altimeter bombs. At least now Adam had something concrete that could substantiate all the rumors. As he studied the pictures there was something vaguely familiar about the bald man with the glittering black eyes. It took only several more minutes before he realized that Swayze resembled Luckinbill's description of the man who bought up pieces of the black box at the crash site. Adam decided to say nothing about that right then. Instead he asked, "Are you aware of the accident report issued by the Mexican government?"

Palmer dismissed the question. "That's about as legitimate as a campaign promise. Somebody was paid off."

"You don't have any idea who, do you?"

"If I were investigating this case, the first place I'd look is the last point of contact with the airplane, which was the airport in Acapulco . . ."

Which was exactly where Adam's office was already investigating. And now it was made easier since he had a photograph. "If what you're saying is true then Danny could be directly involved with the murder of those two pilots."

"And whoever else was in that third basin," Palmer said shrewdly.

"I've already thought of that," Adam said.

"Someone drove that truck off the road."

"Either that or someone helped get that truck down that ravine."

"I can't help thinking Danny was involved . . ."

Something bothered Adam. "Are you aware that your daughter is expecting his child?"

"Of course I am," Palmer said quietly.

"Doesn't that change anything?"

Palmer seemed to choose his words carefully. "There's something very comforting about your religion, Mr. Singer," he began. "A child is automatically given the religion of his mother because there's never any doubt who the mother is . . ."

It occurred to Adam to ask how he knew he was Jewish but he decided there were more important things right then. "Are you suggesting that Vidal isn't the father?"

"Not at all, what I'm suggesting is that the baby belongs to my daughter. It's her child, my grandchild and the rest of it doesn't matter."

The two men talked some more about Swayze and his past involvements with the Montoneros, and about Coriander's infatuation with Danny, until Palmer announced that he had another appointment. The men chatted a few more minutes about the case, each promising to keep in touch, until Palmer and Adam stood and walked together to the door. As Palmer was about to leave he seemed to need to get back to something. "Whatever happens here," he said quietly, "I want you to understand that this baby is a gift, it's a new beginning for all of us . . ."

After the man left Adam sat at his desk and tried to concentrate on all the documents, papers and photographs that Palmer had left with him. He found himself distracted, thinking about Coriander and the whole unresolved situation with Danny. More than that, he kept hearing Palmer's words, which made him realize how much he wanted to be the one to offer that *new beginning* to Coriander and her baby.

Chapter Fourteen

The mobile general store was parked on the side of the driveway leading to the emergency room, the usual line of people waiting to buy everything from batteries to chocolate bars to hero sandwiches to coffee. The cab drove right up the ramp and stopped in front of the sign that read, BROOKLYN GENERAL—EMERGENCY. While Adam was searching in his pockets for change, the driver was talking. "You gotta be nuts to come here at night unless you're dyin' and then it's the only game in town, I got it written right here on my trip pad that if I'm shot, take me right here to Brooklyn General trauma and resuscitate 'cause I want all the heroics they're givin' over here . . ." Adam smiled slightly as he counted out what would be a generous tip. "You a doctor?" the cabbie asked. Adam shook his head. "You ain't no cop," the guy went on, "I can tell that by the tip." Adam didn't answer, he wasn't in the mood. Opening the door, he got out of the cab and headed for the entrance. Walking through one set of automatic doors and then another he found himself once again in the emergency room, redolent of pine disinfectant. It wasn't quite nine on the clock overhead and as he moved through the area he noticed that tonight it was crowded although nothing that looked particularly life-threatening. He continued down several long corridors, the stained linoleum polished to a glossy shine, the graffiti on the walls looking as if it had been scrubbed clean. Every several yards there were armed guards who sat on high wooden stools, leaning against what resembled pulpits. Adam was surprised that they barely paid attention, never even glanced up or asked for identification or checked his pockets for weapons.

As the ratio of uniformed policemen to the number of people who milled around in the halls increased it was obvious that he was nearing the trauma area. Friends, family, or perhaps only the curious stood against the walls, smoking and drinking coffee and whispering among themselves. English and Spanish signs were posted on a pair of swinging doors, advising that only medical staff could enter.

Through the glass portion of the doors there was bedlam, stretchers lined up in the holding area waiting to be wheeled into overcrowded treatment rooms, staff rushing around, uniformed and plainclothes police officers milling about, paramedics trying to quiet those patients who were conscious enough to cry and scream and several nurses shouting into telephones to make themselves heard over the din. Adam wasn't quite sure if he should walk inside or ask someone to tell Coriander that he was there. The decision was made for him when a woman in scrubs pushed out through the doors. She looked familiar. "Excuse me," he said, "I'm looking for Dr. Wyatt." The woman stopped. "You're from the D.A.'s office. You don't remember me, do you?"

He thought about it. "Of course I do," he said, "we talked when I came here that first time . . ." Only three weeks ago, he thought to himself, it could have been a lifetime.

Holding out a hand, she introduced herself, "I'm Lottie Bruner." Walking ahead of him, she held open the door. "Coriander told me you were coming. She's running a little late because we had two MVAs tonight, epileptic driver rammed into three pedestrians."

"Oh . . ." he murmured, aware of the chaos as he entered the unit and too flustered to think of anything more intelligent to say.

"Don't stop, just keep moving," Lottie advised, walking briskly through the mayhem. Adam followed, taking everything in, catching a fleeting glimpse of Coriander as she worked over a stretcher in one of the treatment rooms. Her hair was pulled back into a ponytail and she was wearing glasses. "Do you want a cup of coffee?" Lottie offered, leading the way into a long and narrow room. A coffee urn and several plates of donuts were on a table pushed against one wall, a refrigerator was on the other side, a corkboard hung above it with menus from a few Chinese restaurants, a sandwich shop and a Mexican take-out. "Thanks," he said, "black."

"Don't be afraid to say something if it gets to be too much," Lottie said as she filled the two cups, gesturing toward triage as she did, "I imagine it's pretty shocking for someone who sees it for the first time."

"I'm all right so far but"—he shook his head—"it's pretty unbelievable." It was more than unbelievable, it was almost surreal, the array of stretchers, blood splattered on the floors and sheets and on bandages that had been hurriedly wrapped in the ambulances on the way in, IVs running into veins, wooden boards supporting possible fractured necks, foam rubber wedged in between legs to secure broken bones until radiology could confirm.

"I don't suppose I should bother offering you a donut?"

Adam declined, saying, "No thanks, I'll just stick to coffee for now."

Lottie sat down, motioning Adam into a chair. "It's hard to imagine it from your point of view since we probably lose our perspective after a while."

"Do you always function at this level?"

"Not always but usually when we think we've figured out the pattern around here something happens and all hell breaks loose." She bit into a donut.

"There seem to be a lot of women working around here."

Lottie smiled. "Maybe because it's a thankless job. We get to save them for the hotshot surgeons upstairs who get them off the table and into recovery. And all the family and friends are waiting upstairs to thank the last doctor who touched them, which means we get nothing . . ."

"Why do you do it?"

"I do it because there's no time to think about anything else."

"What about Coriander?"

"You'll have to ask her . . ."

"How long have you known her?"

"We met on the first day of our surgical rotation about eight years ago when we were both residents."

What the hell, he could ask. "How well did you know her husband?"

"I only met him a couple of times."

"From what I gather they had a good marriage." Again he asked to hear what he didn't want to know.

"She certainly convinced herself they did."

"You mean they didn't have a good marriage?" Adam tried to sound offhand.

Lottie leaned forward. "What do you want me to say, that he was a typical macho Latin who treated her badly or that he was the most adoring husband in the world and they were the happiest couple I ever saw?"

Adam was surprised by her apparent irreverence. "Well, which was it?"

"A little over three years ago when she called me up to tell me she was getting married she couldn't stop crying and I kept thinking to myself, hmm, what's this about, why all the tears . . ."

"Did you ask her?"

"According to her she was happy."

"Did you believe that?"

"No."

"Did you tell her?"

"Of course I didn't tell her."

"Why not?"

"She wouldn't have listened. She had her own reasons for marrying him."

"I don't suppose you'd care to give me a hint." It was crazy to put himself in a position to have to listen to that again.

Lottie eyed him closely. "I always had the feeling that she didn't expect it would last."

"Why go into something if you're at least not deluding yourself of success?"

"You've got to be kidding . . . Most people do everything in life without being sure and getting married is probably the least sure thing of all since you're not just dealing with an unknown quantity but an unpredictable one too."

"I get the feeling it had a lot to do with unfinished business."

"Then you know the story."

Adam nodded. "I'd like to hear it from your perspective."

Lottie said it as if she had been called upon to recite it for years. "It was very simple, they were together ten years ago and he dumped her and suddenly there he was in New York begging to come back into her life." She shrugged. "Vindication is every woman's dream."

"Was he in love with her?"

"How could I answer that?"

"Did he seem happy with her?"

"What he seemed mostly when I saw him was nervous . . ."

"Do you think he's dead?"

"Let me put it this way. I hope he's dead and don't misunderstand that I wish it on him, not that anybody died from wishing or got cured from wishing either. But if he isn't dead and you manage to find him, I don't know how she's going to handle it."

"Why are you giving me such honest answers?"

"Because you ask honest questions."

"That's not a reason."

"I care about her," she said quietly, "and I hope you've got a better poker face in the courtroom."

"What do you mean?"

"You walked in here with your feelings written all over your face."

"Maybe they're feelings of concern."

"What I'm seeing goes beyond concern," Lottie said wisely, "and don't bother denying it because when it comes to other people's lives I'm an expert."

He was smart enough to know they had reached an impasse where discretion discouraged any more answers and tact discouraged any more questions.

Lottie stood and tossed the coffee cups into the trash can. "Would you like to go inside and see how we play God?"

"Is that the same as watching Coriander in action?"

Lottie smiled. "Follow me," she said, leading the way into triage.

Coriander looked so taut, so steely-eyed as she moved from one bed to the next, calling out orders to her staff, tending to the patients, wavering between eerie calm and downright savagery. She had finished examining the pedestrians who had been mowed down by that epileptic driver and was in the middle of a work-up on a wild-eyed young man when Lottie and Adam entered trauma. Moving close enough behind Coriander to hear the exchange they tried to stay out of her range of vision.

The patient had non-specific pain that was so "excruciating" that he fell writhing to the floor, was picked up by two orderlies and placed on the table. After several more attempts at a physical examination, Coriander finally said, "Point to the spot where it hurts the most."

He pointed. All over his body. "In my neck, doc, in my throat, it's burning in there like knives are cuttin' up my chest, shootin' all the way to my shoulder, squeezin' my brains right outta my head. I can't stand it no more, I'm dyin', doc, my left leg is numb, I need somethin' for the pain . . ."

"Open your mouth," Coriander instructed before peering down his throat with a small flashlight. "I don't see anything."

"It's down there, doc, keep lookin', it's there, like I'm swallowing glass and like there's blood in there, I can taste the blood."

"You've had a CAT scan and a chest X-ray. You're refusing to have blood drawn . . ."

"I got pain, doc . . ."

"I still don't understand how it happened."

"On the job, doc . . ."

"He says he ate a cookie and there was glass in the cookie," the nurse explained, rolling her eyes.

"On the job?" She looked at the man.

"I work in the Captain Chippo cookie factory and one of the cookies had glass in it."

This one was more imaginative than most, not only specific pain but an injury that could get him workers' compensation payments. She had a hunch. "If you had a choice, what do you think would alleviate the pain?"

The man glanced around nervously. "Morphine."

She could have bet on that one. "Give him two Tylenol III and a prescription for six more." The patient's reaction was predictable; she could almost count to five before it would happen. "What the fuck kinda doctor are you anyway? Tylenol III ain't gonna touch my pain, I need somethin' stronger you fuckin' bitch."

She was unruffled. "Tylenol III is what I'm giving out today. Take it or leave it."

"Fuck you," he raved back, "what kinda fuckin' hospital is this, I'll sue, what kinda fuckin' doctor, you ain't no doctor, you're a quack . . ." On and on until security moved in although she stopped them from putting on restraints just yet. "Either you take this prescription or you don't take it but if you want something stronger you're going to have to take a full blood test."

"Come on," the guy whined, obviously intimidated by those two burly guards who seemed only too willing to subdue him, "you're a nice lady."

"That's right and nice ladies don't deal drugs," she said as she walked away.

"Fuck you, Dr. Quack," the patient shouted.

Coriander was about to move on to the next patient when she noticed Adam and Lottie. "How long have you been here?"

"Long enough to decide not to eat Captain Chippo cookies again," Adam answered, noticing that she looked even more appealing with circles under her eyes, obviously exhausted, and with her glasses pushed on top of her head.

Lottie shrugged. "I told him that it was unusually tense tonight."

"I'm afraid I'm going to be another half hour or so," Coriander apologized, "Do you mind?"

"Not if I can follow you around."

Coriander glanced at Lottie. "What do you think?"

"If he faints he's in the right place for treatment."

Coriander smiled. "Do you intend to faint?"

He looked around. "At least not until there's an empty bed."

She smiled slightly before looking at Lottie. "I hope you're going home before you get roped into anything else around here."

"I just wanted to deliver your visitor," Lottie said, before extending a hand to Adam. "Take care of her," she added, motioning to Coriander who was already on the other side of the unit. A look passed between them. "Thanks again," he said, avoiding any issue before he wandered over to where Coriander stood, keeping out of the way while he observed. She nodded slightly, gesturing in the direction of the stretcher as she picked up a chart attached to the metal bed-frame. A conversation was already in progress between one of her least favorite residents, who was describing the patient's injuries, and a policeman who was taking notes. The case was rape. Arrogant, this particular resident had a penchant for talking to patients in incomprehensible medical jargon and to women in too comprehensible sexual innuendo.

"Victim was hanging around the entrance to Prospect Park," the resident explained.

Coriander moved closer to the bed to check the tube that was running into a vein in one of her hands. "Was she conscious when she came in?"

"Conscious enough to need restraints."

"Violent?"

"It's in the chart, patient was *generally uncooperative.*"

The policeman interjected. "Listen, doc, we get three or four of these a night, you know that."

"And each one is different, you know that. I've got to go through it." She turned back to the resident. "What does *generally uncooperative* mean?"

He said, "From the track marks on her arms and the lesions under her tongue she's an addict and addicts tend to be *generally uncooperative.*"

She asked, "Is that relevant to the rape?"

"Maybe what's relevant is that she's got a whopping case of gonorrhea."

She made a note. "I don't see the connection, Doctor."

"In my opinion the gonorrhea discounts the rape."

"Am I correct in assuming that you believe a rapist checks out his victim's venereal status before he attacks her and because this one would have flunked the test she was spared the rape?" The cop laughed. The resident turned red.

"Gonorrhea—hooker, hooker—addict, and statistically we all

know about rape in those instances, those kinds of people have different standards about what a rape is . . ."

Coriander almost laughed out loud. "And what do we call it, date rape? She saw that the resident was about to say something, which was when she turned her attention back to the policeman. "Who called it rape in the first place?"

"We found her unconscious at the entrance to the park," the policeman explained, "undressed from the waist down and in this general condition."

Coriander leaned over the bed. "Someone certainly did *something* to her against her will."

The resident rallied. "First of all, she's in obvious shock from an overdose, which could explain the delusionary behavior or the delusionary behavior could be a result of the fever from the gonorrhea."

"What about the contusions, cuts, fractures?" Coriander wondered.

"I wasn't there, Dr. Wyatt, were you? Anyway, there was no mention of any rape when she was first brought in."

"Since when is there a time limit for a delusionary patient to report a sexual assault?"

"She was lucid enough to refuse blood and urine tests."

"Make up your mind, Doctor."

"My mind's made up, she tried to avoid a drug charge."

"Did you get the lab report back yet?"

"No."

"Then how do you know the patient's even got GC and not some pelvic inflammatory disease?"

The resident blushed. "I made a diagnosis based on my examination."

"Did you do a pelvic?"

"Yes."

"Then you must have noticed physical evidence of rape."

"Hard to distinguish between the presence of sperm and infection."

"Forget about sperm and forget about infection. This is a living person, Doctor, not a case out of *Gray's Anatomy.*" He started to say something but she kept talking. "Is there or is there not topical confirmation of rape?" She reached for the chart then and noticed out of the corner of her eye that Adam had moved closer. But before she could start reading the resident offered yet another opinion. "This whole rape thing is getting out of hand, every hooker who comes in here swears she's been raped . . ." Coriander ignored him. "Vaginal tear on left labia," she read out loud, "cervical swelling, evidence of forced entry, contusions and abrasions around inner thighs on both sides, abdomen and right breast contused with evidence of cigarette burns around left nipple."

She looked up and this time caught Adam's eye. She kept reading. "Patient has swelling on left cheekbone and right temple, which could explain the dilated pupils. Has she had a scan to rule out any subdural bleeding?" The resident shook his head. The glasses that she had on while she read were now in one hand as she gestured toward the bed. "In conclusion, Doctor, and from a purely diagnostic point of view, I don't care about drugs or venereal disease as it pertains to this woman or to our society at large."

The resident found his voice again. "In my opinion, Doctor," he said, "you're turning this into a political issue."

Coriander was exhausted, impatient, and fed-up, oh was she fed-up. "When a woman says she's been raped, Doctor, we believe her until it's proven that she's lying, whether she's an addict or a hooker or even the wife or girlfriend of one of our doctors." She looked at the policeman. "When she's able to talk, you can question her," she said before repeating, "I want a scan done right away and then get her moved upstairs into medical." Nodding briefly to both men, she turned to leave.

Adam lingered bedside another couple of seconds before he

walked away, followed by the cop. The resident caught up with Coriander just as she stopped at the desk to sign out. He was furious. "That wasn't a consultation back there," he accused, "or even an evaluation, that was a castration."

She seemed surprised. "Of whom?"

"Of me."

"That's impossible, Doctor," she replied evenly, "I don't do micro surgery."

Adam thought about it afterwards, all the way to the parking lot where they went to get her car. When she handed him the keys and asked him to drive, he thought that he shouldn't have come to the hospital. He should have met her anywhere else, in his office, on the street, in a coffee shop, anywhere but there, anything not to see her in yet another light and realize more than ever that she absolutely took his breath away.

Chapter Fifteen

Adam took Coriander's arm as they walked slowly toward the car in the parking garage under the hospital. "Can I ask you a personal question?"

She nodded.

"How do you handle such pressure every day?"

"I suppose I'm used to it."

"Are you ever afraid?"

"All the time."

"How do you overcome it?"

"I've got my own hierarchy of fear."

"What do you mean?"

"When I was a child I was afraid of never making friends every time we moved and one day we stopped moving and my mother died." She paused. "When I first came to New York I was afraid of flunking out of the resident program and then I started doing surgery and was afraid of making a mistake and killing someone." Again, she paused. "I loved Danny for all those years and I was afraid I'd never get over him and then he came back and we got married." She looked at Adam. "And now this . . ."

"Were you ever afraid he'd leave you again?"

"I didn't think about it. When you promise to start over you concentrate on making it work and not on all the negative things that could happen . . ."

"Was he the only man you ever loved?"

What was it about him that made her trust him . . . "The only one . . ."

"There was no one else, not even during those ten years?"

"Does that sound strange?"

"Maybe not strange but certainly not usual."

She didn't answer as she handed him the keys. "Will you drive?"

He followed her around the car to open the door and waited until she was seated before he walked around to the other side. They drove in silence until they were out of the hospital parking lot and through a succession of narrow streets called New York, Flatbush and Nostrand Avenues. They passed Hondas and Chevrolets carrying working-class men and women coming or going from factory shifts or offices while white Nissan Maximas with blacked-out windows and coked-up occupants passed them, tires screeching as they cut in and out of traffic. "Those are the middle-level drug dealers," Coriander commented. "At least their life expectancy beats top-level dealers by about ten years. Eighty percent of all dealers end up in my unit at least once in their lives with gunshot wounds. Fifty percent never come out . . ."

"Aren't you afraid driving around here alone at night?"

"There's a certain system around here, you learn to let everybody pass or cut you off." There were other guidelines to survival in the streets as well, she went on to explain, where traffic lights at every corner were potential death traps. He interrupted her, "Leave enough space for a quick getaway, is that it?" She smiled. "There's nothing worse than being trapped between cars at two o'clock in the morning without a clearly planned-out escape route."

"Wasn't your husband worried about you coming home at all hours of the night?"

"Everyone asks that question."

"What's the answer?"

"We didn't talk about it."

"Now *that* sounds strange."

"It's hard to invent conversations or rules for people because the dynamics are always different in each relationship."

"Did he love you as much as you loved him?"

She felt as if cold water had just been dumped on her head. "Why don't we talk about something else and maybe you could build up to that question . . ."

"I'm sorry," he said, feeling foolish. "Who named you Coriander?"

She kept her eyes straight ahead when she answered. "Everyone always asks that question too," she said with a small smile.

"What's the answer to that one?"

"My mother was Argentinian and she wanted something spicy and not something typically New England, which my father would've named me if it had been up to him. Mother used to tell me how she always thought in colors when it came to people and apparently I reminded her of red." She smiled slightly. "Or she saw red when she saw me." Her gaze drifted out the window. "Have you ever tasted coriander?"

He answered it straight although he wondered. "Probably without knowing it."

Approaching the expressway entrance to Fort Hamilton Parkway, they drove through streets called Linden and Caton where the original residents had been German Jews who perhaps tried to recreate the old country when they named them.

"Tell me about your marriage," she said suddenly.

"Wouldn't you rather hear about my divorce? I can promise you that it's more interesting."

"Why don't we go in order . . ."

"Well, I told you about Eve and the FBI . . ."

"Eve?" she interrupted. "You're kidding."

He shook his head. "I'm not kidding but that's another story."

"Maybe I'd rather hear that one."

He smiled. "Maybe."

She leaned forward. "So, what happened to Eve . . ." She shook her head. "I can't believe it."

"It all started when Eve woke up one morning about six months before she met the guy." He looked embarrassed. "She said she wanted to see other people."

"You should have told her there were no other people."

He laughed. "If I had thought of it I probably would have." He went on to tell her about getting shot and meeting Eve in the hospital and the anger he felt when she left him although now he believed that it was more out of pride than any profound sense of loss that he mourned the relationship. His biggest regret was that he couldn't wake up every morning and have his child right there.

"A girl or a boy?"

"A daughter."

"Does she live with your ex-wife?"

"Yes, and her new husband, but I see Penny as often as possible. What about you," he turned it around, "why did you wait until now to get pregnant?"

If she was upset by the question she didn't show it. "It's sort of a living example of the Lord giveth and the Lord taketh away, wouldn't you say?"

He wanted to reach over and touch her hand, that perfectly lovely hand that just happened to be right there between them on the seat. "It's good that you're close to your father." Adam was fishing.

"I hadn't seen him in three years before this happened."

"Why?"

"He disapproved of my marriage."

"Yet, he ran to your side . . ."

"Blood is thicker than ashes," she said softly.

A series of long piers appeared, strutting astride the polluted harbor that separated New York from New Jersey. "My instinct is to be completely honest with you about everything and that isn't always the best thing to do . . ."

"For me or for you?"

He wanted to tell her about her father's visit to his office. But he had made a promise. "I've got a lot of conflicts in this case."

"We've all got conflicts."

"Mine are interfering with my job . . ."

"Mine are interfering with my life . . ."

"Do you want to tell me about your conflicts first?"

"Uh-uh, because if we can solve yours I've got a feeling mine will just disappear."

He looked at her a minute and almost smiled before he began nodding slowly in agreement. "There are so many questions I want to ask you about your husband and I stop myself. With anyone else, I'd just hammer away with anything that came to mind."

"What do you want to know, if we were happy, close, the same things you've been asking me and everybody else since the accident?"

"For instance . . ."

"Maybe we were both so busy with our careers that we forgot to talk or maybe that's just an excuse and Danny had no intention of telling me anything about what was going on in his life."

"Coriander, for a lot of reasons I'd like to understand the whole story."

"Why don't we eat and we can talk about it over dinner." She smiled. "That way we can make it three out of three."

"What do you mean?"

"Every time we've been in a restaurant together I've lost my appetite."

"It's the atmosphere. Should we give it another chance?" he asked softly.

She said, "Absolutely, but let's go somewhere near my apartment so we can put the car in the garage while I still have a garage. There's a small pub that's not too bad."

"Not Chinatown?" he wondered, "Szechuan or Cantonese?"

"Given the choice I'd rather eat aesthetic."

"Not authentic?"

She told him that she had nothing against Chinese as long as it was someplace small and cozy and quiet without fluorescent lights and linoleum floors, a place that served good food where the egg roll fillings weren't questionable.

"Aesthetic it is," he said right away.

"There's a place near my house."

"When we get close, just direct me to the garage."

They headed west and then up Eleventh Avenue. As they approached 23rd Street, they began to see an interesting collection of women. Some were young and pretty and dressed in lingerie worn as outer garments while others were decrepit and bloated from too many years on those same corners. "Their average life expectancy is about forty so the ones who look old are probably only in their thirties."

"How do you know so much?"

"Before I went on staff at Brooklyn General some of those women were my patients. I used to work at Roosevelt Hospital two nights a week. It was heartbreaking."

"You can't save the world, Coriander."

"No," she said sadly, "not even my own world."

They ended up at that Chinese restaurant near her apartment. It was unpretentious but comfortable with only moderate air-conditioning, not the usual blast of frigid air that made people shiver upon entering and swelter upon exiting as was so common in New York during July and August. It was exactly what they both wanted, Cantonese, Szechuan and Aesthetic all at the same time with dim lights and linen tablecloths and egg roll fillings that weren't questionable.

They were shown to a corner banquette, which presented the first major dilemma, whether to sit side by side or facing each other. Coriander slipped in first and immediately piled her purse and several packages on either side, which eliminated any choice. He faced her. Seated and settled with tea ordered and served, appetizers served as well, they were finally alone.

"I love him," she said without warning. Announced like a challenge, a help-me-get-over-the-pain, prove-that-he's-alive, prove-that-he's-dead, get-me-out-of-limbo but don't-ever-forget-the-ghost-in-our-midst; come here, go away, stay, leave, make love to me, don't dare try; she was giving out signals faster than a distressed ship at sea.

What could he say? "What can I say?"

"Words won't make me stop loving him."

"What can I do?"

"You can tell me what that million dollars means." Her eyes were startling, amber and almond-shaped and filled with pain.

"That's part of this whole conflict," he said, running his finger around the rim of the glass, "I can either lie to you or tell you the truth. Which do you want?"

"The truth."

"That's what I was afraid of . . ." He looked at her with enormous tenderness and tried to speak as gently as possible. "Do you remember when I told you in Mexico about finally having a witness who was prepared to testify against your husband?" It was her turn to nod, her eyes still fixed on him. He didn't say anything, merely reached inside the inner breast pocket of his jacket and pulled out some papers. Silently, he offered them to her across the table, the sections that she was to read highlighted in yellow. It was Fernando Stampa's deposition, the portions of it that dealt with those five blank checks that he signed totaling one million dollars, how Danny Vidal approved those checks without the funds in the account and cashed them before walking out with a million dollars on that Thursday afternoon before the July 4 weekend. She looked as if she had been slapped in the face. Still, she read. And re-read. And read it all again, every last line on all three pages before she stopped. Putting the sheets down and to the side of her plate, she looked at him. "My husband is alive," she said quite calmly. "He knew when he left the bank that day that he wasn't coming back." A little *too* calmly perhaps. "He planned this, all of it," she went on, nodding slowly, her unpainted lips parting as she did. "He's alive," she repeated.

"Not necessarily," Adam said, although it was undoubtedly better not to prolong the uncertainty.

She dismissed his words with a wave of her hand. "How can you say that when you don't believe it yourself, when you never believed it—even before this." She held up the deposition. "From the beginning you believed he was alive."

"If I've changed my opinion it's because I don't want to see you hurt more, that's of greater importance to me than proving my case."

"Death isn't an opinion, Adam, it's a condition."

He said, "You mean a great deal to me."

When she answered her tone was gentle. "And for some reason I depend on you more than on anyone else, but that doesn't change the reality."

"Maybe there are several different levels of reality around here."

"Why would he do such a thing?" she asked, choosing the most relevant one.

"He risked a lot for that million dollars. Obviously he thought it meant a lot to you."

"Then he had no idea what meant anything to me." She looked at him. "How can two people be that close and not have a clue about each other?"

"Unless both people didn't feel the same amount of closeness," he said quietly, reaching across the table to touch her hand. With his hand still touching hers, he went back to the subject of the money. "Did Jorge say when he'd turn over the cash?"

She withdrew her hand. "He said he'd be in touch."

"When?"

"He didn't say except that he was leaving for Mexico and he'd either be in touch before he left or after he came back."

"I don't want to question him until he's actually handed it over."

"Then you'll have to see me again or at least talk to me . . ."

He shook his head. It was crazy, as if he could stay away. He stuck to the subject. "Did you ever meet a man named MacKinley Swayze?"

"No, I don't think so."

"Did your husband ever mention him?"

"Not that I remember."

Adam reached into his pocket and pulled out a photograph. "Do you recognize this man?" he asked, showing her a picture of Swayze.

She studied it a moment. "No," she said firmly, "I've never seen him before. Who is he?"

"He's a suspect in this case," Adam replied evasively before posing yet another question. "Did your husband ever give you reason to believe that he was using Inter Federated money for political reasons?"

The question she dreaded had been asked. There were so many things she sensed but had no way of knowing for certain if they were true. What she knew was about the beginning in Cordoba when Danny left her to go to Buenos Aires. She understood the reasons why he had disappeared instead of *disappearing* with the others in the basement of the Naval Engineering School. And when she met him again in New York she believed that things were different and that what had happened back in Argentina was over. How much did she know? Instead of answering Adam, however, she asked a question of her own. "Are you telling me the truth about everything?" Their eyes met and for several seconds neither spoke.

"No," Adam finally said, "I'm not." And then, "Are you?"

"No."

"Then we're even."

"I need air," she said abruptly, and without warning moved to the side of the banquette, gathering up her things on the way. Adam didn't even bother to ask for the check, merely reached into his pocket to pull out a wad of crumpled bills—thirty or forty dollars—leaving the money on the table before he stood up. Stopping only to retrieve the deposition that she had left behind, he caught up with her and held her arm as together they walked to the exit of the restaurant and out the door.

His arm still gripping hers, they continued in silence. There were no words between them, only movement, for she had somehow gone quite deaf from the realization that there was so much more that she didn't know; mute from the possibility that the one person she trusted in this mess wasn't telling her everything. What frightened her most was that she knew nothing and too much at the same time. . . . She was drenched in perspiration one minute, freezing the next, trembling, fighting back tears, overcoming the temptation to laugh out loud in celebration of Danny being alive until she remembered that he had left her without even a word . . . Leaning on Adam as she walked, she forced herself to remain on the outskirts of this nightmare. It was the longest three blocks of her life; *keep walking, girl, if you can make it home you can make it anywhere.* They reached the building finally and stopped. Discreetly, the doorman stepped inside the lobby from his post on the pavement. She turned to face Adam, about to say something when he said it. "Do you want me to see you upstairs?" She nodded. Again, he took her arm to accompany her inside, to the elevator, up the fourteen floors until the door opened into a private foyer with silk on the walls, marble on the floor, a bronze lantern overhead, beveled mirror on the wall. He released her while she fumbled for the key in her purse and opened the door, stepping aside so she could enter first.

Briefly, she wondered if she had given him any advance warning or if one moment she was standing there perfectly sane and normal and the next she was in his arms, weeping all over his seersucker jacket. He said nothing, only held her, and for that she was grateful. He didn't mumble any of those typical inanities that some would have mumbled more to soothe their own discomfort. It was only after the sobs subsided and she drew back a bit, although not enough to leave his embrace entirely, that her whole life with Danny unraveled in her head. She wanted to tell Adam the entire story in a few sentences just to get it over with; how she met this handsome Argentinian who was charming and educated and cultured and how it had been one long passionate embrace from the very beginning until the very end. Instead, she moved away from him and into the living room where he followed to sit in a chair opposite her. He took her by surprise when he said so simply, "I'm in love with you."

On the one hand she was frightened and on the other she was terrified. "This wasn't supposed to happen . . ."

"Maybe it's just another reality to cope with . . ."

She picked a piece of lint or two from the arm of the chair. "I can't seem to justify my feelings for this one either . . ."

He asked, his eyes crinkling into a small smile, "Just exactly what are we talking about here?"

There was hope that she hadn't quite lost her sense of humor. She smiled. "My feelings for you," she said, so softly that she noticed he had to strain to hear.

"Why do you have to justify anything?"

"Because it's all wrong."

"What was right, falling in love with Danny Vidal and living through this hell?"

"That's different," she argued, "I'm married to him."

"If he's dead you're widowed and if he's alive the last thing you should be is married."

"Either way, you should run like hell away from me and this whole mess."

"Do you really mean that?" And when she didn't answer he added, "I'm leaving for Houston tomorrow."

Halfway to panic, she asked, "How long will you be gone?" And what she saw on his face was that same expression of incredible concern and caring mingled with just the smallest amount of regret. "Until tomorrow night unless something comes up but I'll call you . . ."

She was a mass of contradictions. "Let me come with you."

If he didn't care so much it would have been tempting. "It's better if I go alone."

"When will you know something definite?"

"Maybe soon," he said. Maybe never, he didn't say.

Nothing fit anywhere, what she needed was to settle down and wait it out, to sort through the confusion and despair. She got up after he did to accompany him to the door. "Find my husband," she said softly. It took courage to ask, more courage to want him found.

Adam kept it up. "I'm trying."

After the elevator door closed, she stood there in that tiny hallway, feeling alone and of absolutely no value. It was where she had started before she found Danny or he found her since their history was no longer clear, neither motives nor emotions nor reasons. Help yourself everybody, she thought as she made her way slowly toward her bedroom, except there wasn't much left for anybody to take.

Chapter Sixteen

Adam arrived on a commercial flight into Houston International Airport in the middle of a scorching afternoon. In his hand he carried a battered brown leather briefcase containing photographs of Danny Vidal, Jorge Vidal and Fernando Stampa, all clipped from an Inter Federated corporate brochure, that he intended to show to the man at the private airfield. He also had a print-out from the pay phone in the lounge at Houston Hobby Airport, that private corporate airfield where the Dassault Falcon stopped to refuel on the night of the accident. According to the report released by Southwestern Bell, several calls had been made to Danny Vidal's home phone on the night of July 3. Adam found himself considering several possibilities that might have accounted for those calls. Vidal could have indeed gotten off the plane when it touched down to refuel, wandered into the terminal to call his wife before getting back on board. In that case his whereabouts were obvious, he was dead. Or, someone else could have placed those calls and even unknowingly boarded a plane that was destined to crash into the hills above Acapulco. Yet, given that million dollars cash the most logical possibility was that Vidal got off the plane when it touched down to refuel, wandered into the terminal to call his wife before disappearing into the night. Coriander said there were several hang-up calls on her machine. What was certain was that Houston had been the last point within the United States or anywhere else where that Dassault Falcon was seen in one piece before it entered Mexican airspace. Put another way, from the moment of take-off into Texas skies, the pilots and whoever else happened to be on board had two hours and forty-five minutes to live.

When Adam called down to Hobby to make an appointment with Kit French, the man who had been on duty on July 3, he was amazed to learn that French had somehow gotten hold of portions of the original Mexican accident report. Based on the contents and his own calculations about certain time sequences and flight patterns the man came to the conclusion that there were too many discrepancies and unanswered questions to accept the Mexican version of events. The more he studied certain data the more he didn't like it—more than not like it, he didn't buy it. Which might have explained why the FAA in Washington and the President's Aviation Department in Mexico City had issued a joint statement citing pilot error as the official cause for the accident. Shortly after that all documents were permanently sealed without further explanation. Ironically, the only investigation that was still pending was the one coming out of Adam's office, which had triggered a federal subpoena. Recently there had been several sightings of Vidal around the country.

Armed with photographs of the Argentinian banker, FBI agents had fanned out all over the United States to follow up on leads as well as to take statements from a slew of would-be witnesses, all of which and most of whom turned out to be a colossal waste of time. Not that some of the stories weren't amusing . . . One bank client claimed that he spotted Vidal stepping into a white Cadillac convertible in Fort Lauderdale International Airport, going so far as to say that when he called out his name the man actually turned around to wave. Another client swore that he saw Danny sporting a beard and sunglasses and in the company of two blondes, all three of them eating pancakes at an all-night truck stop in New Orleans at five o'clock in the morning. But the best was a story that someone told about spotting Danny Vidal in the waiting room in the office of a well-known Beverly Hills plastic surgeon with his face all swathed in bandages. In that case the sighting had been meticulously checked out to reveal that the patient in question was definitely not Vidal but rather a minor television actor who had once doubled for Raul Julia on the screen.

On the way from the gate to the car rental counter, Adam tried to imagine Danny Vidal's thoughts, fears, impressions, regrets. It was a process that wasn't completely unfamiliar given that Adam had been living inside the man's head for months. Walking through the airport, Adam wondered if Vidal had passed through that same stretch of terminal on July 3 and if so if he had noticed some of the same sights that Adam now noticed.

The airport was a strip of fast-food stands and neon lights with billboards suspended overhead offering practically anything that anybody could possibly want to help them get by in life. Dial-A-Prayer was the most prominent, as easy as punching in the 1-900-999-Lord. Or, if a relationship was the problem the answer was as near as dialing the 1-900-999-Love while depression was easily remedied by calling the 1-900-999-Help not to be confused with the 1-900-999-Pain which brought relief in the person of a chiropractor.

Electric carts cruised the smooth airport floor, blue-haired ladies with swollen ankles cuddling small dogs were seated next to red-faced men cuddling duty-free bags of Tequila. Advertising posters lined the walls giving departure details for Juarez where one could Get Hitched or Unhitched; photographs of Indian girls wearing long braids and short skirts beckoned visitors to the brand-new convention center; other libidinous placards featured blondes in skimpy bikinis posing poolside at motels and health clubs.

But as he paid for his newspaper he kept thinking about Coriander, imagining her reaction to everything that was so typical of America, so atypical of New York.

Houston Hobby Airport was a single-story redwood building with a sign that advertised Charters, Rentals, Hangars and Lessons. Parking the rental car in a space in front of the building, Adam took it from the beginning, wandering out onto the tarmac, imagining the Dassault Falcon parked where a Piper Cub now stood. Counting the steps back to the entrance of the terminal, he walked inside. In one corner of the reception area was a long formica counter on which was a microphone on a stand and a telephone; on the other wall were a tweed sofa and a couple of canvas captain's chairs with a low table in between that was covered with magazines ranging from Penthouse to Playboy, National Geographic to National Enquirer; piles of aeronautic journals were stacked to one side. Opening another door, Adam left the reception area to enter the lounge itself, which was slick and shiny and smelled like the inside of a brand-new New York taxi.

A middle-aged man wearing jeans, cowboy boots and a red windbreaker stood up when Adam walked into the room. Tall and lanky with pockmarked skin and a full head of white hair, he carried some papers and a postal tube under one arm, as he approached Adam. "I'm Kit French," he said, "and you must be from the D.A.'s office."

Adam introduced himself and shook the man's hand before following him to a corner grouping of chairs and a low table. "Is it always this quiet?" he asked after they were seated.

"Bad times, hardly anyone can afford to lease private equipment anymore on account of the high cost of fuel on account of those camel fuckers . . ."

Adam ignored this remark and tried to turn the conversation to his reason for coming to Houston. But he couldn't get to the point until he had listened sympathetically while the man talked about his friendship with Roy, the co-pilot, and the personal loss he felt.

Placing his briefcase on the table, Adam snapped it open and pulled out the manila envelope. Reaching inside, he took out three photographs and spread them out in front of the man: Danny Vidal, Jorge Vidal and Fernando Stampa. "Do you recognize any of these men?"

French didn't hesitate. He pointed directly to the photo of Danny Vidal. "That's him, that's the guy who got off the plane."

"What about the others?"

The man shook his head. "Nope, never saw them." He studied Danny's picture another minute.

Adam decided to move on. "I understand you talked to him," he began. "Who started the conversation?"

French motioned to another grouping of chairs and tables across the room. "I was sitting over there having coffee with my buddy Roy when the guy asked me if he had any phone messages, said something about expecting a couple of business calls."

"Did he?"

"Nope, nothing."

"And if I understand correctly you told Luckinbill that you heard him making some calls."

"That's when he went into the phone booth so I didn't exactly hear him since he kept closing the door. I saw him making the calls, and when he opened the door I heard him dialing and hanging up. It was real quiet in the lounge and real hot, the air-conditioning is turned down when there's not a lot of business, energy shortage, you know." The guy shrugged.

"How long was the plane being serviced?"

"I'd say about forty-five minutes."

"What happened then?"

"I could see out the window over there when the lineman was finishing up with the fuel truck. The pilot was in the john and Roy and me had finished our coffee. That's when the guy came out of the booth and started saying something about having business troubles in Houston."

"Was there a question of him having to stay in Houston?"

French looked a little embarrassed. "I guess I began pushing for a layover because business is so bad and I was hoping for a hangar fee. I even offered them a good price."

"When did he let you know?"

"He never did because that was when that other guy showed up, friend of his I guess, and the two of them walked outside and talked for about fifteen minutes or so. I got the feeling that the other guy showed up to straighten out whatever business problem he had, sort of like the meeting was arranged in advance . . ."

Adam made a couple of notes. "Can you describe him?"

"He had no hands, just a couple of metal hooks . . . Tall, thin, more than thin he was gaunt with black hair, maybe early thirties, hard to tell . . ."

"What happened then?" he asked, looking up.

"See that microphone on the counter over there?" French gestured to the reception area. "Well, I had it turned high so if the phone rang I could hear it over the loudspeakers if I was here or even if I was outside. Call came in about another small plane landing for some kind of emergency service and they needed to use my truck and lineman. I got caught up in that . . ."

"Where was everybody else?"

"Roy was already out near his plane with the pilot and the passenger was still talking with that guy out on the tarmac, halfway between the plane and the lounge."

"How long were you on the phone?"

"About five minutes but then I had trouble finding landing forms so all in all I was wrapped up in there for about fifteen, maybe twenty minutes."

"What kind of a plane was it that came in for emergency service, do you remember?"

The man thought a minute. "A twin-engine Cessna."

"Do you still have those landing forms?"

"They're on file over at the main airport."

"Would you recognize the pilot?"

"I never saw him, I just talked to him over the radio."

"What do you remember about him?"

"Only that he spoke bad English . . ."

Adam's heart pounded. "Spanish?"

"Nope, it wasn't Spanish, it was more Slavic or something, he had a thick foreign accent but it definitely wasn't Spanish."

"Who got off that other plane?"

"No one."

"And you didn't see anyone get on?"

"I didn't see too much . . ." The man looked embarrassed.

"What happened when you went back outside?"

"Roy's plane had already taxied down the runway and was sitting on the apron out there waiting for clearance from Houston International."

Adam felt drained, as if he had gone step by step through the whole forty-five minute refueling stop with leg irons on his ankles. "Did you see the passenger anywhere around the terminal or out in the parking lot?"

French shook his head. "Nope, nowhere, but to be real honest, I didn't exactly go looking all around for him either because I assumed he was on the plane or they would've worked out that hangar fee."

Adam gathered up the photographs that were still on the table. "You mentioned that you had portions of the accident report . . . How did you happen to get it?"

"It doesn't matter how I got it, what matters is that nothing makes any damn sense."

Adam nodded. "What do you mean?"

"It's just too simple to give the cause of the accident as pilot error especially since the bodies are cremated, death certificates are signed and all the other proof has conveniently disappeared." He studied Adam before continuing. "Like I told you on the phone, I just don't buy any of it."

Adam leaned over for a better view of what appeared to be a map. "Why don't you go through it with me slowly?"

French nodded as he began. "Let me show you what I did here, I took an aviation map and drew a line through it that simulates the contour of the earth up to 155 miles from Acapulco. Then I sketched in the arrival chart which is this here dotted line that looks like a staircase and that's called the *norte arrival code* or *north arrival code* which is nothing more complicated than an approach pattern for pilots flying under instrument conditions."

"What makes you think they were flying under instrument conditions?"

"Everything at night is instrument," French replied, turning back to the graph. "Which means the pilots adhered to this flight code and did exactly what the computer told them which means they followed this staircase." He traced his finger down the series of dotted lines. "And this staircase clears every last contour way above any of those mountains surrounding Acapulco." French put his hand on the manila envelope. "Now, the part of the transcript right here from the accident report helps prove my point which is why I made the graph."

"Is it possible for me to make copies?"

"I'm going to give you everything," French assured Adam, "I already made them."

"That's great . . ."

French rubbed his chin. "What I thought I'd do first is explain how the cockpit radio works." He paused. "Unless you already know?"

"Just assume I know nothing and you'll be giving me more credit than I deserve." Adam grinned.

"In a word here's what it is. There's something called the *line of sight* in all *VHF* transmissions which means *if you can see it you can talk to it.* So, right here at 29 miles from Acapulco," he continued, turning his attention back to the graph, "is a place called *torro intersection*. Every airplane that flies over here is forbidden to go below 13,000 feet . . ."

"Who forbids them?" Adam interrupted.

"Air traffic safety." He turned the graph around so that it faced Adam right-side up. "The portion of the transcript I've got here," he patted the envelope, "says the pilots made radio contact with Mexico City at 14,000 feet or at 35 miles out of Acapulco which keeps the plane within those *torro regulations*. So far so good . . ."

Adam nodded slowly, his eyes narrowed in concentration. "Where does the discrepancy begin?"

"Right out there at 14,000 feet."

"But I thought that was within radio range."

"Ordinarily it is except whoever invented that little piece of theatre forgot about the mountains." He smiled slightly. "They block the transmission tower . . ."

"*If you can't see it you can't talk to it,*" Adam repeated the rule. "What about pilot error?"

"That's what the Mexicans want everybody to believe and that's where it begins to make even less sense. The accident report puts the whole flight profile below any VHF *line of sight* except for the last point of radio contact which would've been at 75 miles out of Acapulco or 35,000 feet up."

"*Was* that the last point the plane checked in?"

"That's debatable although what the Mexicans are claiming is the pilot misread his altimeter and reported he was at 35 miles out and 14,000 feet up instead of 75 miles out and 35,000 up which was one helluva mistake."

"What about pilot error at that point?"

French shook his head. "That possibility is so remote it's almost nonexistent."

"Why?"

The man settled back to explain. "There's this point over Mexico City called *terminal control area* where air traffic is always dense. Any flight over that area is required to check in with the control tower every few minutes. At that point the Falcon was under constant scrutiny by Mexico City." French sat forward again. "Follow me here, the plane is reporting in every few miles over Mexico City until it passes over that point and by then it's only 120 miles from Acapulco which in air time is about 25 minutes."

Adam began nodding slowly, the whole thing coming together. "Go on . . ."

"What the Mexicans are trying to make everyone believe is that after reporting in correctly the entire time over Mexico City, the pilot suddenly makes this huge mistake. Instead of saying he's 75 miles outside of Acapulco he says he's 35 miles outside which is about an eight minute differential or almost a 50% error from his last confirmed position over *terminal control area.* French shook his head slowly. "If that pilot was coming in after crossing the ocean and Mexico City was his first check-in point I could understand a mistake as big as that. But not when he's been reporting in every few minutes . . ."

"That's a mistake of 45 miles," Adam said thoughtfully, his eyes fixed on the man.

"No way in hell he's going to do that. And if he was out of phase someone would've picked it up way before, when he was flying over Mexico City, which means someone's screwing around with the data."

"How many people would it take to alter facts in a case like this?" Adam asked.

"That depends," French replied. "Someone who has the power to request all the information *after the fact.* Look, most guys sitting in the control tower have more planes than they know what to do with, they're not going to remember one private aircraft . . ."

"Even if it crashed?"

"Not unless they pull their data . . . And if the data has already been pulled by someone involved in a cover-up, they've got no way of knowing."

Adam thought about it before turning back to the graph. "Go back to the accident . . . I'm confused about the point of impact or at least about what the Mexicans say was the point of impact. After all, there were all those mountains, you can't deny that."

"Go on, what's the point of impact?"

"7600 feet," Adam answered.

"Or 45 miles out," French said.

"That's right," Adam agreed, "isn't it possible the plane rammed into those mountains there?"

French leaned over the graph once more. "Look here, say I'm willing to go along with everything the Mexicans claim about the plane making contact 35 miles out and say I'm willing to make an exception about the *line of sight* and those mountains being in the way, maybe there's a hole in the terrain that I'm missing that the pilot found so he could dip down and make radio contact . . ."

"Then what?" Adam asked carefully.

"How the hell can a plane make contact at 35 miles outside of its destination and then crash at 45 miles out unless the pilot first called in before taking the plane back up through the clouds to crash?" He shook his head. "No way, that plane was already in a descent pattern."

It made sense. "What's your best guess?"

"Explosion."

"Bomb?"

"Well, let me put it this way, it's unlikely that it's a fuel line since the plane was almost on empty by then."

"But why here," Adam persisted. "Why would someone take a chance and wait until the very last leg of a trip to blow it up?"

"You've got the answer," French said, "it's a lot easier to have a cover-up in Mexico than in the States." He paused. "And there's something else, you've just hit on one of the biggest ironies of all."

"What's that?"

French smiled slightly. "The Mexicans counted on pilot error while the bomber counted on pilot accuracy."

"What do you mean?"

"The bomber was counting on the plane reaching those exact levels of altitude over precise places so that the bomb would go off at exactly 10,000 feet at that point in the flight."

"Which means that even if the plane was forced to make an emergency landing for some reason in Mexico City, the bomb would still go off before," Adam said slowly.

"Exactly, since Mexico City is at 7,000 feet . . ."

"What kind of a bomb goes off like that at a pre-programmed altitude?" Adam asked, certain of the answer.

"Something triggered by an altimeter and a clock that sets off the explosive."

"What's the most effective explosive?" Adam continued, trying to keep his tone level.

"Probably TNT."

"Which explains why all those trees were standing," Adam said almost to himself. He looked at the man. "Just like Luckinbill said, if the plane had plowed into the top of that mountain, all the trees would've broken like matchsticks."

"Everything points to a mid-air explosion," French said sadly.

The men were silent for a few moments, each lost in thought before French said, "I've got to get going. I've got another plane coming in about ten minutes." He stood, offering his hand. Adam stood as well, shaking hands before watching him roll up the graph to slip it back inside the tube. "Here," French said, "this is for you along with the transcript. I've got copies . . ."

"I really appreciate this, and I'll keep in touch. I'll let you know what we make of this thing." He paused. "If you hear anything, I'd appreciate you getting in touch with me."

"One piece of advice that I'm sure you already know."

"What's that?"

"The only way you're going to disprove that it was pilot error is to find that black box."

"We're trying, Mr. French. It's in our interest to disprove that pilot error theory too because what we're dealing with goes beyond a plane crash . . ."

"Damn shame," French said, shaking his head. Clasping Adam's shoulder, he said, "Just do what you can and keep in touch with me."

"Thanks," Adam replied, "and you do the same."

The whole story was heartbreaking. Adam just stood there for a minute or two before he wandered over to the phone booth. Again, he just stood there for a minute or two before he slipped inside and sat down, closing the door, opening the door, wondering, deciding . . .

He knew the number by heart. Picking up the receiver, he dialed, waiting for the electronic voice of the operator to come on the line so he could enter his credit card number. He listened as the phone rang—one two three rings—before he heard her voice. She sounded breathless. "Hello."

"Why aren't you at the hospital?"

"Is that what you called to ask me?"

"No," he said, "I called . . ." Why the hell did he call except to hear her voice. It was epidemic around that phone booth . . .

"Are you in Houston?" she said, filling the silence.

"I'm about to come home." Home. He sat there, his chin against the mouthpiece, the receiver between his chin and shoulder.

"You sound terrible," she said, a note of concern in her voice, "What's the matter?"

He could see her face so clearly, that wrinkle between her

brow, head tilted to the side. He closed his eyes, the receiver still balanced between chin and shoulder. "Maybe I'm tired," he said, "not that I know what tired is anymore since I have nothing to compare it with."

"I feel guilty when you say that."

He sat up in the booth, hitting his knee on the shelf that held the phone. "I'm the one that's supposed to feel guilty, I'm Jewish."

"The moving cartons arrived today . . ."

"Now I feel guilty. If you wait a day I'll help."

"Thanks, but what I'm doing now nobody can do. I'm sorting . . ." A life, she didn't add.

He took a breath. It was incredible how much he missed her, a woman he barely knew in terms of time yet about whom he could recite almost every physical detail. "I've got something interesting to show you," he said, before explaining briefly about the graph and French's theory. He needed to see her, if only to talk about the case . . . "Are you working tomorrow?"

"Only half a day," she said lightly, "twelve hours."

"Don't you think you should cut back a little?"

"It's keeping me sane."

"Is it keeping you healthy?"

"I'm not sick, Adam, I'm pregnant."

He felt a pang. It could have been different for both of them —he could have loved the mother of his child a little more and loved the mother of someone else's child a little less. "What if I call you when I get in and if it's not too late maybe I'll stop over."

"It can wait, Adam," she said, that note of concern back in her voice. "Why don't you go home and get a good night's sleep and we'll talk tomorrow."

It didn't escape him that an intimacy had developed between them. "Let's see how I feel when I get in," he said, leaning his head back. But then he remembered. "By the way, do you know anyone or did Danny ever mention anyone with hooks for hands . . ." He heard her gasp. "What's the matter?" "Adam, come home," she whispered, "please . . ." He sat up in the phone booth. "What's the matter?" he repeated. "Just come home, I'm waiting for you . . ."

He sat there in that phone booth for several seconds holding the receiver after she had already hung up. What the hell was that about . . . Every day there was something else to embroil him deeper into this thing, to make him accept with a kind of regretful inevitability that absolute attraction she held for him. And what made it even more difficult was that nothing that anybody had done had broken her, not anything that happened so far had extinguished that light of rebellion in her eyes. Not yet . . .

Part III

". . . They chose Patagonia for its absolute remoteness and foul climate; they did not want to get rich."

In Patagonia by BRUCE CHATWIN

". . . A man can only live one great passion in his life."

JUAN PERON when asked to compare EVITA to ISABEL

Chapter Seventeen

Metal hooks for hands. Coriander could think of nothing else as she sorted books and papers into moving cartons or into the trash. There was a part of her that rejected even the possibility that Hernando was alive and another part that believed it almost as if she had seen for herself. She was smart enough to know that it went beyond Hernando and her own hurt feelings that he never contacted her between his release and his "suicide," or his release and his disappearance. It went beyond her own guilt that she could have saved his life by sacrificing her own happiness. There seemed to be a slight confusion somehow since her husband was no longer missing and presumed dead but rather dead and assumed missing.

She stopped to look in the mirror as she made her way to the foyer. There were smudges of dust across one cheek and on the tip of her nose and her hair was loose, uncombed and falling everywhere. She didn't even bother to wipe off the dirt or smooth her hair as she opened the door. Adam wasn't in the apartment more than an instant when she took his hands and began explaining, "I know who that man is, the one in Houston with the metal hooks . . ."

He tried to calm her, "Take it easy."

But she was too agitated. "There's no doubt in my mind that Danny's alive . . ."

He turned his hands around to hold hers. "How do you know that?"

She rambled on. "The man with the metal prostheses, the one at the airport, is someone who was so close to both of us back in Argentina." She shook herself free. "Don't you understand, that's Hernando . . ."

He didn't remember . . .

"My friend, the one I was with the night he *disappeared.*"

"But Danny told you he was dead, committed suicide . . ."

There was something almost comical about it. "*Dead* to my husband means something different than what it means to most people."

There was no argument there. "But you told me . . ."

"No, Adam," she began pacing, "I lied . . ." She amended it, "By omission, I lied."

"Take it easy, Coriander, and try to explain it to me slowly."

"When I met Danny in New York years later one of the first things I asked about was Hernando . . ."

"That's when he told you about his hands?"

She nodded. "And when he told me that he committed suicide shortly after that . . ."

"And the body?"

"I didn't ask, I didn't think to ask." She was beside herself. "We were so desensitized by then we never expected a body . . ."

"And now he shows up in Houston."

She took a step closer until she was in his arms, her head leaning against his shoulder. "I'm so tired," she said.

Adam held her. "I know," he soothed. "We all are."

She picked up her head and looked at him. "Should we go sit down somewhere?"

"If we can find a place to sit in this mess."

Making excuses for the disarray, she led him through the apartment, the long way around, more to gather her thoughts than to show him what had been her life. On highly-polished marble floors they walked where an occasional Oriental rug was scattered, through corridors where sketches of Piranesi and Ensor lined the walls, through a small salon where antiques stood in various stages of crates to be shipped back where they came from, underneath a Gothic arch and into a larger salon where paintings were already unhooked and resting on the floor. It was there that they paused at a row of windows that took up one entire side of the room. "Are you sorry to be leaving this apartment?"

"There are so many things I'm sorry and sad about but that isn't one of them."

"When are you moving?"

"Next Sunday."

"So soon?"

"I can't afford to stay here another month and even if I could I wouldn't want to. Sunday is the only day that I've got any time."

"Where are you going?"

"Back where I came from," she said with a touch of irony.

"Buenos Aires?"

Not that she hadn't considered that option briefly . . . "No, I'm going back to my old apartment on the West Side where I lived before Danny found me."

"Is that a good idea?"

"I don't know any more. I feel like I'm reeling out of control."

"I think you're doing just fine."

Neither spoke for several moments as they gazed out the windows. City lights sparkled white and glittered gold in all directions, south toward a collection of skyscrapers where, on the top of one, time and temperature changed by second and degree; west across Central Park and over the eerie nighttime silhouette of the Metropolitan Museum of Art and that playground *where the children will play, querida.* "Do you see that playground over there?" she pointed.

He moved closer, "Yes, why?"

"I put all my hopes on that playground once. I used to stand here and imagine my children were there. I would invent my schedule so that I wouldn't miss one day with them when I got home from work . . ." She gazed out. "I really believed that we could have it all—love, a family, security . . ."

"Do you know what I think?"

She shook her head.

"I don't think you ever believed that . . ."

She focused on the park in the distance once again. "Maybe I wanted it so much that it became real to me."

"Were your parents happy?"

"My parents either drank when they were fighting or toasted each other when they made up."

"Always in front of you?"

"Enough so I grew up determined that my life would be different. I was convinced that if I gave up the passion I'd have the sanity and then when I met Danny I thought I could have it all." She smiled vaguely. "The passion, the sanity and of course the guilt . . ."

"About?" He touched her cheek tenderly.

She turned around so her back was against the window pane. "Because of the choice my father gave me that night, that if I left Danny and came home he'd do what he could to get Hernando released."

"So you convinced yourself that if you married Danny at least what happened to Hernando wasn't for nothing, is that it?"

She nodded. "That's it," she said softly before taking his

hand. "Come." She led him out of the main living room and down another long corridor where miniature paintings lined one wall and a few South American and Mexican primitives lined another. She stopped when they came to a blown-up picture of a child who couldn't have been more than five or six. She was wearing Coriander's smile and a smocked pinafore. On her feet were adult high-heeled shoes, and over one small and fragile arm was a cumbersome pocketbook. "That's me," Coriander said from somewhere behind Adam.

Turning, he studied her, as if to compare the child with the woman, before turning back again to the picture. "How old were you?"

"That was taken only last year, before all the problems. Do you think I've aged?"

Grateful for the moment of humor, he relaxed a bit. "You've got the same face, maybe a little older, but I'd know you anywhere." Again, he turned to look at the photograph. "You're going to have a beautiful baby, Coriander Wyatt," he predicted, aware that there was so much more he couldn't say because there was so much more she couldn't hear.

"I've wanted this baby for so long . . ."

"That's another good thing that came out of this situation."

"I'm almost afraid to think so."

"Nothing bad is going to happen anymore," he said firmly.

"Danny once told me that."

"I'm not Danny."

She didn't answer right away, at least not until he promised, "I'm here for you, Coriander, no matter what happens and until you don't want me around."

It was all too familiar. "I need time."

"I'm not in a hurry."

They continued down the remainder of the hallway and into a paneled room that had been Danny's study. She told him that if some people used guns her husband's weapon of choice was a telephone. He used it constantly, at all hours of the day and night, working his way across one time zone and into another. She motioned Adam over to a long brown suede sectional sofa while she moved to where an array of crystal decanters stood on one of the bookshelves. "Would you like a drink?"

"Are you having one?"

"In about six months."

"Can I buy it for you?"

"If you haven't run like hell by then . . ." She turned then and without asking what or how, poured straight whiskey into a brandy snifter and carried it over to the sofa. "Why are you looking at me like that?" she asked as she handed him the glass.

How could he explain that it had everything to do with the ongoing conflict he had about finding Danny Vidal, especially after listening to the tape that Palmer had given him. How could he tell her that he had spent most of the night cutting out those intimate moments on the tape, portions that had nothing to do with politics, money, or murder and only with love. How could he describe what he had heard without humiliating her—those muffled cries, whispers, uneven breathing, the obvious rhythmic creaking of a bed, a night of love-making in La Boca after Hernando had been taken by the secret police or a tryst at his office in between classes . . . What was incredible was that her father hadn't erased those portions before turning the tape over to him. When Adam asked about it the following morning, Palmer's response at least had been honest. He was afraid that he would have been accused of tampering with evidence had he tried to cut things out. He was also honest when he admitted that his only interest was in bringing Danny Vidal to justice, even at the expense and sacrifice of everything else, including his daughter's privacy.

"You could have left your briefcase in the foyer," Coriander remarked, noticing that he had carried it with him through the house.

"There are things in here I want to show you."

"Should I be afraid?"

"Not if you rely on that hierarchy of fear that you told me about."

"What do you mean?"

"Once you told me Danny wasn't a thief, you were absolutely certain about that, remember?"

She nodded. "In Mexico . . ."

"Now that you know about that million, have you changed your mind?"

"What are you saying?"

He wanted to hold her. "Is it possible that your husband blew up that plane?"

"I can't allow myself to believe that."

"Tell me something, Coriander, is there a safe in the apartment or a closet that he kept locked that you had no access to?" He felt like hell because he knew he was badgering her.

She hung in . . . "Sometimes he locked the door to his study."

"And that didn't strike you as strange?"

"Nothing struck me as strange because he always had a logical reason. He said he didn't want the maid rummaging around the desk."

"And now?"

Her face was flushed. "Yes, now it strikes me as strange."

"I'm not trying to put you on the spot."

She glanced away. "Why don't you just tell me what you found out in Houston?"

Instead of answering, he reached down to open his briefcase and take out the accident report and graph that Kit French had given him. Spreading everything out on the table, he started by telling her about the mountains as they pertained to the *line of sight,* explaining how communication between cockpit and control towers functioned, which made it doubtful that the plane crashed on its own into a mountain, how it was likely that someone had planted a bomb on board so that it exploded in mid-air.

"Someone but not Danny." She was adamant.

At worst, he admired her loyalty. "I want to play you a tape."

"Is this the bad part?"

What the hell could he say? He said nothing. Her eyes never left him while he reached down into the briefcase again to take out a small tape recorder, which he placed on the table. Glancing at her, as if for permission, he pushed down the *play* button, noticing that she started the moment Danny's voice filled the room. Within seconds it was clear; Danny Vidal was describing the murder of Matthew Johnson, how he fired a single bullet into the man's right temple while he was on his knees with his hands tied behind his back. Coriander went pale. Adam stopped the machine. "Are you all right?" he asked. "Play it," she whispered. Adam pushed down the *play* button and again Danny's voice filled the room as he continued to explain how, along with several others, he had wrapped the body in a Montonero flag before tossing it over the wall of the American Embassy. It certainly made an unforgettable impression, "Mac" pointed out on the tape. Coriander and Adam looked at each other, realizing that Danny was speaking with the man called MacKinley Swayze. Adam and Coriander listened as Swayze went on to say that all of Argentina would see that the Montoneros were back in business and not the least bit fearful of creating an international incident; this time around it wasn't about money since there was no shortage coming in after that kidnapping and ransom coup of sixty million dollars; this time it was about pride and honor and above all a message directed at that pompous ass in the American Embassy, the man who believed that they were "nothing more than a band of savages." Adam shut it off.

"How did you get that tape?"

"Someone gave it to me."

"Who?"

"Coriander, don't . . ."

She studied him a moment. "Only the military could have made that tape."

"It doesn't matter anymore."

"Everything matters," she argued, "because suddenly everything's a matter of life and death."

"Let's just leave it that it was someone who cares about you."

There was a flicker of understanding in her eyes. "What we do for love . . ." She looked at him. "I would have liked to be loved a little less in my life."

"How about loved a little differently?"

In an instant she was next to him, her head resting on his shoulder and in an instant more he had gathered her in his arms to hold her. "It's almost all over," he said soothingly, his mouth buried in her hair.

"Not yet," she whispered.

"At least the confusion is almost all over."

"Find him," she whispered again.

"I'm not sure I want to, Coriander," Adam said simply.

She sat back. "That's not a solution."

"I've been thinking that maybe it's better if I bow out."

She picked up her head to look at him. "What is it about me that makes men leave when things get tough?"

He smiled. "I'm not leaving, I'm just suggesting I turn over the investigation to someone more objective."

"When you have a case with such a potentially spectacular ending objectivity goes out the window."

"You're such a contradiction, Coriander Wyatt Vidal, you either reason like a child or you're the biggest cynic I've ever met."

She nodded slowly. "Without sounding like a child, what's going to happen?"

"In the abstract or in the real?" he hedged.

"Both."

"In the real world we wait until Jorge gives you the money and in the abstract we wait to see how you feel."

"I wonder . . ."

"Tell me something," Adam began without even stopping to consider, "if we never find him, are you going to spend the next ten years the way you spent the last ten years?"

"What do you mean?" But she knew.

"Alone and unwilling to let yourself love someone else."

"He's still the father of my child."

There was no argument there. "Maybe I'm being too simplistic but he should have remembered that before he took off and killed three innocent men."

"I still can't accept that . . ."

"However the outcome, he should never have jeopardized you or put you in this position."

"I'm a grown-up woman, Adam, I put myself in this position. He didn't put a gun to my head."

Not yet, Adam didn't say.

It had been a long day and an even longer night. Whatever each of them knew and recounted was already history. And while they had run the gamut of emotions it neither excused nor explained what happened at the door as they waited for the elevator. For him, it marked a turning point in his life when he took her chin gently in his hand and kissed her face, damp near the corners of her hair. A small sigh as he gathered her against him, involved suddenly with her lips, her tongue, her arms. His breathing changed and in a moment she felt his body pressed against hers. He was big enough for her to disappear in his arms and how she would have welcomed that. "I'm sorry," she whispered very seriously when their lips parted. "I love you," he whispered just as seriously before stepping into the elevator. "Forgive me," she murmured as she shut the door to the apartment.

Chapter Eighteen

The only sound was the wind slamming a gate open and shut in the distance. Danny Vidal sat in a black leather sloped chair in a pre-fabricated cabin on a sheep ranch in Ushuaia and read about his own death. He was growing a beard and his hair was longer than it had been in years. Wearing tight jeans, loafers, no socks, and a V-neck sweater he looked more like an Italian film star playing an urban guerrilla than the real thing.

Of the immediate repercussions of his disappearance, the newspapers knew quite less than he would have predicted. Speculation about Danny Vidal varied by country and level of publication. The tabloids reported that he had committed suicide because of impending financial disaster and in the process had blown up two innocent men. Weeklies offered the possibility that he worked for several secret services ranging from Israeli to Irish to South African. The dailies focused their reports on the bizarre coincidence that the banker was killed on the eve of financial ruin. The *Wall Street Journal* made the most interesting point in a series of articles on the bank's demise. Although Jorge Vidal had been privy to most of his brother's financial machinations there was no concrete proof that linked him to anything criminal. He had never signed a single bank document or loan authorization nor had he sat on any credit committee. And in a statement made through his lawyer, Jorge Vidal proved the paper's point by claiming that his connection to Inter Federated was limited to his ownership of several thousand shares of stock, which made him as much a victim as anyone else.

Inter Federated had been closed for weeks, with all records, files and assets impounded by the District Attorney's office and the New York State Banking Commission. Although the FDIC guaranteed deposit accounts of under one hundred thousand dollars, there was talk of a takeover by Republic Exchange—coincidentally the bank Fernando Stampa had used—which would protect depositors without the necessity of a payout by the government. Danny was less concerned about any takeover by Republic than about Fernando Stampa. The man evoked sympathy in every article written about the scandal; he was consistently portrayed as a victim who had been left with five bad checks totaling a million dollars. And in every such article there were statements made by that Special Investigator from the District Attorney's office, the man who seemed to be keeping Coriander under such close watch.

How well he knew her, his Coriander, so well that he could almost hear her arguing that between deception and death she would gladly choose death. There wasn't a day or an hour that passed where he didn't think about her or their life together. The wind blew the smell of damp earth and pungent plants around the campsite and he thought of her. Two oxen yoked to a cart and he thought of them. The vast pampas stretching endlessly in the distance and he thought, with a shudder, of his loneliness and the loss of his own life.

Across the room a fire blazed in a stone hearth above which hung a boar's head, slashes of red paint around its mouth. Out of one window was an ochre-colored fence and the biting wind whipping around bare trees and shrubs. Out another window in the far distance was the Beagel Channel and the ragged outline of the Hoste Islands, the Murray Narrows beyond it, reaching toward the Straits of Magellan and the Horn Archipelago, all approaching Antarctica. Legend had it that thousands of years before, Patagonia had tumbled down a mountain and into a prism of blue ice in one of the many lakes to arrive in perfect condition at its bottom.

How well he knew his Coriander, so well that he could predict her reaction when confronted with that million dollars. Again, if it wasn't too much to ask, she would have preferred a choice between knowing just what the hell was going on and a suitcase filled with a million dollars in crisp one hundred and five hundred dollar bills. And frankly, she would have opted to know just what the hell was going on . . . In my absence, *querida,* for you in the event of my death, security for you and the child although it was never intended as an apology. Throughout every day he had imaginary conversations where he answered her questions about how he passed the time. It was always the same, he would tell her that he rarely socialized, hardly ever went out, mostly just sat and read or watched the wind.

He missed her like hell, his blood went crazy when he thought of her. Patagonia was the only place on earth where eternity had boundaries and forever took on shape and substance. He liked to believe that his only possessions were a hunting knife, a gun, a list of grievances, and his memories of her. What they had together was a love affair, the difference between *cosmic passion* and a *cheap thrill,* and even around this outpost to nowhere there was plenty of opportunity for the latter. On at least six occasions Swayze planted a girl in his bed and each time that he opened his eyes to be confronted with the temptation to forget, his reaction was the same. He rejected the girl with a vaguely paternal air that caused concern among his peers. They wanted him happy, satisfied, and without remorse. They might as well have wanted him in pieces in that basin in Chilpancingo. Danny opened his eyes and glanced out the window. Swayze was standing next to a fire that burned logs and sticks under a metal grill, about to drop two limp rabbits into a pot of boiling water, undoubtedly on his way inside to talk . . . Turning his attention back to the cabin, Danny took inventory of what had become his prison until the next phase of the plan when he would leave for Havana.

English antiques cluttered the room, the pieces not old enough to be of any real value, not new enough to be considered junk. The cabin itself was on the grounds of a sheep ranch on varied and rolling terrain that included steep hills, plains, forests, streams, and *vegas* or damp meadows, with gravel driveways leading up to each structure on the property.

Danny looked up when Swayze entered the cabin. Shaking off his anorak, the man warmed his hands briefly over the fire before he sat down. He got right to the point. "Your brother contacted Coriander about the money. The minute he gives it to her he implicates himself."

"The bills aren't marked."

"The guy from the D.A.'s office is just waiting for that million dollars to turn up somewhere. Be sensible, how many different million-dollar bundles are floating around New York?"

"Which one of them is the liability?"

Swayze didn't hesitate. "Both of them," he said before adding, "and then there's Stampa."

Danny stalled. "What more can he do?"

Swayze shook his head, studying Danny as if he couldn't believe his naiveté. "You're not thinking clearly," he began, "he's the one who carried six hundred thousand dollars to Havana every month and he's the one who can decipher all the codes in your files. You underestimated him or maybe you overestimated both of them when you left Stampa with five bum checks and made your brother the delivery boy. What you've done is handed over the two weakest links."

"Stampa implicates himself if he talks about delivering that money to Havana every month."

"Maybe the whole problem here is that you just don't understand the American judicial system." Swayze separated the words as he said them. "He'll-make-a-deal."

Danny was impatient. "I know all about the American system and I'm very aware about making deals but if he does they'll expect him to tell them where we are and he can't."

"He knows you're not dead."

"What do you want me to do?"

"Tell Jorge to get rid of the money. Tell him to dump it in a river or burn it. The last thing we want is for the D.A. to realize you were doing some last-minute estate planning."

"Where's Jorge now?"

"Somewhere between New York and Acapulco."

"Why did he go back down to Mexico?"

"I sent him there to meet my men when they came down from the mountain with the rest of that black box."

"Did they get it all?"

"All of it. You see, *hombre,* I've covered my end of things." He waited for a compliment.

Danny allowed him that much. "That's certainly a relief."

"Tell Jorge to dump the money," Swayze repeated.

As if there was one chance in hell that he would comply. "If that's what you want . . ."

Swayze seemed satisfied. "You know, Danny," he went on, "she's still not convinced that you're dead although for the life of me I can't understand what she'd do with you if she found you except kill you herself." He laughed. "But as I predicted, they've become very close, Coriander and that Special Investigator."

Swayze had him on every level: practical, legal, emotional. "How much is Stampa telling them?" he asked, changing subjects. His mind was racing to find solutions that had only to do with her. Coriander. Before it was too late.

"He's talking like a crazy man because he's scared to death of going to jail and frankly, *hombre,* at his age, who can blame him?"

Gazing off into the distance, Danny took a long drag on his cigarette. "That's the whole point, isn't it . . ."

Swayze shrugged in agreement. "He's old and sick, his life isn't worth much anymore."

"And what about Jorge?" he wondered, making an attempt to sound nonchalant, "what if I can't reach him in time?"

Unfortunately, Swayze couldn't make any promises although he could absolutely assure him that as long as that million dollars was destroyed there would be no problem. "He's your brother, *hombre,* make sure you reach him in time."

"That's not an answer, Mac."

"It's the three of us, Danny—you, me, and Hernando."

"And what about my wife?"

"Cor-i-an-der," Swayze said the name, rolling it into four distinct syllables. "She's not your wife, *hombre,* she's your widow." He paused, and as if he just thought of it, added, "Maybe she'll run off with that glorified cop and live happily ever after. By then, they'll forget about looking for you—*con suerte,* they'll forget all about you."

Danny controlled himself from jumping up and grabbing Swayze by the throat. *With luck,* Swayze would fall into that pot of boiling water along with those rabbits.

"Actually, it's got nothing to do with *suerte,* Danny, it's got to do with time; in time women get over everything. The only problem is that the smarter the woman the longer it takes and your woman is very smart." Danny's gaze wandered outside as Swayze continued talking. "What about you, Danny, I worry about you." His voice took on a paternal quality. "What's it going to take to make you start living again? You know that girl is only seventeen, she's very sensitive, her feelings get hurt every time you throw her out of bed." He tried a smile. "You could give her a complex."

"Tell her I don't like girls."

"She'll never believe you're a *maricón*."

"Who said anything about *maricón*? Tell her I only like women."

"She won't understand."

"When she grows up she'll understand and when she does I won't throw her out of bed."

"Try her," Swayze coaxed, "let me send her to you tonight."

His head ached, his heart pounded, he saw Coriander's face, he read Swayze's mind, it was a matter of disconnecting past from present. His hands shook so that he avoided bringing the cigarette to his lips. It was worth it, what the hell, let Swayze send the girl, anything to make him feel more secure about his state of mind. Men like that needed to share the same woman, like dogs who marked their territory after other dogs. *"Por cambiar las ideas,"* he agreed, "send her." Swayze got up and actually hugged him. How little it took to make the old goat happy, the promise that he wouldn't throw some teenage hooker out of bed. For ten minutes more he listened to abstractions about how Jorge presented no problem as long as he was contained, as long as he was never put in a position of functioning alone or having to make unilateral decisions or choices about saving his own skin at the expense of the rest of them. . . . But that problem appeared to be solved as well and what a relief since he had been consumed with that million dollar delivery that could have cost them everything they had accomplished up until now. As far as Stampa was concerned, he wasn't even worth discussing although once he had hoped the man would be able to settle down to a life of quiet retirement, living off the income from his wife's hand-knitted sweater business.

For ten more minutes Danny listened to hypotheses at dictation speed about how there was no room for individual desires or obligations if they were going to achieve everything they had planned. Swayze bragged about the small army he had in place, a couple of good men who happened to be in New York right now, ready to do anything that was necessary to preserve their goal. Swayze stood. There was nothing to worry about as long as they agreed on how to handle things. At least the emotional part seemed to be under control and in the process of healing; Coriander had her whole life before her and it was doubtful that she would spend it either in mourning or alone. He wished her well . . . As for the three of them here in Ushuaia, in the middle of a Patagonian winter, plans had changed. Things were calm enough for them to leave for Cuba sooner than expected. The plan was that Swayze would leave first with the money, Danny and Hernando would follow with the files and computer equipment.

There was no doubt in Danny's mind as he listened to Swayze that he had to get to her. Coriander. Before it was too late. Danny followed Swayze to the door, remaining passive as the man clutched his shoulder; remaining silent as Swayze expressed his pleasure about how Danny was about to join the living. If fucking was living then he was about to be reborn . . . Swayze hugged him again, put on his anorak, and said it again, that nothing would ever stand between them because they were a team, a family. After he left Danny just stood there and considered how all of it sounded vaguely familiar although right then he couldn't quite place where he had heard it before . . .

Silent signals, Danny considered as he smoked, unspoken words except there was something that still bothered him. Clearly, Swayze was right about certain things, that Stampa was old and sick and living on borrowed time, that his life was meaningless. The most pressing problem, however, was that million dollars and how to manage Jorge without Swayze suspecting he had failed to cancel the delivery. The version could be that he had tried and that Jorge wouldn't listen, something about his having a late-blooming feeling of obligation and responsibility since Coriander was pregnant. Or, that he tried and couldn't reach his brother . . . As long as the money got to her he didn't care what happened afterwards. Floating this way and that he conjured her up. She was lying on the bed and looking at him while he kissed those favorite places: eyes, nose, ears, neck, and mouth and again and then once more, *Goodbye baby.*

Of his life apart from Swayze as it concerned Coriander the man never understood the extent nor the depth of his feelings, no one did except the boy. Settling back in his chair, he waited for Hernando to return from town, having already decided to talk to him about the problem with the money. Hernando would come up with a solution since it had to do with Coriander. After all, he once loved her too . . .

Curiously, an overwhelming sensation of desire came over him. Dozing, his thoughts turned to that teenage hooker before he awoke with a start, drenched in sweat, his mind whirling in a thousand different directions. He was suddenly aware of what struck him as so familiar. It was Matthew Johnson all over again, it was that same familiar Montonero thing about pride and honor and murder.

Chapter Nineteen

The District Attorney was getting pressured by the New York State Banking Commission, which was getting threatened by the Federal Deposit Insurance Corporation in Washington, which was getting harassed by the Office of the Comptroller of the Currency. Everyone wanted indictments handed out to every last member of the board of Inter Federated, members of the bank's credit committees, and Jorge Vidal. But what they wanted most was concrete testimony by Fernando Stampa against Danny Vidal. What was frustrating was that although he had been offered total immunity, Stampa was only giving them meager tidbits with the promise of more, feeding it to Adam in little bites that made it almost impossible to mount a case quickly. The D.A. sent word down to Adam that the time had come to play hard ball. They would worry later about making the indictments stick.

Adam got the news when he arrived at the office, which meant that in addition to wading through the mounds of paperwork he now had to spend double time playing dentist with Fernando Stampa. It would have been easier to pull teeth . . .

Accompanied by his wife, the man arrived forty minutes

early and still managed to get Adam out of a meeting within five minutes of their arrival in the lobby reception area. To the surprise of the guard on duty Adam came rushing down himself to greet them. Stampa stood silently while his wife spoke for both of them, explaining that she was only there to make sure that her husband wasn't unnecessarily upset by the questions.

On the way to the bank of elevators in the back of the marble lobby and up to the fifth floor where the District Attorney's office was located, Adam chatted with the Stampas about the weather and the air-conditioning that had finally been repaired. Holding open the door, he invited them to step inside, arranging the chairs in a semicircle around the coffee table, gathering up files, papers, law journals, and several heavy legal texts before offering coffee along with excuses for the disarray. When he got everyone settled he excused himself. What he didn't mention to the Stampas was that he had asked Coriander down to the office to go over several of Danny's personal files and checkbooks. Before he walked back into his office, he instructed his secretary to buzz him the instant she arrived. Sitting down, he observed Elsa Stampa.

She was a small woman with delicate bones, lovely features and what must once have been beautiful red hair. Now it was heavily streaked with gray, still fine and fly-away as it wisped around her brow and neck, coming loose from a bun that was wound at the back of her head. Her face was lined, her eyes still china-blue although the expression they held was world-weary, that of a woman who had seen and suffered far too much to care about masking any pain. Of her husband it was apparent that she was protective, the way that she glanced over when he spoke, patting his hand when he paused, interrupting to inform Adam that this whole nightmare had taken its toll, not on her but on him as his heart was weak and his stamina nearly depleted and could they get this over with as quickly as possible . . .

Adam began slowly, giving the reason for this sudden meeting. "I'm afraid the D.A. is getting impatient," Adam explained gently.

Elsa Stampa answered for her husband. "Perhaps you could explain to your D.A. that my husband isn't a well man."

"He knows that, Mrs. Stampa, and he sympathizes but there's pressure from Washington."

"You can tell that to your friends in Washington too, my husband isn't strong."

Adam assured her that the sooner they could get started the sooner it would all end and he took her silence as agreement. Adam began slowly and in chronological order, alluding to certain incidents that he had learned from Palmer Wyatt's tape although not mentioning how he happened to know them. Stampa admitted everything, beginning with the plan to kidnap that executive back in Buenos Aires and ending with the scheme where he personally carried six hundred thousand dollars out of the bank and into Montonero hands every month. The man spoke haltingly, stopping every so often to run his tongue over parched lips or to take a sip of water that Elsa had provided, smiling weakly at his wife in an effort to reassure her that he was able to continue. The woman interrupted only once and that was to make sure that regardless of the extent of her husband's involvement with Danny Vidal and events in New York and Buenos Aires he would still have immunity. Adam assured her that he was absolutely protected as long as he told the truth. Stampa resumed his story. "The briefcase was prepared in advance. During the first week of every month Danny would call me up to his private office to pick it up."

"Did he always give it to you himself?"

"Always. Sometimes when he was in the middle of a meeting he would even come out to see me personally and remind me to call the minute I got back."

Elsa Stampa had taken out her knitting, the needles clicking together as they looped and pearled stitches in neat rows. Glasses perched on the tip of her nose, she listened to her husband, putting down her wool every so often to check Adam's reaction before turning her attention once again to what she explained would be a sweater. It reached the point where Adam only relaxed when he heard the needles clicking against each other as she knit.

"I would take a taxi in front of the bank to Kennedy Airport where I'd get a direct flight to Montreal. There was always a thirty-five or forty minute delay for the plane to Havana. Danny always insisted that I never stay overnight, which I never did, which meant that everything was perfectly timed. When I arrived in Havana I was rushed through customs by someone from the government who drove me directly to a house along the beach where someone would be waiting for the briefcase."

"Who owned the house?"

"I don't know."

"How did you know the briefcase contained money?"

"Because it was always opened in front of me and the money counted before I was given a signed receipt to take back to New York."

"Where are those receipts now?"

"In Danny's personal files written in code."

"Do you understand the code?"

"Yes."

Adam made a note on a pad of paper that was balanced on one knee. "And was the amount the same every month?"

"Yes, it was always six hundred thousand dollars packed in that same briefcase in large denomination bills."

"Did you know the person who took the money?"

"Yes, he's one of the leaders of the organization and a surrogate father to Danny ever since his own father died when he was very young."

"What's the man's name?"

"MacKinley Swayze."

Adam didn't react. "Do you have any idea where he is now?"

"The last time I saw him was about a year ago in Havana."

"And was that the last time you carried in money?"

Stampa nodded. "After that the bank wasn't making enough profit to skim off any interest."

"Which was when Vidal began stealing entire deposits?"

Stampa nodded. "By then, Danny began to get very suspicious and paranoid, he didn't trust anyone anymore. He decided to handle all money transfers alone."

"How?"

"From what I could gather he was moving out small amounts of cash in a suitcase every day."

"Didn't anyone at the bank wonder what was in the suitcase?"

"If they did they didn't say anything."

"Why not?"

"He was the boss so unless people were prepared to go to the authorities what was the point of confronting him?" Without looking up from her knitting, it was Stampa's wife who offered a more logical explanation. "You don't know how charming he was, how warm and caring, how he remembered everyone's name, asked about their families, knew if they had a backache or if their aging mother was ill. He made it his business to be involved and informed about everyone so that people believed he really cared about them." Elsa looked up over her glasses. "He charmed them into silence."

"Why would anyone challenge him as long as they didn't miss a paycheck?" Stampa added.

"And he always met the payroll," Adam said softly, marveling at the man's talents.

"That was his first priority."

"After himself," Elsa added, her attention turned once again to her knitting.

"Did he ever actually tell you that the money was destined for Havana, Mr. Stampa?" Adam asked.

"He told me that when he had the full amount he intended to hire a private plane to fly down there with the money."

"In your opinion was that what he was intending to do on that July 4 weekend?"

"As far as I know the plan was for him to go to Havana with a stop in Acapulco to pick up Jorge."

"What did he intend to do with the money while he was in Acapulco?"

"I don't know."

"I thought you said he went looking for a house."

"No," the man admitted. "That was just the official story for anyone who asked."

"How could fifty million dollars fit in two suitcases?"

"It wasn't fifty, it was forty-six million, four hundred thousand. Don't forget I had already carried out six hundred thousand a month for six months . . ."

Adam tried not to sound annoyed. "How can forty-six million, four hundred thousand fit into two suitcases?"

"Danny figured it out to the last dollar."

"What you're saying is that Danny had the money with him when he left New York and boarded that plane."

Stampa had tears in his eyes. "It was a horrible twist of fate but that's what happened."

When the phone buzzed the couple looked up questioningly. Reaching over to answer it, Adam listened. "Give me a couple of minutes," he said, and after he hung up, used the interruption as an opportunity to change the subject. "Are you familiar with the Matthew Johnson case?"

Elsa Stampa stopped knitting. "My husband had nothing to do with that," she blurted out.

"Nobody said he did, Mrs. Stampa," Adam replied evenly. "Besides, your husband is still protected under the same terms of that immunity agreement."

"Yes," Stampa said quietly, "I'm familiar with the case. Johnson was the American Honorary Consul in Cordoba."

Adam sat back in his chair and crossed his arms. "Did Danny Vidal murder him?"

Stampa didn't even bother to glance over at his wife for approval as he set forth the facts, which matched almost verbatim what Danny himself had described on that tape. When he finished Adam judged that it was the time to bring the conversation back to the present. "You were obviously very close to Danny."

"Yes, which makes this so difficult."

"He was part of a very painful past," Elsa added softly.

Carefully, Adam proceeded. "You understand, Mr. Stampa, that this office is not investigating the murder of Matthew Johnson. The only reason I brought it up was to understand the whole person a little better, this man you were so close to and trusted, the same man who left you at risk of criminal indictment."

"I never would have come to talk to you in the first place if Danny hadn't put me in that position," Stampa agreed with visible emotion.

For a moment Adam thought about Coriander sitting out in the reception area, imagining what would happen when he called her in. He had already formulated the plan. "I want you to know that I understand this was one of the most difficult decisions you've ever made." He paused. "You see, if it weren't for your close relationship with Danny, I'd be absolutely certain that he faked his own death," he lied. "The fact that you *were* so close makes me believe that Danny would never have done something like that with those checks unless he had every intention of straightening it out." Again, he paused. "Which is why I believe that he perished in that crash."

Although Stampa accepted Adam's conclusions almost gratefully, it was Elsa who voiced her own doubt. "I've spent sleepless nights trying to figure that out how he would have covered those checks."

"That's something we'll never know."

"I don't believe Danny ever intended to hurt me," said Stampa obstinately.

"Which gets back to my original question, Mr. Stampa. Why didn't you wait before coming down to talk to me?"

The man looked ashamed. "I was scared," he said softly.

"You had doubts, is that it?" Adam asked gently.

"My wife . . ." he began.

Elsa spoke calmly. "We went through enough . . ."

"It was a shock," Stampa interrupted.

"A million dollars is a lot of money," Adam agreed, certain that Elsa Stampa had forced the issue.

"I'm an old man . . ."

Adam nodded. He had to choose his words carefully now since timing was everything and he had only one chance once he brought Coriander into the office. "When was the last time you spoke to Danny Vidal?"

"About a week before the plane crash."

"Are you absolutely certain that you had no conversation with him after that or even when his plane touched down in Houston?"

"Absolutely not."

Adam shrugged. "You see, Mr. Stampa, if we can show that Danny is dead it looks better for you. Otherwise somebody might get the idea that you were in on the thing together until he left you holding the bag with that million dollars. If there is anything that you know that proves or at least makes it difficult to believe that he would fake his own death . . ." Mrs. Stampa seemed suddenly to forget about her knitting. "What about immunity?"

"Immunity can be canceled like this," Adam snapped his fingers, "the first time anyone suspects your husband of lying or not telling the complete truth." So what if he was inventing rules, the guy was a liar not to mention that he had a searing pain in his gut and wanted to get this over with as quickly as possible.

"They were expecting a baby," Stampa announced without emotion, barely taking his eyes off the floor as he did.

"Something planned?" Adam wondered.

The man looked up. "How can I answer that?" he asked miserably.

"When did Danny tell you about expecting a baby?"

"Weeks ago," Stampa said without even considering.

Adam stopped. He heard what he suspected all along, what he had hoped to hear and what he had dreaded at the same time. There was no way that Stampa could have known about the pregnancy weeks ago. He had to have heard the news on the day Danny left for Acapulco—at the earliest—which meant that he had to have talked to him after learning about those bounced checks. And if that was the case then the question remained why the man had come down to the District Attorney's office on that holiday weekend unless those checks weren't part of the deal and the man panicked. Adam excused himself and reached over to pick up the telephone. "Ready now," he said into the receiver as an overwhelming sadness came over him. Hands crossed over his chest, he said nothing while he waited for the door to open and Coriander to enter the office. Somehow he didn't have the stomach for these games anymore.

She walked in before either Fernando or Elsa Stampa could ask just what was going on. Actually, everybody looked surprised. "You all know each other, don't you?" Adam said, looking from one to the other.

"Yes, of course," Coriander said, the first one to regain her composure. Walking over to the woman she extended her hand, "I'm so sorry about everything, Mrs. Stampa," she said before turning to her husband. "Mr. Stampa, how are you?"

It was her incredible dignity that impressed Adam. He asked the question immediately. "Coriander, when did you tell Danny that you were pregnant?"

Her expression registered confusion for only a moment before she replied, "On July 3, the day he left. Why?"

"Because Mr. Stampa says that Danny told him about it weeks ago."

It took only an instant for her to understand. Her gaze moved from one to the other before she spoke in a soft voice. "Where is he?" Stampa looked as if he had been slapped. Elsa turned white. "Please tell me where my husband is, please, I know nothing will happen to you if you do." She looked beseechingly at Adam. "Didn't you tell them that?"

Adam said nothing, a muscle twitching in his jaw. Coriander first looked at Stampa and then at his wife. "Please, if I only knew if he was really dead I could accept it, this way is sheer torture . . ."

It was Elsa who spoke. "Do you have any idea what we've been through?"

Coriander took a breath. "Of course I do, what I don't understand is why you're protecting the one person who's put you through this." It didn't escape her that it was the first time that she actually blamed Danny for anything.

"I blame your father for what happened to our son, he entertained those murderers in your Embassy."

It was Cordoba all over again although this time she had answers. "Even if my father hadn't been in touch with the military would it have changed anything for your son?"

"Perhaps my son would be alive if your father cared to intervene."

"My father did what he could."

"Your father's life wasn't at risk."

"No, but he believed that mine was which is why he maintained relations with the military. You would have done the same to protect your son if you had the chance."

For the first time in years she actually understood her father's motives.

Adam interrupted then. In a voice that was deliberately neutral he said, "This is all irrelevant, it has nothing to do with what's going on now at the bank."

"If it weren't for my son's death we never would have been involved with the bank because we never would have come to New York," Elsa insisted.

"You were involved with Danny before your son was killed and before that Danny tried to help you find him," Coriander argued.

"Until it wasn't convenient for him anymore."

Again, Coriander found herself defending her husband. "It had nothing to do with convenience, Danny was one man against an army."

"We believed he had the power to save our son's life," Stampa said.

"No, you wanted to believe that, Mr. Stampa, and I can't blame you. No one really understood what was happening in the beginning. Danny gave you hope. He gave us all hope."

"The tragedy is that we believed Danny and he fooled us all because everything he did was for the money. How can we forget that he disappointed us by disappearing, just like he disappeared now except now we have recourse."

It was then that Fernando Stampa seemed to try to enlist her support. "Can you forget what he did to you? Can you forgive him for leaving you and your baby like this?"

With tears threatening to spill from her eyes, Coriander spoke softly. "What I'm asking you is to give me the right to know how I should feel. If he's dead I want to mourn him, if he's alive I want the right to be angry."

"Why should we give you a choice when we never had one?" Elsa asked bitterly.

"Then why are you protecting him?" Coriander cried.

"We're protecting ourselves."

She was no longer calm. "How does it help you by not telling me where he is or what you know?"

"What makes you so sure that we know anything?"

"The only thing we know is that I've got to clear my name," Stampa added.

"Everything my husband tried to do was only to get back at the people that killed your son, he had no other motive."

Elsa asked, "And now?"

Coriander just shook her head. "I don't know . . ."

But the woman was once again gathering momentum. "All I know is that my son died because we were unimportant and you're alive because your father was the American Ambassador."

"You're right," Coriander said softly, "I can't argue that . . ."

"I think this is enough," Adam cut in. "We have a deal here, either Mr. Stampa talks and answers honestly or his immunity is canceled and he's indicted along with everyone else."

"We have nothing more to say," Elsa Stampa said as she put her possessions into her pocketbook. "We intend to get a lawyer." Ashen, her husband stood as well, his gaze focused on the floor as he waited for his wife to collect everything so they could leave. There was nothing more to say.

Elsa Stampa took her husband's arm to guide him out the door. Before leaving, she turned. "Maybe your husband didn't love you enough."

But that was an old story. Still, Coriander answered, "Or maybe I loved him too much."

Adam did nothing to prevent Fernando Stampa from leaving. There was time later to serve him and to rescind his immunity, time to pin him down to details even if Adam was convinced that it would only lead to more lies. He wandered over to the window and gazed out, his back to the room, listening as they slammed out the door, their heels clicking against the marble floor as they headed toward the elevator. It was only then that he turned around and walked slowly toward her to take her in his arms. Coriander leaned her head against his shoulder, offering no resistance. "She's right, you know."

"About what?" He stroked her hair.

"He didn't love me enough." The tears came again.

"How about if I love you too much?" he whispered.

They just stood there, the two of them, holding each other . . .

Chapter Twenty

It was six-thirty in the morning when the car first appeared on the northeast corner of Third Avenue and 68th Street. It was a four-door Honda, either beige or gray, it was hard to tell the color with all the mud caked up to the door handles and over the license plates. The car headed up Third Avenue, on the right side of the street, cruising at no more than twenty or twenty-five miles per hour before turning east on 70th Street, proceeding down Second, turning west on 63rd to head back up Third. There were several more tours around the block, never at an accelerated speed although taking the turns at different corners between Second and Third Avenues. At precisely six-forty-two the car stopped on that same northeast corner of Third and 68th Street with its engine idling.

The owner of the Korean market on Third and 69th Street had arrived several minutes before six-fifteen and began arranging the cut flowers for display in the outdoor cases. Several yards north was a newspaper stand at which the owner, having arrived at about the same time, was busy stacking additional copies of the Sunday New York *Times* that had just been bounced off the truck onto the sidewalk. Across Third Avenue, a modern high-rise took up almost the entire block between Lexington and Third Avenues on 67th Street. The building was set back from the sidewalk with a circular driveway leading up to the entrance and down a ramp to the building's garage. At six-thirty-eight an elderly man walked out of the building to make his way slowly toward Third Avenue before he would turn north as he did every morning at approximately the same time to buy oranges and a newspaper. Wearing a tan windbreaker, beige trousers, tinted glasses and tan sandals with dark brown socks, he looked like a foreigner, at least that's what someone would say later. Walking up Third, he reached the corner of 69th Street just as the light turned green, allowing him to cross. He never made it to the other side.

The moment that he stepped off the curb that Honda accelerated up Third from where it had been standing on 68th Street, swerved over to the left and aimed directly for him, hitting him full force. The impact caused the man to fly through the air, slamming head first into a parked car before bouncing onto the pavement seven feet away. Without backing up or losing any momentum, the car screeched west on 69th Street until it was out of sight.

Before the man was even thrown clear of the car, a woman watching from a second floor window began screaming and yelling for the driver to stop. Seconds later, the Korean ran out into the middle of Third Avenue and watched helplessly as the car screeched around the corner and west. Seconds after that the newspaper vendor rushed out from behind his stand to the corner pay phone to call the police. Within minutes all three witnesses including the woman, who had run downstairs in a bathrobe with her baby clutched in her arms, stood on the corner of Third Avenue and 69th Street, staring at the crumpled figure on the pavement. He was dead.

*　*　*

Coriander entered the hospital and nodded at the three guards
who milled around the first set of swinging doors waiting for their
shift to begin.

"Hiya doin' Doc."

"Lookin' good, Doc."

"Hey Doc," one of them said, clutching his side, "my appen-
dix, they're yours . . ."

"Is," she corrected, sailing past.

The corridor smelled of pine disinfectant and the permanently stained linoleum floors were polished to a shine. Even the
graffiti looked as if it had been scrubbed clean. Walking through
emergency, Coriander smiled at the staff behind the glass-enclosed
bulletproof reception area as overhead Roy Orbison twanged out
"Running Scared." The lyrics struck her, *If he comes back, which
one would you choose.* Stopping at the vending machine, she
dropped in the correct change and waited for coffee and a splash
of milk to fill the cup. The waiting room was almost deserted
except for a few people who were there for their daily methadone
cocktails or insulin shots. Sunday mornings were usually calm
except for maternity, as if ghetto babies knew enough to be born
on the Sabbath cease-fire, that short respite before combat resumed mid-week only to escalate into full-fledged warfare by Friday night. Sixteen new residents were due to begin her service this
morning; six third-year medical students, two subinterns, three
interns, one second-year resident, three third-year residents, and
one fourth-year resident.

Carrying her coffee, Coriander pushed through the swinging
doors leading into trauma where she was immediately stopped by
one of her outgoing residents. "Are you giving your morning
lecture in the auditorium or in the chief's office?"

"Are you actually going?" she asked with a smile.

"Wouldn't miss it, Dr. Wyatt."

"How come you always missed my talks when you were on
my service?"

"When I wasn't working I had ten to fifteen minutes to sleep," the resident teased.

"Wasn't that tough?" she said, smiling. "Check on the board, but I think it's in the auditorium." Shifting her shoulder bag to the other side, she continued through triage, past the examining rooms and down the hall before reaching the small office in the rear of the unit. The speech she would deliver was in her head, notes were never necessary since she took everything from actual events and situations that happened in the preceding weeks on her service. What she always maintained was that it was crucial to give these eager new doctors an idea of reality, especially since they believed that more lives were miraculously saved around there than foolishly lost. How wrong they were . . .

Closing the door, Coriander walked over to the locker to put away her purse, pausing a moment to lean her forehead against its cool metal surface. Today was the first day she felt queasy, a touch of morning sickness although the fatigue she felt was less physical than it was emotional.

Since that confrontation with the Stampas her sympathy and patience had diminished except for those innocent victims who passed through her service. There was no need for anyone to tell her that it was bad policy to make value judgments about patients. Medicine was like sex, if it was lousy it counted for ninety percent and if it was good no one dwelled on it. She undressed slowly, hanging up her clothes inside the locker before slipping on a pair of blue scrubs and white coat. Sitting down at the desk she began the same routine, rummaging in a drawer for a couple of pens and a small flashlight, which she stuck into her breast pocket before draping her stethoscope around her neck.

Out the door of her office and through triage, Coriander walked swiftly down the corridor to the elevator. Stepping inside, she considered that perhaps it was all a question of judgment and if so, she was the last person to know how much to feel about whom. After all, she had fallen in love with a man, taken on all his anguish and pain, trusted him, married him, shared a life, planned, hoped, only to find out that nothing about him was real . . . Stepping out of the elevator she could only be grateful that she hadn't been called upon to talk about the rewards of marriage. Entering the auditorium filled with at least fifty or sixty people, she wondered how it happened that Adam Singer had become such an important part of her life. Or was that just another example of bad judgment.

Last month Hermine Mashavas won the Sheraton Hotel Employee of the Year Award in a small ceremony in the employees' dining room off the kitchen. As far as Hermine was concerned the most valuable prize was that she got to choose which shift she would work for the following year.

Hermine picked the day shift from eight in the morning until four in the afternoon, which meant that she could pick up her baby from her mother's and go home to prepare dinner so that the whole family could eat together after her husband came home from work. Hermine also chose to work Sundays with a day off during the week so her child could have one day alone with each parent and her own mother could have two full days of rest.

The last few hours of this particular Sunday shift were more hectic than usual. Thirty-four members of the Allied Insurance Company had checked out at noon and twenty-six executives from Barnum and Bailey Circus were due to check in at four. Hermine and two other housekeepers worked quickly to prepare the rooms for the supervisor's scheduled inspection at two o'clock. Word had already come up from the reception desk that some of the Barnum and Bailey people were having complimentary drinks in the lobby bar, anxiously waiting to get upstairs.

At exactly one-thirty-four in the afternoon, Hermine shut the door to room 1636 and counted only four more rooms to finish: 1638, 1640, 1642 and 1644. Pushing the linen cart down the hall, she stopped it between rooms 1638 and 1640 and took out her passkey to open the door to room 1640. Knocking first and counting to thirty to make sure it was vacant—Sheraton rules—she turned the key and stepped inside.

The room was dark with the double draperies drawn across the windows. Off the small entrance corridor where she entered was a bathroom. Switching on the lights, she noticed that it appeared not to have been used. The towels were folded on the racks, the soaps and shampoos were unopened on the counter near the sink, and even the sanitary paper band around the closed toilet seat was unbroken. But Sheraton Hotel rules called for sheets and towels to be changed after every checkout even if they appeared to be unused and the bed untouched. What Hermine wondered, however, was if one of the other two girls on the floor had already serviced the room. Walking out into the hall and down to where the others were working, she stopped in each room to ask, learning that neither one had made it up.

Once again Hermine entered room 1640 and walked into the bathroom to gather up the towels before walking out to deposit them in a laundry bag hanging on one side of her cart. With fresh towels in hand she entered the bathroom and placed them on the shelves above the sink before closing the bathroom door to head into the bedroom. Bumping her leg against a chair, she made her way cautiously over to the right side of the windows to pull back the blackout shades. Daylight filtered underneath the regular drapes. Hermine was about to walk to the left side to open them when she happened to glance over to the bed. Horrified by the sight and too shocked to run, she just stood there screaming uncontrollably. The sheets were soaked with blood as were the pillows as was the body of the man lying on his back, his eyes staring vacantly at the ceiling, his throat slashed from ear to ear.

* * *

Near the conclusion of her lecture Coriander reached over to take a sip of water just as the doors opened at the back of the auditorium and a man entered. It was Adam.

Coriander was having trouble concentrating with Adam sitting there. Something must have happened or he wouldn't have come. Cutting everything short, she announced that she would take questions. A dozen or so hands went up and, as she listened and answered, she glanced toward the back of the auditorium every few moments. Finally, after having called on everybody, she thanked the group for attending and welcomed her new residents once again, adding that she was always available for any help or questions they might have.

The applause was long and loud, rows of clapping hands blurred before her eyes as she took off her glasses. The applause continued even after she stepped out from behind the podium, walked across the stage and started down the three steps leading to the audience. Her thoughts were only on Adam. Putting her glasses on, she stopped to shake hands with several of the staff doctors and a few of the residents who gathered around to tell her how much they enjoyed the lecture. Adam was no more than four feet away by then, obviously as eager as she for everyone to leave. He looked upset. After several more interminable minutes everyone finally dispersed and she was able to make her way over to him. "What happened?" she asked anxiously.

Taking her by the elbow he led her up the aisle. "Let's get out of here."

She felt herself being propelled out the doors at the back of the auditorium, having trouble keeping up. "What's wrong?" she repeated, trying to read his face as they walked toward the elevators.

Instead of answering, he complimented her. "That was an interesting speech, no wonder you get such a crowd."

Slightly out of breath, she answered, "You didn't come here for the speech. What happened?"

When they finally reached the elevators, he took hold of her shoulders and said it quickly, "Stampa is dead."

She paled. "How?"

"Hit and run."

"Where?"

"*Why* might be a better question," Adam said just as the elevator arrived. Guiding her inside the crowded car, they rode in silence, their eyes locked until they reached the ground floor. "Why?" she asked the instant they stepped out. Holding her elbow, he guided her along the hall leading to trauma. "I'll tell you everything when we can sit down someplace in private."

She was visibly shaken as she tried to keep up with his long strides. "Let's go to my office."

Striding through the swinging doors and into the holding area without acknowledging anyone, they finally reached her office at the back of the unit. Opening the door, she walked in with Adam following. They weren't inside for more than two or three seconds, barely long enough for her to shut the door, when he announced, "You can't be alone."

"Why?"

"It's not safe."

"Adam, what are you talking about?"

"Jorge is dead too."

She clutched the back of a chair. "What?" she gasped.

"He was found in a hotel room this afternoon by one of the maids." Adam paused. "His throat was slashed."

Stunned, she sank down into the chair. "I don't believe it," she whispered. "Why?"

Adam knelt down in front of her. "Now do you understand why you can't be alone?"

Her voice trembled. "What are you saying?"

"I'm afraid they'll find you."

"Who?" she asked, her head spinning. "I thought we were the ones looking for someone."

He took her hands. "Two men are dead," he said, enunciating the words. "Murdered. Don't you understand what's going on?"

She said it without thinking. "Why would Danny hurt his own brother? It doesn't make any sense."

"This isn't about sense, Coriander, this is about dollars, millions of dollars."

"What does that have to do with me?" she said, almost pleading.

He sounded exhausted. "I'm not sure but I think Jorge was murdered because of that million dollars."

"But it was Danny who arranged it."

"And probably Swayze who saw the stupidity . . ." Adam got up, took a chair and swung it around. He sat down, his arms resting on the back. "Listen to me, Coriander, your life is in danger. These two men were murdered because one of them told us about five bounced checks and the other told you about a million dollars. Don't you see? It connects two separate events to make it clear that Danny planned to give you a million dollars because he knew he was never coming back. It proves he's probably alive, that he planned everything, which implicates him in three murders."

She repeated the question. "But why would he want to hurt me? He loved me."

"Enough to leave you like this, pregnant?"

She was suddenly furious. "Abandoning me is one thing, damn it, that's hard enough to accept, but plotting the murder of two pilots as a way for him to escape is another, unbearable for me to imagine, and now you want me to believe that he had his own brother and some pathetic old man killed?"

He was offering no comfort that day. "You forgot about that torso in the basin, but why are you so surprised, did you forget about Matthew Johnson?" Still holding her hands, he shook them to get her full attention. "These people are ruthless, Coriander, and he's one of them."

As if in a trance she said "I'm moving today . . ." As if that made a difference.

"I'll help you move and I'll either stay with you or you'll stay with me at my apartment."

"And what about my job and your job and my life and your life and everything else . . ."

Nothing mattered. "They're going to have to do without you for a while around here," he interrupted. "As for my life and your life and everything else, that's another issue."

"I can't hide forever," she said softly. She stood. He was on his feet as well and within an instant she was in his arms. "Nothing is forever, Coriander," he said before his lips found hers.

Coriander reached up to link her arms around his neck as they kissed tenderly. When the kiss was over their eyes met. She reached up to touch his face. "What would I do without you?" she whispered. He gathered her close to him again. "It makes no difference because you're not going to be without me."

Nothing is forever, the words went around in her head. But she said nothing . . .

Chapter Twenty-one

He had the face of a cadaver, gaunt and pale with eyes that were flat, the expression lifeless and bored but not as if he had seen it all, rather as if he didn't care even to begin. He moved gracefully, his limbs fluid, his step sure, like a classical dancer with a permanent adagio playing in his head. Tall and thin, he walked slightly forward on the balls of his feet, his trousers hanging around his hips and buttocks, pulled high up on his waist and giving the vague impression of a hip bone protruding under each pocket. Taking long strides, he continued along the steep streets of Ushuaia.

He had his own ideas about what had transpired in New York. There were limits as far as he was concerned. Robbery was one thing, kidnapping as well, even murder if it was committed against enemies and only if there was no other way to make a point, launch an offensive or create a defense. But killing an old man—running him down like an animal—was on the same level of inhumanity as what those monsters used to do. And Jorge, regardless of his morals or other traits of a less-than-sterling character, slashing his throat in an anonymous hotel room was a brutal and senseless act of violence. Danny had gone into a state of depression, even worse than after Alicia died.

It had been months since Hernando had come into Ushuaia and as he made his way along the streets he realized why it always depressed him to come into town in the middle of winter. There was no one in sight except for the stray dogs that wandered or huddled in doorways, abandoned by those who had come to work on limited contracts for one of the state-owned construction or electrical companies.

The wind was fierce as it blew off Ushuaia Bay, patches of ice on the ground making it nearly impossible to walk if it weren't for the ropes and metal railings along the sidewalks. There was nothing appealing about the town itself except for the view of the mountains and forests that bordered it and the vast expanses of water that stretched toward the Navarino and Hoste Islands on the Chilean side of the Beagle Channel. Regardless of how much time elapsed between visits everything remained in that same suspended and unfinished state of repair along the waterfront. Snow-covered cranes and dumpsters stood idle, waiting for the spring thaw before construction could begin again, then there were only a few short months of working time until the brutal winds of fall and winter resumed.

He continued past the row of small wooden houses covered with corrugated iron and those typical gingerbread designs so reminiscent of Czarist Russia that had somehow found their way into this southernmost country on earth.

It had been on his mind to contact her and, ever since he made the decision to do it, he had thought of nothing else. He had discussed his intentions only with Danny, although he presented it as something he would do regardless of Danny's opinion. There was something fatalistic about Danny's reaction when he left everything up to him, preferring to decide what to do in the end when the end was upon them. He was only sorry he hadn't thought of it from the very beginning. It would have saved Jorge's life, that was certain. There never would have been the question of that million dollars. But there was no point belaboring the obvious or lamenting the past. Time was running out. Swayze was preparing to leave for Havana today with two suitcases filled with over forty-six million dollars because the situation was suddenly judged safer in Cuba than in Argentina. They were scheduled to follow him on Sunday.

Changing direction, he crossed several streets, the architecture taking on a different look. Instead of houses in the style of the Czar there were now concrete structures and imported Swedish pre-fabs in the style of the workers, wooden shanties that were crowded together along the sidewalk. Over and over he rehearsed what he would say to her. Even if she was there he would keep it brief and without emotion, refusing to answer questions or give explanations on the phone. Other than date and place of the meeting he would say nothing else. And if she wasn't there he would simply leave a message that only she would understand.

The Tierra Major Travel Agency was just beyond the corner on the Avenida San Martin, not far from the best and largest hotel in Ushuaia, the Albatross. If all went according to plan, Marie Ines hadn't gone to lunch and was waiting for him, the appointment having been set for noon. It was just three minutes before the hour when he arrived at the door of the agency, opened it to the tinkling of glass chimes hanging from fishing wire. With relief he saw that his friend was indeed there and expecting him. Looking up from her desk, she smiled and turned the telephone around so that the dial faced out. "*Hola*, Hernando," she greeted him, "I hope you have lots of time to get your call through." Hernando understood. Sometimes the wait for an overseas call took hours, especially in winter when there were so few operators and limited telephone lines. However long it took was better than standing in the street and asking someone to help him feed *cospeles* into a temperamental pay phone. Sitting down at the desk, Hernando thanked Marie Ines before he embarked upon the first step in a long journey back in time. Picking up the receiver, he dialed the operator with the metal hook of one prosthesis and waited for her to come on the line to give her the number of Brooklyn General Hospital. There was only one obstacle in an otherwise flawless plan and something that Hernando couldn't have known then. As always, Swayze was still the perfect commander, prepared for any deception. He had already ordered the murders of Stampa and Jorge, ordered Hernando to be followed, already arranged with the travel agency's owner for a record of the call—not only time and charges but also name and number of the party called. It was only a question of hours after Hernando hung up before Swayze would undo the damage that had been done. Once Swayze made up his mind about something he rarely failed.

The plan was dinner at some neighborhood restaurant before Adam would spend the night at Coriander's new apartment. He understood that she wasn't on duty and was only going to the hospital to talk to the attending about taking a leave of absence.

She was late, not seriously, only about ten minutes, but enough to make Adam anxious. Logic told him it wasn't unusual. Instinct told him something else. He tried not to worry. After all, she had often been delayed at work. Chances were that the attending had detained her or she was caught in traffic somewhere along the way. Out of sheer nervousness he began dialing her home number, hanging up several times on the machine before finally leaving a message that he was in the office and hoped he hadn't confused the time and place for their meeting.

At six-thirty, when she was thirty minutes late, Adam decided the hell with it, he would call the hospital and have her paged—something he would feel foolish about doing if she was still in a meeting.

Lottie answered Coriander's page. "I was just about to call you," she said. "Is Coriander there yet?"

"Not yet, that's why I'm calling you. I was getting a little worried."

"Don't worry, I saw her earlier when she was going downstairs to wait for the cab."

"Then why were you going to call me?"

"Because I've been picking up her pages and she got a really strange message or at least I think she got it if she picked up her page earlier."

"Why do you have it if she picked up the page?"

"Because they always send a computer printout to follow the page and I happened to be in our office when it arrived." She laughed nervously. "Around here, they're either overly efficient or they run out of blood at the blood bank."

"What's the message?" He leaned back in the chair, tilted the receiver, and took a deep breath out of range of the mouthpiece.

"The operator said a man called and didn't leave his name, just said that he'd meet her on Friday." She hesitated. "The day after tomorrow."

"That's all? He didn't say where?"

"That's why I was about to call you, doesn't that strike you as strange?"

More than strange. Adam sat up in the chair. "What about the page operator, can you transfer us down there?"

It took only seconds for Lottie to effect the transfer in such a manner that she and Adam were on the line. The operator was embarrassed. Actually, she did remember the call for Dr. Wyatt and not only because it sounded long distance and the man spoke English with an accent but because of what he said. In fact, she had told Dr. Wyatt the whole message even if she didn't put it into the computer. The woman hoped she hadn't caused any trouble but there were so many calls from crackpots and lunatics that it was hard to know sometimes what was real, not to mention all the personal calls from the wives and girlfriends of the doctors, all of which made it impossible to keep everything straight. "What was the rest of the message?" Lottie asked. Get to the point, Adam willed the woman, just say it. Finally the telephone operator explained, "The man said something about meeting her where the dwarf was . . ."

By the time Adam showed up at the brownstone on West 76th Street Coriander was already gone. He walked downstairs and around to the side where he pressed the brass button on the door leading to Miranda Malone's apartment. "Who's there?" a British-accented voice came through the intercom.

"It's Adam Singer, a friend of Coriander Wyatt's, I was here last night . . ."

"I know who you are, luv, just hang on, I'm coming."

He tried to calm down but it was useless.

"Take a minute, luv," the voice went on, "all these locks and bolts and chains . . ." Wearing a flowered kimono and velvet embroidered slippers, her red hair tied up in an even brighter red silk kerchief, gray roots visible, fingernails painted blood red as well, Miranda Malone opened the door and announced, "She's gone, luv."

His heart sank. "Where?"

As if she didn't hear the question. "She left an hour ago."

Again he asked, his voice unnaturally low. "Do you know where she went?"

Miranda thought a minute before opening the door wider. "Come inside, it's too bloody hot."

Adam followed the woman into the cluttered apartment, stepping over several grocery cartons filled with bottled water that stood in the middle of the foyer. "They won't even carry them into the kitchen," she complained. "They think they're doing you a favor if they deliver."

"Why don't I take them inside for you," Adam offered.

Miranda didn't hesitate. "Right this way, luv, down the hallway and watch the litterboxes."

Adam lifted one carton on top of the other and followed the woman down a dimly lit hallway and into a large kitchen with copper pots and pans hanging from hooks over the stoves and counters. He set everything down on top of the kitchen table. "Where do they go?" His stomach was a mess, he felt like hell. "You're a gentleman," she said, "just leave them and I'll cope with them later."

He got back to her. "Do you happen to know where she went?"

"To the airport."

Adam took a breath. "Buenos Aires?"

Miranda shrugged. "I warned her about marrying him, I told her women never get over them, they're like hepatitis, the way they lie dormant, you know what I mean? Want a cup of tea, luv? You look a little pale."

It was nothing personal except that he had to control himself from losing his patience or his temper or his mind. "Buenos Aires," he repeated, "is that all?"

"Funny girl she is, smart girl, except when it comes to him." She paused to scoop up one of her cats. "Lucifer here has more sense than Coriander . . ."

Although there was no doubt in his mind that he had the beginning of an ulcer there was all the doubt in the world that he could survive this. He'd remember this case forever regardless of how it turned out, he'd remember her forever regardless of where she ended up . . .

"Did she tell you that she was going to meet him?"

"Not exactly, luv, but she wasn't going there to visit her father, that's for sure. And I saw the look in her eye when she came to say goodbye to me. It was written all over her face, sheer folly. Frankly I never believed he was dead, did you?"

He never believed anything, especially that he would have

fallen in love with her. "Did she say where she was meeting him in Buenos Aires?"

Miranda shook her head. "No, luv, nothing, just that she was going to Buenos Aires."

He was sweating in that freezing air-conditioned kitchen in Miranda Malone's basement apartment. "Could I use your phone?" She not only told him he could use the phone but sat him down in a comfortable chair in her sewing room with a beer and a telephone directory. He called Aerolineas Argentinas, but its flight taking off in forty minutes was fully booked, not that he could have made it anyway. The reservation clerk refused to tell Adam if Coriander was a passenger. Hanging up, Adam tried calling several other airlines that flew to Buenos Aires until he was finally able to book a reservation for Friday, which was the day after tomorrow. That accomplished, he just sat there for a few minutes before Miranda came back into the room. "You intend to follow her down there, don't you?" He nodded. "You're in love with her, aren't you?" He nodded again.

If her question about being in love struck him as presumptuous, his question must have struck her as bizarre. "She didn't happen to say anything about a dwarf, did she?"

Whatever Miranda might have been she was a lady with deep sensibilities who passed judgment on no man or woman. Shaking her head, she looked at him sadly, almost maternally, and said, "Now don't go imagining things, luv, I'm sure that once she gets him out of her system she'll realize what a good man you are, so don't go thinking there's someone else, not a giant or a dwarf . . ."

What could he say except to thank her for her kindness. He left the brownstone like a man in a trance, not quite alive but not dead either. How the hell was he going to find her in Buenos Aires; he could just picture himself roaming around the city looking for a dwarf.

Chapter Twenty-two

There she was, back in Buenos Aires and wandering along Corrientes as if all the years away could fit into the past month. Long before Coriander said her first farewell to Danny, before she welcomed him back into her life for the last time in New York, before their existence together became the fiction he created, she had happy memories of carefree times spent in this city.

Corrientes remained the very pulse of the city with its lights and music and laughter. She expected that Hernando would arrive late or not at all and she was prepared to relive all the uncertainty from that day so long ago when she lost him and then refused to sacrifice enough to get him back.

She had made the plane by twenty minutes in New York and arrived in Buenos Aires on Thursday morning, checking into a small hotel in Recoleta by the same name. It was near the cemetery, which was the only place she went on that Thursday, to visit her mother's grave. What she remembered about Recoleta cemetery as she wandered the small streets and alleyways of that neighborhood filled with the well-bred dead was how typical it was of Argentina. So eclectic with its many different styles of architecture, representative of the many diverse cultures and nationalities. Some of the mausoleums had filigreed iron gates and brass bells; others had glass doors and winged angels perched on their roofs; all had names and professions of the occupants posted on the stone facades. Coriander always had the temptation to ring, as if the person who resided within would actually rise up to answer.

Wandering through Recoleta made her momentarily forget her sadness for her mother; wandering back to her mother's grave made her momentarily forget her sadness about Danny. The rest of the time she stayed in her hotel room, afraid to go out in case she ran into someone she knew.

It was Friday and a cold August winter morning on the day she was supposed to meet Hernando. She began wandering Corrientes, combing the single room bookstalls that opened onto the street. There wasn't the slightest doubt in her mind where he intended for them to meet.

She who was not known to be particularly punctual found herself at the right place at the precise time, give or take twelve hours since it had been unclear whether she was supposed to be there morning, afternoon or night. Wandering in and out of the stores, she glanced at the newspapers, magazines, books on sale, books on stacks, books on lists until she wound her way around and out to begin yet another tour. Down the long block she walked to where Avenida Callao merged with Corrientes. Democracy had indeed returned to Argentina, the streets were a mass of potholes, homeless lined the boulevards, beggars appeared from the shadows around the marble statues that separated the enormous avenues that went on forever. Stores were kept locked, cars had signs in their windows telling would-be robbers that there was nothing of value to rob, people walked along eating fast-food. There seemed to be no more leisurely lunches or siestas. Where were the men in crisp military uniforms who drove around to collect bodies and trash at the end of a demonstration? She felt an overwhelming distance from this place that had once been her home. She didn't belong here any more than did the other *Porte-nos,* those citizens of Buenos Aires whose very name implied that they had immigrated into the Port from faraway places. Perhaps she was different, perhaps she belonged there more than the others. Her blood was here, her ancestors had been here since the nineteenth century, her mother was here for eternity, buried within one of those pink marble crypts in Recoleta; her father was here as well, his photograph hanging in the American Embassy with those of other former Ambassadors.

She headed back down Corrientes again, past the old cafés with their tall, wood-framed windows that opened onto the street when the weather was warm, past the movie houses playing American films and past several fast-food chains. She wrapped her coat tighter around her in defense of the wind. She was cold, tired and frightened and she wished Adam were with her, but that was another story . . . Right then all she cared about was seeing Hernando and Danny although it still wasn't clear whether she would see either of them ever again. She was taking a chance.

All her life she had been accused of having no sense of humor, a serious girl, they said, studious and intense, not like the other young people who danced and flirted and fell in and out of love. Coriander moved through life with purpose, dedication and resolve, they claimed, mature beyond her years, which made Danny the last person they imagined this serious woman would take into her heart. She took them both in, Hernando and Danny, one for his mind, the other for his soul. And then there was Adam. Maybe it wasn't too late for the girl with no sense of humor to have the last laugh . . .

There was nothing more depressing than a nightclub in the middle of an afternoon, as bleak as the beach at Punta del Este off-season. La Verduleria's bright lights revealed the stains in the carpet, the frayed edges of the red velvet curtain, the faded tablecloths and the dust on the plastic plants and flowers. The musicians looked pasty and the singer's arms looked flabby without the soft pink spotlight to cast its youthful glow or the dim yellow beams to reflect off her sequined dress.

They were kind enough to allow her to sit inside the club and wait. The dwarf was at the far end of the bar looking older and wizened with his shirtsleeves rolled up and his hairless arms leaning over the counter. There was nothing hot to drink, no coffee or tea, it was too early. Positioning the chair so she could see the street directly outside the club, she sipped a glass of mineral water.

For several hours she sat and waited until the sun set and the lights dimmed and several men rolled the piano out onto the stage. A few of the musicians sat around and tested their flats and sharps as the dwarf donned his red jacket with the brass buttons and his black patent-leather cap. *Welcome to La Verduleria, señoras y caballeros, cumbias, sambas and tangos begin at three o'clock in the morning . . .*

She was off the bar stool and through the swinging doors, standing outside on the street. There he was. Without a word, she took his wrists gently in her hands and kissed each one, above the metal, holding them as she looked into his eyes. Tears welled in her own and she couldn't speak. As for him, he smiled with the sheer pleasure of seeing her again despite his every effort to appear so sullen. Within moments the tension between them was gone, his shoulders slumped down and he seemed to relax. It was so obvious that all the years apart were forgotten as he began their old routine, testing her for those spot quizzes in her anatomy classes. Pointing to places on his body and face, he asked the names of the bones beneath. Laughing through her tears, she called them out in Latin, "Tibia, zygomatic, temporal, humerus . . ." He loved her still although Coriander-the-woman carrying the child of his mentor gave Hernando an uneven joy. "He told me about the baby," he said when their game stopped. She had made every effort not to mention Danny for the first six or seven minutes and now dissolved with something beyond relief that all the doubt was finally gone. What she didn't feel was surprise . . . "Why did he leave?"

"He had no choice, Coriander, but he always intended to send for you."

"He should have told me, he should have explained."

"He couldn't trust you to understand then because there was too much at stake."

"You're so naive," she began sadly. He was so thin, so pale. She touched his cheek. "You're the one who doesn't understand."

He turned his face and his tone was angry. "Why don't you tell him that when you see him."

"Are you taking me there?"

Still looking away, he nodded.

She turned his face gently with her hand so he was forced to look at her. "And you, why didn't you contact me all these years?"

For an instant he looked twenty again, the boy with the *bandoneon* who became the warrior. "Could I play music for you anymore?"

"But you were alive . . ."

"Do you think that's everything?"

"Of course it's everything given the alternative . . ."

He shook his head. "I was twenty years old when I lost my hands and for what?" She didn't dare breathe. "Was I stealing? Had I killed someone?" Tears rolled down his emaciated cheeks and he was suddenly every last one of them who had suffered or *disappeared* at the hands of the Junta. "What was it? What was my crime?" She stood there without moving until she held out her own hand somewhere in the air between them. "Hernando," she said, her voice breaking, "it was their crime, not yours." And again she understood all the rage, inhumanity and cruelty of what had transpired except now she understood that it only mattered for the ones who had suffered directly and not for those who had lived it on the periphery. "And Danny?" she asked.

"He told me to come and fight . . ."

It was insane. "Come and fight," she repeated softly before asking, "Fight what, Hernando, why?"

"So it wouldn't happen again . . ."

"You're living in another time," she said, begging him to understand. "What you believe now isn't founded in any reality."

He shrugged. "The reality is that we're leaving for Havana on Sunday. Doesn't that make a difference?"

Nothing made a difference or everything did, it depended on the moment. This time around she judged the reasons to be illogical and irrational although for Hernando there seemed still to be justification. It wasn't hard to understand that he needed to keep it alive in order to survive. Her husband was another story; the idealist who had gone corporate, the executive who had gone criminal. "Where is he now?"

"He's at my parents' *estancia* in Ushuaia. We're going to drive part of the way and then fly from Bahia Blanca."

There was no possibility that she wouldn't go with him. She had to see Danny again, if only to understand everything that he had never bothered to explain.

Adam arrived in Buenos Aires on Saturday morning, two days after Coriander. It was the cab driver who suggested that he stay at the Alvear Hotel, which was inside a shopping plaza called the Galeria Promenade and centrally located in the heart of the Barrio Norte. Ironically, the hotel was so close to Recoleta Cemetery that it was merely a question of crossing one street and walking through the well-tended park that surrounded the city of the dead. Had Coriander visited her mother's grave today there would have been every chance that Adam would have seen her.

As he was checking in Adam asked the concierge "If someone told someone to meet them in Buenos Aires where there was a dwarf, would you have any idea where that might be?" The expression on the clerk's face as he stood behind the gleaming mahogany reception desk made Adam consider that perhaps he should have waited until *after* he was checked in before posing the question. "That's the bungled message I got from someone," he went on with an embarrassed laugh. But the man was completely professional when he nodded as if he understood the problem. "I'll check for you, Señor," he said before summoning the bellboy who had been standing off to the side, waiting to take Adam's valise up to his room. As an obvious courtesy, the man spoke to his colleague in English, repeating the question, maintaining an impassive expression and a benign tone. But the bellboy understood immediately. "You must mean La Verduleria," he said. "It's a well-known nightclub on Corrientes where a dwarf stands at the door." He turned to the concierge then and added something in Spanish to which the man responded by smiling and shaking his head. "Of course, La Verduleria, it's quite well-known," he repeated. "But you know, Señor, if you are going there to dance the tango or the samba, you must wait until three o'clock in the morning. Dancing begins only then." Adam thanked him, remembering Coriander's description of the night she spent with Hernando—dancing until she began to worry about Danny at five o'clock in the morning when they finally left the club, standing on Corrientes when that car screeched up and the police jumped out to take Hernando away . . . Following the bellboy through the gleaming lobby and into the elevator, which was a restored old-fashioned cage, Adam decided to go directly to La Verduleria. It was not quite noon, more than twelve hours early to dance and probably a day late to find Coriander.

As the taxi drove through Buenos Aires on the way to La Verduleria, Adam looked out the window, fascinated by everything that he saw. The city was as magnificent as Coriander had described with enormous boulevards, mounds of well-tended grass on which were benches separating each side. The buildings that lined those boulevards were either in the old-world European-style or were modern glass-and-chrome skyscrapers. Ornate statues of ancient Greek and Roman figures in chariots or single marble figures of Argentine liberators and heroes stood in circular paved courtyards leading to several office buildings and apartment houses. Driving along, Adam noticed churches and outdoor markets, red Mercedes city buses, small glass-fronted stands called *kioscos* all aglow with neon lights. He asked the driver what they were and learned that although they were no larger than a medium-sized closet they were open twenty-four hours a day and sold everything from cigarettes to soap to lottery tickets. There was something eerily familiar about the city even though he had never been there before. It struck a chord of recognition deep within him and all because of her and everything she had told him about her life there; more because she was so deeply embedded in his heart and mind . . .

There was no doubt where they were as soon as the driver turned down Corrientes. Again, it was exactly as she had described—the street that never sleeps—with all the movie theatres and crowds, traffic and restaurants and nightclubs, bright lights on the outside even in broad daylight, music coming from the inside. The cab pulled up in front of La Verduleria and stopped. Involuntarily, Adam shivered as he paid the driver and stepped out. It struck him then, how everyone in Buenos Aires who was fourteen or older had either been *born during* or *lived through* or *suffered from* the Junta. When he walked in and saw the dwarf sitting at the far end of the bar it was like seeing a link between then and now, someone who had been witness so long ago to an incident that set off a series of events that had changed so many lives . . .

Adam had brought a photograph along with him to show people when he inquired about her. The dwarf remembered seeing her only yesterday and he pointed to the exact place where she had been sitting. How could he forget, she was there for hours, waiting for someone. Before they invited her inside she had been walking back and forth on Corrientes, around the block, coming back to stand in front of the club. Nobody else in La Verduleria could offer anything more since apparently she spoke to no one except the bartender and then only to ask for several bottles of mineral water. When her friend finally arrived she raced out the door, barely remembering her coat.

The owner of the club was concerned. He approached Adam to say that he hoped he wouldn't have any trouble with the police since he had never seen the woman before. He was only being kind when he allowed her to wait inside, he didn't know anything about her. Adam assured the man that it had nothing to do with the police but rather only with something personal between them. Relieved, the man nodded and smiled, mumbling something about *son cosas del corazon,* not that it amused Adam to be judged the jilted lover or jealous husband. He continued to ask questions; could anyone describe the man or the car, had anyone overheard a conversation about where they were going. No one had heard anything. It was only when Adam was about to leave that the dwarf came up to him. There was something else no one had mentioned or perhaps they hadn't noticed, something touching. When the woman ran out into the street to greet her friend she kissed his hands. Adam must have looked shocked because the dwarf hastened to explain that it wasn't exactly his hands that she kissed but rather his wrists. You see, the man didn't have hands, only metal hooks.

When Adam first arrived in Buenos Aires he had no intention of telling Palmer Wyatt that he was there. After leaving La Verduleria he changed his mind.

When he got back to the hotel he stopped at the desk to see about messages—as if someone would have called him—before he rode the elevator to his room. Once inside, he sat down on the bed and telephoned the former Ambassador. Wyatt answered on the second ring.

It took only several minutes for Adam to bring him up to date and explain just exactly what he was doing there. The man listened without interrupting or asking a lot of questions that Adam couldn't answer—at least not yet.

"What do you know about this man that she met at the club?" Adam asked.

"That's the man I told you about. His name is Hernando Sykes and I've got a file on him from years ago when he was arrested."

Adam held his breath, hoping that the man had access to that file given that it had something to do with that tape from Danny's house, which had everything to do with Coriander. Palmer told him that he would check and call him back. Within ten minutes the phone rang. "His family owns a sheep ranch down in Ushuaia," Wyatt said, "and from that I gather they're decent, hard-working people."

"How do I get there?"

"How do you even know that's where they've gone?"

"I don't, but it makes more sense to talk to the man's family than chase around Buenos Aires."

Adam was fully prepared for the argument that followed. Wyatt had all the logical reasons for why he should accompany Adam down to Ushuaia. In the end Adam was able to convince him that it was better for everyone if he waited at home. There was too much at stake to dredge up old hostilities and Wyatt brought back memories of a painful period in these people's lives.

Although there were two flights a day out of Buenos Aires for Ushuaia on weekdays, there was only one flight a day on weekends. The Saturday flight had already left. Adam booked a seat for Sunday morning, which would put him in Ushuaia six hours later or at about five in the afternoon. He promised to call Wyatt the moment he knew anything; they would decide then whether he should come down. If something happened and Adam wasn't able to call, at least Wyatt knew where he was.

Chapter Twenty-three

The Aerolineas Argentinas 737 dipped down over the Beagle Channel whose choppy waters washed over the scattered mounds of small islands. The plane rocked unsteadily from side to side as it cut between the jagged mountain peaks that bordered the narrow path of air space. Flying over the calmer waters of Ushuaia Bay, the craft made its final approach onto the shortest and most dangerous airport in the world. Bumping down onto the runway, the pilot instantly threw on the brakes, causing the plane to screech to a stop.

Inside the terminal near the luggage area Coriander stood and waited. The interior of the structure was covered with posters warning of cholera, drawings of fruit and vegetables boiling in vats of water; other posters warned of *meria roja,* the killer disease that attacked sea and shellfish during certain months of the year. On the wall over the Lade, Austral and Aerolineas Argentinas counters there were blown-up photographs of sheep grazing on rolling lush green hills and wood-hulled sailboats tied to unfinished docks, amber-colored wildflowers dotting the shore line in the distance. Glancing overhead, she saw wires dangling from spaces in the ceiling in between metal pipes. She gathered her coat around her against the freezing wind that blew in from underneath patches of plywood that covered holes in the walls.

From a window on one side of the plane Adam could see stretches of barren land, miles of untouched snow on which were scattered red-roofed houses and small enclaves of construction sites, scaffolded buildings and rusted machines, pick-up trucks half-buried in the snow. From the other side of the plane he could see a low corrugated metal structure with a rounded roof that resembled a command post in an army barrack; several other crudely-constructed barracklike buildings were off to the left. As the plane taxied toward a waiting set of stairs on the tarmac, Adam noticed a twin-engine Cessna. A man sat on the steps leading from the door of the craft. He had no hands.

There were only several other people in the terminal, all of them milling around a *kiosco* that sold duty-free perfumes and makeup. Hernando had already called the *estancia* to speak to Danny, who assured him that he would be waiting when they arrived.

Coriander half expected that he would be there when they drove up to the terminal. Now her eyes scanned every exit in the room for fear of missing him. She had never been so terrified in her entire life although it was less the fear of seeing him than of making a decision she would live to regret.

"Coriander, *querida.*"

She jumped at the sound of his voice and turned around. He looked different somehow or perhaps she was the one who saw him differently. His hair was longer and he had a scruffy beard, his eyes glittered intensely and he was wearing the same black trousers and turtleneck that he had on the day that he left her.

It was impossible for her to say anything then, the shock of seeing him overwhelming her relief that finally she knew for certain that he wasn't dead, that he had only abandoned her without bothering to give a reason or offering any discussion before he simply disappeared. Trembling, she just stared, aware of her pounding heart.

He didn't hesitate, but acted as if he had been waiting for her for weeks, as if she had been the one to leave without warning. Gathering her in his arms, he pressed his lips against her ear. "Thank God you're here . . ." His words sounded vaguely familiar, that same bizarre expression of gratitude that he once used when she told him she was expecting his child. Involuntarily, she stiffened. "Maybe you shouldn't have come, *querida* . . ."

Wrong, she screamed silently, still too overwhelmed to speak, maybe you shouldn't have left . . .

"Maybe I'm being selfish to want you with me . . . Maybe it's better if we had left it . . . I only want what's best for you . . ."

He was still making excuses, vaguely justifying his actions as he had always done, for the good of something or someone, never for himself, always under the guise of selflessness and altruism. But this time it wasn't quite enough; all the pain and sorrow flowed together within her to emerge as unadulterated rage. She flew at him, pummeling his face and chest with her fists, tears running down her cheeks, screaming "How could you have done this? How could you have put me through this . . ."

If he was surprised by her violent outburst he didn't show it. He merely took her wrists and held them in the air as he talked soothingly, "I tried to protect you, don't you see, I didn't want you involved in anything."

She took a breath to calm herself and only then did he release her hands, taking a step back as he did.

"You promised me, Danny," she wept, "you swore that you'd never get involved in anything like this again . . ."

His instincts were on high, that much was obvious, the way he gauged her reaction, fighting for the right words to calm her. "I loved you too much to let you go."

"You lied to me . . ."

"My only crime is that I wanted you so much . . ."

"You made our whole life together meaningless."

He went back to the beginning of the story. "I can't survive without you . . ." Somehow she felt herself standing outside of the situation, more as an observer than a participant, more on the periphery of an emotional scene that had to be played until the end. As she listened she could feel the tears well in her eyes and her hands tremble and her knees grow weak. "How could you believe that I could?" he asked.

Her jaw clenched as she fought back more tears. "How can I ever trust you again?"

"Because this is a new beginning."

"No, it's just another ending."

"This is the beginning of forever, darling, with our baby . . ."

But she wasn't listening to his promises. "You murdered Matthew Johnson," she accused, choking back the tears, "and you lied to me about Hernando and you knew that plane was going to blow up after you got off it in Houston . . ."

"All those people were tragic casualties of the revolution."

Again, her rage was choking her. "What revolution?"

He stiffened. "All over the world."

"What are you talking about?" she cried, an inch from lunging again. "It's pure insanity . . ."

He spoke slowly, his eyes burning into hers. "You don't understand, *querida,* this is my life, this is what I'm committed to, I tried to explain it to you years ago."

She stood there staring at him, for the first time feeling an enormous wave of pity for what he had become.

"The only mistake I made was to imagine that I had to sacrifice the only person in the world I loved." He paused. "You taught me that long ago in Cordoba, don't you remember?"

She spoke slowly, as if to a child. "Danny, we're talking about murder, those people were human beings . . ."

But he was talking about his cause. "How can I convince you that the threat is back? There may not be uniforms or marching bands or rallies and there may not be allusions to *fatherland, juntas,* or *Nazis* but nothing's changed. During every political campaign all over the world it appears somewhere with a perfectly acceptable façade. It's the new face of fascism . . ."

It was horrifying because there was a shred of truth in what he was saying, even more horrifying that he was able to use it to justify what he had done. "You stole innocent people's money."

"Never for myself."

She could barely breathe. "When does it end?" she whispered.

He held out a hand. "With you, it all ends with us together, I need you, come with me . . ."

He was a murderer, a liar, a thief. He was her only lover, her husband, the father of her unborn child.

She moved closer and took his hands in hers to try and explain it again, as if he might understand so she could follow him anywhere to live happily ever after. "It doesn't excuse what you've done and it doesn't justify anything. Don't you see that you're as bad as *they* are when you do these kind of things?" The tears were running down her cheeks. "I love you," she said, her voice breaking, "I've always loved you but I can't be a part of this . . ."

"You're carrying my child."

"What did you imagine when you left me?" A new-found calm had suddenly enveloped her.

"I never intended to leave you forever."

Her voice was sad. "The problem is that you never intended any of it to be forever . . ."

"That's not true," he protested, but his voice sounded less sure.

She could have brought up the plane crash and the bank and a million other excuses or dollars to offer to support the argument that he fully intended to leave her forever. Instead she allowed him to take her arm to lead her outside. He was still explaining. "They murdered thousands," he said, tears brimming, "they took away the best and the brightest because those were the ones who had the strength to oppose them . . ." Even if she had wanted to answer there was no chance. Hernando was walking toward them and asking in Spanish if she was coming along. The wind was kicking up and the pilot was getting nervous. Holding out his hand, Danny implored, "Come with me . . ."

I am grieving, she thought to herself, I am the confused widow grieving for the living husband, filled with my own madness. Both of them saw the disbelief in her eyes, the sorrow and the pity as she looked from one to the other. Danny took a step closer, still pleading his case, "Whatever I've done or however I've hurt you I've always loved you, you're the love of my life."

It came to her suddenly and she wondered why she hadn't realized it before. Shaking her head, she just stood there. "No, Danny, I was never the love of your life . . ." It was all so clear. "It was always Alicia, it never stopped being Alicia . . ."

He looked pale and all he could whisper was her name, not even a denial. But it didn't matter since it went beyond anger or hurt with each having his private agony and guilt about having survived the *dirty war* when others hadn't. It worked in his favor, actually. The cold-eyed passion that she brought with her to the hospital when she treated other victims was gone. Once she was capable of being dedicated and distant at the same time; now she trembled as she walked between them toward the small aircraft. It worked in his favor, actually, or at least it almost did . . .

Adam was running toward her in what seemed like slow motion with his hair blowing and his jacket billowing out. He wasn't more than six feet away, shouting against the wind, "Coriander, wait . . ."

She felt a wave of panic and relief at the same time. "What are you doing here?" she cried.

But he spoke only to Danny. "Let go of her."

In response Danny only clutched her arm tighter.

Adam moved closer.

"Adam," she began, "don't . . ."

"She's coming with me," Danny said in a firm voice.

"Is that right, Coriander? After all that you know and after all that he's done, you're still going with him?" He took another step closer.

"She's my wife . . ."

"Then why don't you do the first decent thing in your life and leave her alone?"

"It's none of your business."

"Adam, go away, please, I'll handle this . . ." Her eyes filled with tears.

"What the hell are you going to handle? How many times has he left you, how many times has he lied . . ."

Hernando moved closer and to everyone's surprise Coriander whirled around to scream, "Stay out of this . . ."

"The wind is getting worse," he pleaded desperately. "In another few minutes Milos won't be able to take off."

Desperately, Adam kept on, "Ask him to tell you about that torso in the basin, ask him to tell you how they shot an innocent man and pushed his truck down a ravine because they needed a body . . ."

But the denial was quick. "I didn't shoot him. I wasn't even there . . ."

"Tell her who did shoot him, why don't you explain how you knew all about it and where you were when it happened . . ." The distance between the two men was diminishing.

"Get out of here," Danny shouted, "you're jeopardizing her life by wasting time . . ."

"Adam, please," Coriander begged, "let me go and I promise I'll come back . . ."

Adam took another cautious step forward. "He'll never let you go and if you try to get away he'll kill you."

"You're carrying our child."

"He didn't care about that before . . ."

"This is our new beginning, *querida.*"

Milos emerged from the plane then, his hands jammed into the pockets of his fur-lined anorak. "We've got to leave, the wind . . ."

"We can't waste any more time, Danny," Hernando reminded him, "the money is already there."

Holding out a hand, Danny asked with infinite sadness, "Are you coming with me?"

She said nothing as she took his face between her hands and kissed him full on the lips. She stepped back then, her eyes filling with tears as she shook her head slowly from side to side. "I can't go with you . . ." And in her head she listed all the reasons, from Alicia to Matthew Johnson, from Jorge to Stampa.

There was no more time. The wind dried the tears that streaked her face as she turned to mouth the words *I love you* because she did and would forever. She watched as he followed Hernando toward the plane, noticing the look in his eye, a flash of regret as he shouted instructions to the pilot, "Milos, start the engine . . ."

Adam was upon her, holding her so tightly that she could barely breathe, shielding her from the wind and the world. But the last thing she cared about was breathing or feeling or seeing anything except Danny leaving for the last time.

The sound of the engine drowned out Adam's every other word, ". . . love . . . forever." The wind swept across her face to dry her tears. Climbing through the ragged-edged white clouds in an ascent pattern toward the peaks of the snow-capped mountains, the Cessna emerged against a sapphire sky, climbing higher and higher toward the shimmering sun that reflected off its silver wings.

The blast ripped through the silence, shaking the very ground on which they stood. Flashes of fire appeared overhead as a series of explosions reverberated around them. Pieces of plane fell to earth, discernible only by the trail of black smoke and an occasional spurt of fire. The twisted and burning mass plunged down into a crevice of an ancient glacier.

Coriander just stood there, her mouth slightly open, her lips dry, her eyes fixed at the unseen horror in the far-off distance. For seconds she was dazed and shocked until a strangled cry escaped her lips and she turned to bury her face against Adam's chest. "Hold me," she wept, "just hold me."

"I'll never let you go, Coriander," he promised, "you're mine forever . . ."

Once long ago in the Hotel el Tropezón on the Tigre Delta she heard those same words. Somehow now they sounded true.